He pitched forward face-first into the water....

From what Phyllis could see of McKenna's face, the man didn't look good. He hadn't been under the water all that long, probably less than a minute in all. A person couldn't drown in that short a time, could they?

Phyllis got to the end of the pier and jumped down to the narrow, reedy beach. She dropped Sam's sneakers and waded into the water, heedless of her own shoes and blue jeans, and leaned down to grab McKenna and help Sam haul him out of the water. A shudder went through her as she saw the man's gray, lifeless face.

"My God, Sam!" she said as he climbed out. Water streamed from his clothes and body. "Mr. McKenna's dead. He must have drowned right away."

Sam pawed his soaked hair back and shook his head. "Nobody drowns that fast. Did you see the way he went in? He was just balanced there on the wall, waiting for somebody like me to come along and knock him in."

"You mean . . . ?"

Sam nodded. "He was dead when he went into the water."

More Praise for the Fresh-Baked Mysteries

"Washburn has a refreshing way with words and knows how to tell an exciting story." —*Midwest Book Review*

continued . . .

"*A Peach of a Murder* runs the full range of emotions, so be prepared to laugh and cry with this one!"
—The Romance Readers Connection

"I really enjoyed *Murder by the Slice*. . . . It's got a nice plot with lots of twists." —James Reasoner

"Christmas and murder. It's a combination that doesn't seem to go together, yet Washburn pulls it off in a delightfully entertaining manner." —Armchair Interviews

Killer Crab Cakes

A Fresh-Baked Mystery

LIVIA J. WASHBURN

AN OBSIDIAN MYSTERY

OBSIDIAN
Published by New American Library, a division of
Penguin Group (USA) Inc., 375 Hudson Street,
New York, New York 10014, USA

Penguin Group (Canada), 90 Eglinton Avenue East, Suite 700, Toronto,
Ontario M4P 2Y3, Canada (a division of Pearson Penguin Canada Inc.)
Penguin Books Ltd., 80 Strand, London WC2R 0RL, England
Penguin Ireland, 25 St. Stephen's Green, Dublin 2,
Ireland (a division of Penguin Books Ltd.)
Penguin Group (Australia), 250 Camberwell Road, Camberwell, Victoria 3124,
Australia (a division of Pearson Australia Group Pty. Ltd.)
Penguin Books India Pvt. Ltd., 11 Community Centre, Panchsheel Park,
New Delhi—110 017, India
Penguin Group (NZ), 67 Apollo Drive, Rosedale, North Shore 0632,
New Zealand (a division of Pearson New Zealand Ltd.)
Penguin Books (South Africa) (Pty.) Ltd., 24 Sturdee Avenue,
Rosebank, Johannesburg 2196, South Africa

Penguin Books Ltd., Registered Offices:
80 Strand, London WC2R 0RL, England

Published by Obsidian, an imprint of New American Library, a division of Penguin Group (USA) Inc. Previously published in an Obsidian trade paperback edition.

First Obsidian Mass Market Printing, November 2010
10 9 8 7 6 5 4 3 2 1

PUBLISHER'S NOTE
This is a work of fiction. Names, characters, places, and incidents either are the product of the author's imagination or are used fictitiously, and any resemblance to actual persons, living or dead, business establishments, events, or locales is entirely coincidental.

The recipes contained in this book are to be followed exactly as written. The publisher is not responsible for your specific health or allergy needs that may require medical supervision. The publisher is not responsible for any adverse reactions to the recipes contained in this book.

The publisher does not have any control over and does not assume any responsibility for author or third-party Web sites or their content.

This book is dedicated to all the people who helped us recover from a devastating wildfire. Family members that went above and beyond, Paul and Naomi Washburn, Bruce and Patricia Washburn, Harold and Jodie Reasoner, John and Norma Kinchen, Eric and Jennifer Washburn, Billy and Amanda Gann, Nina Henderson, Elmo and Billie Wright, Ricky Wright, Gayle Rotton, Sidney and Wanda Brantly, Mike and Sabra Torok, you will never know how much your help meant. We would have been lost without all of you. And to all the rest who offered prayers and words of encouragement, thank you so much. I would also like to thank all our friends and neighbors for being there for us. There are so many who helped that to list them all would take another whole book! To everyone who sent us books to replace our lost library, thank you! Kim Lionetti, you are the best agent out there. Thanks! Brent Howard, I'm lucky you are my editor and thank you for being so understanding. The fire was terrible, but it taught us how many good people there really are in the world. Thank you for all your love and support.

Chapter 1

$\mathcal{A}$n early-morning calm lay over the water, broken only by the plaintive cries of seagulls as they wheeled over the glassy surface. The sun wasn't quite up yet, but a half circle of pink and orange glow was visible at the horizon, far out over the Gulf of Mexico, as Phyllis Newsom stepped out onto the porch of the old three-story house that faced the sea. Only rarely had she ever seen anything more beautiful, Phyllis thought as she raised a cup to her lips and took a sip of coffee.

Nor was there anything more restful and peaceful than these moments just before sunrise. She would never wish ill on anyone, but right now she was almost glad that there had been complications with the birth of her cousin Dorothy's first grandchild. If Dorothy and her husband hadn't had to go up to Dallas to be with their daughter, they wouldn't have asked Phyllis to come down here to Fulton, Texas, and look after their bed-and-breakfast for a while. Mother and baby were doing just fine now, but Phyllis suspected that Dorothy would want to stay up there and play proud grandma for as long as she possibly could.

The door behind Phyllis opened. She knew without looking around that Sam Fletcher had come out onto the porch. He liked these early mornings, too. Phyllis's other two friends who had come down here with her from Weatherford, Carolyn Wilbarger and Eve Turner, were still inside the house. All four of them were retired schoolteachers, so they were used to getting up fairly early after decades of having to arrive at school before the students did. Since retirement, though, Eve had taken to sleeping in, and Carolyn had never been much of one for the glories of nature. She was probably in the kitchen by now, interfering with Consuela's attempts to fix breakfast.

"We've been down here three days now," Sam said as he moved up beside Phyllis, a cup of coffee in his hand, too, "and I'm not tired of that view yet. I wonder if the people who live here ever get tired of it."

"I don't know," Phyllis said. "Can you imagine living here and going somewhere else for your vacation?"

"You mean like to Weatherford?" Sam shook his head. "That's pretty hard to picture."

"But I'm sure it happens. People would get tired of being anywhere, even paradise, and want a change of scenery."

Paradise was a pretty good word to describe this area along the Texas Gulf Coast. There wasn't nearly as much traffic and pollution as people in the Dallas/Fort Worth area had to put up with, and life moved at a slower, friendlier pace. At this time of year, early autumn, the weather was still summerlike along the coast, with warm days and comfortable nights. Every now and then, there would be a hint of the coolness to come in the breeze. You really couldn't ask for better weather, though.

Tall, lean Sam rasped fingers along his jaw and laughed. "Things are so laid-back down here, it's hard for a fella to even remember to shave. Reckon if I stay here very long I'll look like an old beachcomber."

Phyllis looked over at him. He wore sneakers with no socks, cut-off blue jeans, and a T-shirt with a picture of a pelican on it that had come from a nearby bar and grill.

His salt-and-pepper hair was tousled, and he had white stubble on his cheeks and chin to go with the mustache on his upper lip. Phyllis laughed, too.

"Too late," she told him. "You already look like a beachcomber. Or a fisherman. Although you'll need a fishing hat for that. You can't go fishing without the proper hat."

"Is that a law in these parts?"

"Evidently, from what I've seen."

"Actually, I thought I might try the fishin' pretty soon." Sam nodded toward the pier that jutted several hundred yards out into the water, starting just across the road from the big house. It was a private pier, belonging to the Oak Knoll Bed-'n'-Breakfast. The little hill that gave the place its name was just inland from the house and was covered with the gnarled, bizarrely leaning oak trees that were common around here.

The house itself was painted a beautiful sky blue, with white trim. It was nearly a hundred years old and had been cared for with diligence and love so that it was still in excellent shape. Phyllis's cousin Dorothy and Dorothy's husband, Ben, had owned it for more than thirty years. It was originally just their residence, but when their kids had grown up and moved out, they had turned it into a bed-and-breakfast . . . much like Phyllis had taken in other retired schoolteachers as boarders after her husband, Kenny, passed away. The big house in Weatherford had been too much for her; she hadn't wanted to rattle around in it by herself. The same feelings had caused Dorothy and Ben to make that change in their lives. A house *needed* plenty of people in it in order to give it personality and vitality. Otherwise it was just a heartless pile of lumber.

Phyllis had been a little unsure of what to do when Dorothy asked her to come down. She didn't have any experience running a bed-and-breakfast. Dorothy had assured her that she had a highly competent staff who would continue doing all the actual work. She had also had a couple of cancellations, so there would be plenty of room for her and her friends. She just wanted someone she could trust, like Phyllis, to keep an eye on the place while she and Ben were gone.

When Dorothy had told Phyllis about the SeaFair and its Just Desserts competition, that had clinched the deal.

The beachfront town of Fulton was nestled side by side with a larger neighbor, the city of Rockport. Both had been in existence and served as Gulf Coast ports for well over a hundred years. Each fall, during the first weekend in October, Rockport had held its annual SeaFair, a huge celebration featuring dozens of vendors, artists, craftsmen, local bands and musicians, a gumbo cook-off, games and crab races and a carnival for the kids, and, for the past few years, the Just Desserts competition. Cooks from all over the area—and beyond— entered their best dessert recipes, and the judging and awarding of prizes was the highlight of the final day of the SeaFair.

As soon as Phyllis heard about that, she had known that she had to accept Dorothy's invitation. And, of course, there was no way to keep Carolyn from finding out about it, and she had jumped at the chance to enter another baking contest. She and Phyllis had been friendly rivals at such competitions for years now. In fact, just a few months earlier they had gone head-to-head again at Weatherford's annual Peach Festival.

Phyllis had been a little nervous when that time came around, because there had been a murder at the previous year's Peach Festival, a murder that had involved Phyllis and her friends. Luckily, this year nobody had died. Carolyn had won the baking contest with her Sweet Peach Rolls, and Phyllis had placed third with her creation, Peachy Bread Pudding. The competition had been spirited, as usual.

Phyllis didn't think the Just Desserts contest would

be quite that intense. Folks in Rockport and Fulton were just too friendly and easygoing for that.

Sam perched a hip on the railing that ran around the porch and drank some more of his coffee. "Care to try your luck?" he asked Phyllis.

"You mean at fishing?" She hesitated. Ever since the previous Christmas, she and Sam had been involved in an informal, low-key romantic relationship. They had their passionate moments, but mostly it was dining out, going to movies, taking walks together, things like that. Fishing certainly fell into that same category, but . . .

"I'm afraid I'm not very good at fishing," she said. "I don't even have a license."

"Well, you can't fish, then. Game warden'd come along and get you, sure as anything."

"I could walk out on the pier with you, though, if you don't mind the company."

A slow grin spread across Sam's rugged face. "I don't mind the company at all. Fact is, I sort of like it."

Phyllis felt herself flush with pleasure at the tone of his voice. Some people thought certain feelings were over and done with once you got to a certain age . . . but some people just didn't know.

The door opened again, and Phyllis glanced over her shoulder to see a thin, gray-haired man come out of the house. He wore a khaki shirt and trousers and an old-fashioned brown fedora. In one hand he carried an expensive rod and reel, in the other a tackle box and bait box. A net with a long aluminum handle was tucked under his arm. The sun had started to peek above the horizon now, and its rays glittered on the steel-rimmed glasses he wore.

"Good morning, Mr. McKenna," Phyllis greeted him pleasantly. "Going to try your luck again this morning?"

Ed McKenna nodded, a somewhat sour expression on his face. "Yeah, even though I don't know why. Haven't caught anything worth keeping all week. Don't feel too good, either. Maybe some sun will perk me up a little."

McKenna had been staying at the bed-and-breakfast when Phyllis and her friends arrived, and he was booked for another week's stay. Phyllis didn't know anything about him except that he was from San Antonio. And that while he was polite enough, he wasn't overly friendly. He had been out on the pier every morning with his fishing gear, but he wasn't in the habit of striking up conversations with the other anglers. Of course, Phyllis had heard that a lot of talking sometimes scared off the fish, so she guessed that might be the reason McKenna seemed a little antisocial.

"I'll be out there in a while," Sam told McKenna. "What's the best sort of bait? Live shrimp?"

"That's as good as any," McKenna answered. He went down the steps from the porch and headed across the road to the pier.

"Not the friendliest cuss in the world," Sam commented when McKenna was out of earshot.

"Not everyone is as amiable as you, Sam," Phyllis pointed out.

"I just try to be myself. I'm too old to be anybody else."

They went back inside, and sure enough, Carolyn was trying to convince Consuela to do things differently in the kitchen. She wasn't getting very far. Consuela Anselmo had been the cook and head housekeeper at Oak Knoll for more than five years and liked to do things her own way, which Phyllis understood. Her daughters, Bianca and Theresa, worked part-time in the mornings as the maids, and Consuela's husband, Tom, worked part-time handling maintenance chores around the place, in addition to his regular job on one of the offshore oil rigs.

As soon as Phyllis came into the kitchen, Carolyn turned toward her and said, "Phyllis," just as Consuela was saying, "Señora Newsom."

Phyllis held up the hand that wasn't holding her coffee cup to ward off both of them. "Whatever this is, you'll have to settle it among yourselves," she told them.

"But Señora Gadsden left you in charge, Señora Newsom," Consuela protested. "It is up to you to decide how things are done."

"That's right, Phyllis," Carolyn said.

"I'm sorry. I have more pressing business right now." Carolyn frowned. "What?"

"I'm going fishing."

With that, she set her empty cup on the counter and left the kitchen as quickly as she could.

She decided that she was dressed all right to go out onto the pier with Sam, in a pair of jeans with the legs rolled up just under her knees, some canvas shoes, and an untucked, light blue, long-sleeved shirt with the sleeves rolled up a couple of turns so she could get some sun on her forearms. She went into Dorothy's room and rummaged around in her cousin's closet—which Dorothy had given her permission to do—until she found a cloth hat that she pulled down over her short graying brown hair.

She went downstairs, figuring that she would avoid the kitchen and wait for Sam out on the porch. As she went through the living room she looked through the arched opening that led into the dining room and saw that several people were already sitting at the long mahogany table. She thought she ought to at least speak to them, so she stepped into the dining room to say good morning.

Bed-and-breakfasts were popular with couples, and there were three of them at the table this morning. With the ease that came from years and years of learning the names of the children in her classes, Phyllis already knew all of them. Nick and Kate Thompson were the youngest guests, in their mid-twenties and married less than a year. The other two couples, Leo and Jessica Blaine and Sheldon and Raquel Forrest, were in their forties, with an ease around one another that showed they were longtime friends. From what Phyllis had heard, they had been coming here for a couple of weeks every autumn for more than a decade.

Phyllis chatted briefly with them. Stocky, redheaded Leo Blaine grinned and said, "You look like you're going fishing, Mrs. Newsom."

"That's right. I'm going to watch my friend Sam fish, anyway. I'm afraid I wouldn't know what to do if I actually hooked a fish."

"You'd figure it out," Sheldon Forrest said. He was tall and somewhat gawky, unlike Sam, who moved with a certain grace despite his size. "Fishing is an instinct. Mankind has been doing it for thousands of years."

"Maybe so," Phyllis said, "but *I* haven't."

She went out onto the porch and found that Sam was already there. He had the same sort of equipment that Ed McKenna had been carrying earlier, plus a big plastic bucket. "For that big red drum I'm gonna catch," he explained.

"You're a man with confidence."

"Might as well be. Otherwise you're halfway to being beat before you start."

There were a few clouds along the horizon, but the sun was well above them by now. The air was starting to get warm. A slight breeze blew, but not enough to disturb the water much. It rose and fell some, but only with the natural rhythm of the sea.

"Is this good fishing weather?" Phyllis asked as they started out along the pier. It had a railing on the right side and a shorter wall on the left where people could sit to fish if they wanted to. Phyllis wasn't crazy about piers, especially the ones where the planks had gaps between them where the water was visible. The Oak Knoll private pier was sturdy and well built, though, so she wasn't particularly nervous.

"Any weather is good fishin' weather if you don't care that much about catching keepers," Sam replied.

"You don't want to keep what you catch?"

"Only if it's something really good, like that red I mentioned. Otherwise I'd rather just reel 'em in, take 'em off the hook, and throw 'em back. As far as I'm concerned, the fun's in the catchin', not in the cleanin' and cookin'. In the eyes of some people, that would disqualify me from bein' a real fisherman ... but I don't particularly care."

Phyllis thought that was a very sensible attitude. She had cleaned fish before. She didn't care for it.

"There's Mr. McKenna," she said, nodding to the hunched figure of Ed McKenna, who sat on the wall to the left side of the pier about five hundred feet offshore. That was approximately halfway out.

"We'll go on past him," Sam said. "You don't want to crowd another fisherman."

That sounded reasonable to Phyllis. "Should we be as quiet as possible?"

"No, that's not necessary. You don't want to go hollerin' and scarin' off the fish, but it's all right to say howdy and ask how they're bitin'."

"You must've fished a lot." Phyllis had known Sam for more than a year, ever since he had moved into the house as a boarder the summer of the Peach Festival murder, but there was still a lot about him she didn't know.

He shook his head. "Nah. Strictly amateur. Mostly lake fishin'. But I've done a little saltwater fishin' like this, too."

They were drawing nearer to Ed McKenna, who hadn't looked around at them even though he must have heard their footsteps on the wooden pier. He was staring out at the water with a fixed expression, obviously intent on his fishing. He wasn't turning the handle on his reel, Phyllis noticed, which struck her as a little strange, but maybe that was some special fishing technique she didn't know anything about.

As they came even with McKenna, Sam paused and

reached down to give the man a friendly slap on the shoulder. "Gettin' any bites?" he asked.

McKenna didn't answer.

Instead, he pitched forward face-first into the water.

Phyllis was so shocked that for a moment all she could do was stand there staring at the ripples spreading out violently from the place where McKenna had vanished beneath the surface with a giant splash. Then her instincts kicked in and she realized that someone should jump in and help the poor man. She started to kick off her shoes.

Sam was already in motion, though. He had dropped his fishing equipment and toed the sneakers off his feet. He sat down on the wall, swung his legs over it, and dropped feetfirst into the water, which was about four feet under the pier. He entered the water carefully because he didn't know how deep it was right here, Phyllis realized.

Sam took a deep breath and went all the way under as Phyllis leaned over the side, resting her hands on the wall. She watched the surface anxiously as she waited for him to reappear. Fear welled up inside her. She was glad that Sam had gone in to help McKenna, but she didn't want anything to happen to him. There might be all sorts of things in that water, like jagged rocks or stingrays or even sharks . . .

With another big splash, Sam broke the surface. He had one arm around Ed McKenna's body, looped under his arms to hold him up. Sam waved his other hand toward the shore and called, "I'm takin' him in!"

That made sense. He couldn't lift McKenna to the pier from where he was. Carrying Sam's sneakers, Phyllis trotted along the pier. She kept pace as Sam swam strongly toward shore, towing McKenna as he went.

From what Phyllis could see of McKenna's face, the man didn't look good. He hadn't been under the water all that long, probably less than a minute in all. A person couldn't drown in that short a time, could they?

Phyllis got to the end of the pier and jumped down to the narrow, reedy beach. She dropped Sam's sneakers and waded into the water, heedless of her own shoes and blue jeans, and leaned down to grab McKenna and help Sam haul him out of the water. A shudder went through her as she saw the man's gray, lifeless face.

"My God, Sam!" she said as he climbed out. Water streamed from his clothes and body. "Mr. McKenna's dead. He must have drowned right away."

Sam pawed his soaked hair back and shook his head. "Nobody drowns that fast. Did you see the way he went in? He was just balanced there on the wall, waiting for somebody like me to come along and knock him in."

"You mean . . . ?"

Sam nodded. "He was dead when he went into the water."

Chapter 2

A heart attack. That was Phyllis's first thought. The poor man must have been sitting there fishing when the crushing pain hit him. That was why he had been sort of hunched over when Sam came along and gave him that friendly slap on the shoulder.

Ed McKenna had died doing what he loved, she told herself.

Then she realized immediately that she didn't know that at all. She had met him only three days earlier and hadn't exchanged more than a few dozen words with him since then. Even though he spent a lot of time fishing, she had no idea if he loved it or not.

Sam leaned over and put his hands on his knees as he took several deep breaths. His face was somewhat gray, too, though he didn't look nearly as bad as Mr. McKenna, of course.

Phyllis put a hand on his arm and said, "Sam, are you all right? You don't look very good."

"Not as young as I used to be," he said. "Never was a great swimmer, either. That was a pretty long haul, towin' him in like that."

"You need to sit down and catch your breath," she told him as she led him toward several wooden benches that were set back a short distance from the water on the grass between the road and the shore. Some people tried to fish from those benches, but mostly they were just for sitting and looking at the Gulf.

"What about McKenna?"

Phyllis glanced at the man's body and tried not to shudder again. "He's not going anywhere," she said. "Right now I'm worried about you."

It was odd, she thought as she sat on the bench beside Sam, who leaned forward and hung his forearms between his knees as he drew in deep breaths. A half mile or so from shore, a couple of shrimp boats were heading in with their morning's catch. Most of the shrimpers went out early, well before dawn. Even farther off shore an oil tanker made its stately way. And closer, a small boat with a couple of fishermen in it puttered along. Cars passed by on the road.

All around them, life went on as if nothing had happened, and yet only a few yards away Mr. McKenna lay, gray-faced and lifeless, his passing unnoticed by everyone except Phyllis and Sam. If they hadn't come along when they did, he might have sat there on the pier all morning without anyone realizing that he was dead. Odd, Phyllis thought, and more than a little sad.

After a minute Sam straightened up on the bench. His voice sounded stronger as he asked, "You got your cell phone with you?"

"No, I left it inside. What about you?"

"Nope, and even if I did, it probably wouldn't work after I jumped in the water that way."

"I hadn't thought about that. I'll go inside and call 911." She started to get up, then hesitated. "I guess we can't just leave him here alone. . . ."

"Don't worry. I'll stay with him," Sam said. "Let's face it. He's not much worse company now than when he was alive."

"Sam!"

"I'm just sayin', ol' Ed wasn't a fella you'd warm up to in a hurry."

That was true, but Phyllis didn't think it really needed to be said, at least not at a time like this.

"I'll be back as fast as I can," she told Sam as she started across the street toward the bed-and-breakfast.

Nick and Kate Thompson were coming out the front door onto the porch as Phyllis started up the steps. They must have been able to tell from her expression that something was wrong, because a worried frown appeared on Kate's pretty face and Nick said, "What is it, Mrs. Newsom? Are you all right?"

They were a nice-looking couple, Nick with a friendly, open face and curly dark brown hair, Kate a brunette, as well, with hair a couple of shades lighter than her husband's and what some might call sultry, even exotic good looks. She was also a couple of inches taller than Nick, and while Phyllis knew there wasn't a thing in the world wrong with that, to someone of her generation it still seemed a little odd to see a wife who was taller than her husband.

She had no idea what they did for a living, but they drove an expensive little sports car so she assumed they were lawyers or something like that. Doctors, maybe. They were certainly solicitous as they moved forward on either side of her. Kate reached out and touched her arm supportively.

"It's Mr. McKenna," Phyllis said.

"That grumpy old guy who never talks to anybody?" Nick asked. "What about him?"

There was no easy way to say it. "He's dead."

The eyes of both young people widened with surprise. "Dead?" Kate repeated.

Without saying anything, Phyllis waved a hand toward the benches and the grassy area across the street, next to the water.

"Good Lord!" Nick said. "What happened? Did he fall in and drown?"

Kate asked, "Is that Mr. Fletcher sitting there? Is he okay?"

"He's just winded from pulling Mr. McKenna out of the water." Phyllis turned to Nick. "But he didn't drown. Sam and I think he must have had a heart attack. I suppose the police and the medical examiner will have to determine that."

"Have you called the cops?" Nick asked.

"No, I was just on my way to do that."

Nick took her arm and steered her toward the front door. "Why don't you let me call them?" he suggested. "Kate, take Mrs. Newsom into the parlor and sit down with her. No offense, Mrs. Newsom, but you look a little green around the gills."

"I *feel* a little green," Phyllis admitted. "I told Sam I'd be right back, though . . ."

"I'll go over there and wait for the cops with him," Nick said as he reached into one of the big pockets of his khaki cargo shorts and pulled out a cell phone. He flipped it open, punched in the three-digit emergency number, and as Phyllis went into the house with Kate she heard him saying in a brisk voice, "Yes, we need the police and an ambulance. I believe a man here has died of a heart attack." He was giving the address as the door closed behind Phyllis and Kate.

The big parlor/living room was empty. Kate took Phyllis over to one of the comfortably upholstered sofas and sat her down. "Can I get you something?" she asked. "A cup of coffee, maybe?"

Phyllis nodded. "That would be nice. Thank you, dear."

Kate hurried out of the room. Phyllis took Dorothy's hat off and placed it on the sofa cushion beside her, then closed her eyes and rubbed her temples. You didn't get to be her age without becoming well acquainted with death. It stalked friends and family and collected its inevitable toll.

And yet it was still shocking when it happened unexpectedly, even to someone you didn't know that well, like Ed McKenna. She had seen too much unexpected death in recent years, Phyllis thought.

Hurried footsteps sounded nearby. Phyllis opened her eyes and looked up as Carolyn and Eve came into the room. "Don't tell me you've stumbled over *another* dead body, Phyllis!" Carolyn said with her characteristic bluntness.

"Carolyn!" Eve said. "That's hardly comforting." She added to Phyllis, "You *do* seem to have a way of finding them, though, dear."

They sat down on either side of her. Eve patted her hand. Phyllis said, "I suppose Kate told you what happened."

Carolyn nodded. "She said you and Sam fished Ed McKenna's body out of the water. What happened to him?"

"A heart attack, I suppose," Phyllis said for what already seemed like the dozenth time, even though she knew it wasn't, of course. "Or possibly a stroke."

"That man looked like a candidate for a heart attack," Carolyn said. "Always with a sour look on his face and not a good word for anybody. You could tell he was in poor health."

Phyllis hadn't gotten that impression of Ed McKenna. He wasn't friendly, true, but he had seemed to be healthy enough. You couldn't always tell by looking at someone, though. She recalled numerous cases over the years of even professional athletes dropping dead unexpectedly from some undiagnosed, unsuspected ailment.

Kate Thompson came back into the room carrying a cup from which tendrils of steam and an enticing aroma rose. "Here you are," she said as she handed it to Phyllis. "I've seen you fixing your coffee before, so I know you like it with cream and a little sugar."

"Thank you so much." Phyllis took a sip of the hot brew and was grateful for the bracing effect of it.

Consuela and her two daughters followed Kate into

the parlor, all of them wearing concerned expressions. Theresa was in her early twenties, Bianca only eighteen. They crowded around the sofa, Consuela asking, "You are all right, Mrs. Newsom?"

"I'm fine," Phyllis said. "I'm a lot more worried about Sam than about me."

"You should get those wet shoes off," Carolyn said. "That can't be good for you, wearing wet shoes."

Leo and Jessica Blaine started through the foyer, just outside the arched entrance to the parlor, but they stopped when they saw everyone gathered on and around the sofa. "Something wrong?" Leo called.

"Mr. McKenna died of a heart attack," Carolyn said.

"You're kidding!" Leo said as he and his wife came into the room. He went on immediately, "No, of course you're not. Nobody would kid about a thing like that. This is terrible. You're sure he's dead?"

Eve said, "Phyllis and Sam pulled him out of the water. They got a good look at him."

"But if he was in the water, couldn't he have drowned?" Jessica asked.

"Who drowned?" That question came from Raquel Forrest, who walked into the parlor with her husband, Sheldon, right behind the Blaines. The two couples had probably been on their way to get an early start on some shopping in Rockport. That was how they spent most of their time, prowling through the numerous seashell shops, antiques shops, and art galleries that lined the streets of the picturesque Gulf-side town.

"He didn't drown," Carolyn said. "He died of a heart attack. Or a stroke."

"Who?" Raquel asked again.

"McKenna," Leo told her. "You know, the old guy who fished all the time."

"Really? That's awful!"

Phyllis was starting to feel a little claustrophobic with so many people bunched around her. She wished they would back off a little. But they were just concerned and upset about Mr. McKenna's death, so she couldn't very well fuss at them.

The sudden wail of a siren outside did the trick. The five guests and the Anselmo women all went to the parlor's front windows to look out, leaving Phyllis on the sofa with Carolyn and Eve. Phyllis drew in a deep breath and then took another sip of the coffee.

"The police are here," Sheldon Forrest announced. "And here comes an ambulance, too."

Phyllis stood up. "I need to go back out there," she said. "I was there when it happened, so I'm sure the police will want to talk to me."

Her son, Mike, was a sheriff's deputy up in Weatherford, so she probably knew more about police procedure than most retired history teachers. Throw in the experience she'd had with murder cases and she knew more than she had ever wanted to about how the authorities investigate suspicious deaths. Thankfully, in this case there didn't seem to be anything suspicious about Ed McKenna's death, only sad and a little tragic.

Carolyn was on her feet, too. "You just sit right back down and let them come to you if they want to talk to you," she told Phyllis. "All this excitement isn't good for a person."

"Nonsense. Like I said, I'm fine." Phyllis set her coffee cup on a coaster that rested on a nice antique end table. She started toward the door.

"I'll come with you," Kate offered.

"Let's all go," Leo suggested. His voice held a slightly festive tone, almost as if he welcomed the excitement of Mr. McKenna's death. Phyllis told herself not to think too badly of him for that. After all, it wasn't like they had been close friends. Mr. McKenna hadn't socialized with the other guests at all.

With Phyllis in the lead, everyone trooped out onto the porch. She glanced up and down the road and saw that several cars had stopped to see what was going on, their drivers' attention caught by the flashing lights of the ambulance and police car. People had come out of the other houses along the road, too, drawn by the sound of the sirens.

Phyllis saw Sam standing beside the bench talking to a tall, white-haired man in khaki uniform trousers and shirt. A few yards away the EMTs who had arrived with the ambulance were kneeling next to Mr. McKenna's body, checking it out to make sure he was dead. That was standard procedure, Phyllis knew, but in this case they weren't going to discover anything that she didn't already know just by looking at the gray, lifeless face.

Another officer stood beside the patrol car's open passenger door, talking into a corded microphone she had taken from inside the vehicle. She was an attractive woman in her thirties with reddish blond hair pulled back into a ponytail. As Phyllis approached, she reached into the car to replace the microphone on its holder, then said, "Mrs. Newsom?"

Phyllis nodded. "That's right."

"I'm Abby Clifton, assistant chief of police. I hear that you were with Mr. Fletcher when he discovered Mr. McKenna's body."

"I was there, but we didn't *discover* it so much as . . . Well, I don't know what you'd call it."

Abby Clifton nodded and said, "Let's go over here and talk about it."

Carolyn and Eve started to follow as Abby led Phyllis toward the pier, away from the crowd. Abby looked back at them and said, "I need to talk to Mrs. Newsom alone, please, ladies."

Her tone was polite but at the same time firm enough to indicate that she wouldn't put up with any argument. Carolyn frowned but didn't say anything. In the past Carolyn had had troubles of her own with law enforcement, Phyllis recalled, so she was always a little suspicious of police officers.

Even without being told to stay back, none of the crowd got too close to the body and the EMTs working on it. They just stood by and looked on with the mixture of horror and curiosity that the sight of a dead body always evoked in people who weren't close to the person who had died. Phyllis knew it was a natural reaction. She had been guilty of it herself.

She and Abby Clifton stepped out a few feet onto the pier. Abby said, "Just tell me what happened."

Phyllis knew why they were doing it this way. They wanted to get her story and Sam's story separately, to make sure that they matched up. It was ridiculous, of course, to think they would have any reason to lie about what happened, but Phyllis knew that if Mike were here, he would tell her not to worry about it, that the officers were just going by the book.

It didn't take long to tell Abby Clifton about it. The young woman listened in silence for the most part, asking only a couple of questions to clarify Phyllis's connection to the owners of the bed-and-breakfast and why she and her friends were staying there. Abby didn't take any notes, but Phyllis had a feeling that she wouldn't forget anything she was told.

When Phyllis was finished, Abby nodded and said, "Thank you. You said that Mr. Fletcher slapped Mr. McKenna on the shoulder?"

"Yes, but it wasn't a *hard* slap or anything like that. More like a friendly pat."

"But it was enough to knock Mr. McKenna into the water."

"It wouldn't have been if he hadn't already been dead. He was hunched forward, and I'm sure he would have toppled on into the water sooner or later on his own, if we hadn't come along."

"But you don't know for certain that he *was* dead at that time," Abby said. "Maybe he'd had a heart attack, just like you supposed, but was still alive until he was knocked into the water."

"Sam didn't actually knock him into the water." Phyllis frowned. It sounded almost like this woman was trying to blame Sam for Mr. McKenna's death, when in reality Sam had done everything he could to help the man. He'd just been too late, that was all.

"Well, I'm sure the autopsy will give us the answers we need." Abby smiled again. "You'll have to come down to the police department and sign a statement."

Phyllis nodded. "Of course. I understand. My son is a deputy in our hometown."

"Really? Then you know something about police work."

"A little," Phyllis said.

She wondered if she ought to mention that she had also been involved in four murders and an attempted murder.

Probably not, she decided. Not unless someone asked her about them. Thank goodness this wasn't anything like that!

Chapter 3

$\mathcal{B}$y this time the white-haired officer had finished talking to Sam, who had moved over to stand well out of the way with Carolyn, Eve, and the guests and employees from the bed-and-breakfast. The EMTs had covered Ed McKenna's body with a rubber sheet and moved back as well. Clearly, they had determined that he was indeed dead, but they were waiting on the medical examiner to make the official pronouncement.

"That policewoman give you the third degree?" Sam asked as Phyllis came up to him.

"She just wanted to know what happened." Phyllis hesitated. She didn't want to worry Sam, but she thought he ought to know about some of the questions Abby Clifton had asked. "She seemed to think that maybe Mr. McKenna was alive when he went into the water."

Sam's somewhat bushy eyebrows rose in surprise. "You mean she thinks I knocked him in on purpose and drowned him?"

"Oh, no," Phyllis said. "She didn't seem to doubt that he had a heart attack or something like that, but she just thought that maybe he hadn't died yet when we came along."

"I reckon that's possible." Sam shook his head. "Doesn't seem likely to me, though."

It didn't to Phyllis, either, and she was confident the autopsy results would confirm that Mr. McKenna had been dead when he toppled into the water. She didn't see how anybody could blame Sam for anything. He'd just been trying to be friendly.

The white-haired man was talking to Abby Clifton now. Phyllis leaned closer to Sam's shoulder and asked him, "Who's that?"

"The local chief of police. Name's Dale Clifton, he said."

"Really?" Phyllis wondered if he was related to Abby. It seemed too great a coincidence to be otherwise, and as she looked at the two of them standing together, she thought she saw a family resemblance. She guessed that the chief was Abby's father, or at least her uncle.

"Yeah," Sam said, "evidently this is a pretty quiet little town, so when a body gets fished out of the water, the chief himself comes to investigate."

The Blaines and the Forrests were standing close by. Leo Blaine said, "This place is quiet, all right, at this time of year. It's a lot busier during the summer. That's why Jess and I started coming in the fall with Shel and Raquel. They told us how nice it is now."

"But it can still get crowded on the weekends, even in the fall," his wife put in. "Especially on SeaFair weekend."

That was coming up in several more days, Phyllis reminded herself. She still had to figure out exactly what she was going to make for the dessert competition. Carolyn probably had her recipe already worked out to the last detail.

A white SUV with a flashing light on its roof but no siren came along the road and pulled off to the side near the benches and the pier. A man got out and spoke to Chief Clifton for a moment, then knelt beside the body and pulled back the rubber sheet. He had to be the medical examiner. After making a cursory examination, he stood and nodded to the EMTs, who moved in with a gurney and a body bag. Phyllis turned her head, not wanting to see the slackness of the corpse as it was placed in the black plastic bag.

Chief Dale Clifton came over to the group of bystanders, trailed by Abby. He had the tanned, weathered face of a man who spent a lot of time outdoors, and Phyllis wondered how much of the white hair was due to age and how much to being faded by the sun. He looked around at them and asked, "Did any of you folks happen to see anything unusual this morning? Other than Mr. Fletcher and Ms. Newsom, I mean."

Phyllis wanted to point out that she and Sam weren't all that unusual, but then she realized what the chief meant. Everyone else must have, too, because they all shook their heads.

"My wife and I were in the house," Nick Thompson said. "We didn't even see Mr. McKenna leave this morning. He goes out to fish before we get up."

"All he *does* is fish," Kate added. Then she caught her bottom lip between her teeth for a second before adding, "I mean, all he did was fish."

Clifton nodded. "Everybody else was inside, too?"

"My daughters and I were working," Consuela said. "I was in the kitchen; the girls were upstairs."

Clifton smiled at her. "How's Tom these days?" he asked. Obviously, he knew the Anselmo family. "Haven't seen him for a while."

"He's fine," Consuela said. Phyllis thought she looked and sounded a little nervous. Some people got like that around the law, whether they had anything to hide or not.

"We were all at breakfast," Leo said, making a vague gesture that took in himself, Jessica, and the Forrests.

Clifton turned to Carolyn and Eve. "What about you ladies?"

Phyllis stepped forward and said, "These are my friends, Mrs. Wilbarger and Mrs. Turner. They came down with Mr. Fletcher and me."

"I see."

"We didn't see anything," Carolyn said. "I was in the kitchen with Consuela."

"And I was in my room putting my face on for the day," Eve added. She gave the chief a bright smile. She had an eye for any eligible bachelor of a certain age, and Phyllis would have been willing to bet money that Eve had already noticed the absence of a wedding ring on Chief Clifton's hand.

"All right, then," the chief said. "We'll canvass the other people who live along this stretch of road, but it seems pretty cut-and-dried to me. I expect the autopsy will show Mr. McKenna died of natural causes. I'm sorry you folks had to go through all this uproar so early in the day. I hope it doesn't spoil the rest of your stay."

He was dismissing them, Phyllis realized. Telling them to go on about their business, only being polite about it. The EMTs were loading the body in the ambulance now, the medical examiner was getting back in his SUV, and in a minute the two police officers would get back in their patrol car and leave. There was nothing more to see.

They turned and began making their way back across the road, straggling out into smaller groups. The Forrests and the Blaines walked together, as did Consuela, Theresa, and Bianca and the four friends from Weatherford. Nick and Kate were the only ones walking alone, talking quietly to each other.

Phyllis paused on the porch to watch the ambulance pull away, followed by the police car. No lights or sirens now on either vehicle. There was no hurry.

Sam lingered with her. "Darned shame," he said. "I don't reckon Ed and I would've ever been buddies, but I hate to see somebody go like that, all sudden and unexpected-like."

"Yes, but he was doing something he enjoyed. At least, I hope he enjoyed fishing. Why else would he do it?"

"Yeah, there's that." Sam paused. "I've given considerable thought to how I'd like to go."

"Sam!" she said. "How morbid."

"Nah, just realistic. I don't care much how it happens, just so it's quick."

Phyllis knew that Sam's late wife had died of cancer, a slow and painful passing that must have been hell for Sam to watch, helpless to do anything about it. She understood why he felt the way he did. He didn't want to put anyone else through what he had endured.

Right now, though, Phyllis had thought about death enough for one morning. She had a pressing problem of her own. The soaked shoes and socks she had been wearing for the past hour had made her feet cold, clammy, and uncomfortable.

"Well, I'm not going anywhere," she said, "except upstairs to soak my feet in a pan of hot water."

Phyllis didn't come back down for an hour. When she did, she felt better, although she was still somewhat shaken by the morning's experience. She found Carolyn in the kitchen, looking through the cabinets. The way Carolyn quickly closed the cabinet door she was holding open told Phyllis that her friend had been checking to see what ingredients Consuela had on hand. Just as Phyllis had suspected, Carolyn was thinking about the Just Desserts contest.

Phyllis didn't let on that she had figured that out. Instead she said, "Where's Consuela?"

"Gone to the store, I believe she said."

There was a giant Wal-Mart about a mile away on the main highway through Rockport. Phyllis had gone in it once and realized that it was laid out almost exactly like the one where she shopped in Weatherford. If they ever opened Wal-Marts in Moscow or Peking—and for all she knew there was already one in both of those places—they would look just like the ones in Texas.

"I should probably do some shopping myself," she said. That ought to get Carolyn thinking. She hoped her friend would assume that she already knew exactly what she was doing for the competition. Their rivalry was a friendly one, but neither of them was above a little psychological warfare, even though Phyllis knew that was a ridiculous term to use in conjunction with a cooking contest where nothing was at stake other than a ribbon or a cheap trophy or some bragging rights.

She went on. "Where's everyone else?"

"Sam went out on the pier to fish. He said he'd left all his gear out there, so he might as well use it."

Phyllis nodded. If it had been her, she probably would have lost all desire to fish after what had happened, but Sam was made of stronger stuff . . . or at least he was more pragmatic. The fact that Ed McKenna had died on that pier wouldn't keep Sam from fishing.

"Eve said she was going to walk down to that shop across from the boat basin," Carolyn went on. "She asked me to come with her, but I was too busy."

"Doing what?"

"Oh, this and that." Carolyn evaded the question, convincing Phyllis more than ever that her friend had been working on her recipe for the contest. Carolyn hurried on. "And don't ask me about that young couple, because they went back upstairs. I imagine they're doing what *they* do all the time."

Phyllis couldn't help but smile. "They've been married less than a year, they said. Technically, they're still newlyweds."

"Maybe so, but they could show a little restraint. There are other things in life, you know."

"Of course there are."

Before that discussion could go any further, the doorbell rang. Phyllis turned and went toward the foyer. She heard footsteps on the stairs and glanced up to see Theresa Anselmo starting down.

"If you're coming to answer the door," Phyllis said, "I'll get it."

"All right, Mrs. Newsom." Theresa went back upstairs.

Phyllis opened the front door and found a heavyset, middle-aged woman with short, curly brown hair waiting on the porch. The woman smiled and said, "Hi. I'm Darcy Maxwell, from next door."

Phyllis recognized her. They had nodded to each other several times without speaking in the past few days since Phyllis and her friends had gotten here.

"Of course," Phyllis said. "Won't you come in?" She stepped back and held the door.

Darcy Maxwell stepped into the house. She wore a short-sleeved blouse and capri pants, which was still suitable attire for the weather in this area during October, at least most of the time.

"I'm Phyllis Newsom," Phyllis introduced herself. "Dorothy's cousin."

Darcy nodded. "I know. Before she left Dorothy told me you were coming down to keep an eye on things while she was gone."

"I'm not sure that was even necessary," Phyllis said as she ushered the visitor into the parlor. "Consuela is so efficient, I'm sure she could have kept everything running just fine without any help."

Darcy laughed. "You don't have to tell me! I would have hired Consuela away from Dorothy years ago if she'd any interest in changing jobs. She's too loyal to do that, though."

Phyllis motioned for Darcy to have a seat on the sofa and offered a cup of coffee or something else to drink, which the woman refused politely. Then Phyllis asked, "Is your house a bed-and-breakfast, too?"

"Oh, no. It's just a private residence. But it's a big

place, too big for me to keep up with on my own. It was different when my kids were at home, but since they've moved out . . ." Darcy shrugged.

It was a feeling Phyllis knew all too well. During that interval after Kenny had died, before she opened the big old house in Weatherford to other retired teachers, she had thought she might go mad knocking around by herself in the empty home.

"Anyway," Darcy went on, "the reason I came over, other than to be neighborly and introduce myself—"

"Was to find out what happened this morning," Phyllis finished for her. She saw the slightly startled look on Darcy's face and hurried on. "I'm sorry. I shouldn't have interrupted you that way. It was rude of me. And after all those years I got on to my students for interrupting one another."

"You're a teacher?"

"I was. Eighth-grade history. But I'm retired now."

Darcy seemed to accept Phyllis's apology. "I admit, I'm curious about what happened. I know the ambulance came and took someone away, and I heard that a man who was staying here had died."

Phyllis nodded. "Mr. McKenna. He had a heart attack while he was out on the pier fishing." She didn't go into detail about how Ed McKenna had fallen into the water and Sam had hauled him out.

"How terrible!" Darcy said. "That poor man."

"Yes, it's a tragedy," Phyllis agreed.

"Did he have family here with him?"

Phyllis shook her head. "No, he was alone."

But he had to have family somewhere, she thought, and that reminded her of the fact that they would need to be notified of his death. Surely the police would handle that, though. That wasn't something she should have to deal with . . . she hoped.

"Is there anything I can do to help?"

"I don't know what it would be," Phyllis said. "Once I've found out about Mr. McKenna's next of kin, I suppose I'll have to gather his belongings and send them. But other than that, I don't think there's anything else I'll need to do."

Before she could say anything else, she heard the back door open and close, and then Consuela's voice sounded in the kitchen, talking to Carolyn.

Darcy got to her feet quickly and said, "I'd better be going. It was nice to meet you, Mrs. Newsom."

"Please, call me Phyllis."

"And I'm sorry about what happened. It must have been terrible for you."

Much worse for Ed McKenna, Phyllis thought, but she kept that to herself. She had already been rude to Darcy once—although that hadn't been her intention—and she didn't want to do it again.

She showed Darcy out, lifting a hand in farewell as the woman walked down the steps. Then she turned and went back along the hall to the kitchen.

Consuela was putting away the groceries she had brought back from Wal-Mart. Carolyn wasn't in the kitchen now, and Phyllis supposed she must have gone up the rear stairs just off the pantry.

"Mrs. Wilbarger said somebody was here," Consuela said.

"Yes, Darcy Maxwell from next door."

Consuela made a face. "Her."

"You don't like her?" Phyllis asked with a frown. "She seemed nice enough, and she spoke very highly of you."

Consuela shrugged and said, "She's all right, I guess. She's just the biggest gossip between here and Corpus Christi. She offered me a job once, and when I turned her down she spread some nasty stories about my girls." Consuela's expression hardened. "You could say I don't like her, all right. I'm glad she's not gonna be next door much longer."

"Why not?"

"Oh, she and her husband sold their house. That's

what I heard, anyway. They said it was too big for them with their kids gone. I don't know when they're supposed to move out, but it probably won't be much longer ... I hope."

"Well, maybe whoever bought the place will be better neighbors."

"Yeah, maybe."

The conversation had roused Phyllis's curiosity. She asked, "What about the house on the other side? I don't recall seeing anybody over there since we've been here."

"That's because it's vacant. The couple who owned it died in a car wreck about six months ago."

"How awful."

"Yeah, and they were pretty good friends with Dorothy and Ben, too. A real shame."

"You don't think about bad things happening in a place as pretty as this," Phyllis mused. "But I'm sure they do, just like they happen everywhere else."

"Yeah, you can't get away from trouble. It follows people wherever they go." Consuela's mouth twisted in a little quirk as she spoke, and the words had a slightly bitter tone to them. She sounded like *she* had been followed by trouble of her own, Phyllis thought, and plenty of it. She didn't recall Dorothy ever saying anything about that, though, and she certainly wasn't going to pry. Whatever went on in Consuela's personal life was private and none of Phyllis's business.

"Well, there ought to be places that are immune to trouble and pain," she said.

"There's one," Consuela said. She made the sign of the cross. "And poor Mr. McKenna's gone there now."

Chapter 4

Not surprisingly, a reporter from the local newspaper showed up before noon. Chief Clifton hadn't said anything about not talking to the press, so Phyllis ushered the woman into the parlor intending to answer all her questions. Sam had just gotten back from fishing, so he spoke to the reporter, too, telling her with a rather sheepish look on his face about slapping Ed McKenna on the shoulder just before the man fell forward into the water.

"Do you feel like you had anything to do with Mr. McKenna's death because of that?" the woman asked.

Phyllis responded before Sam could say anything. "He most certainly did not! Sam was just being friendly. He didn't push Mr. McKenna or anything like that. Anyway, I'm convinced that Mr. McKenna was already dead when Sam and I walked out on the pier."

"Isn't that up to the medical examiner to determine?"

"Sure it is," Sam said quickly, and Phyllis wondered if he had noticed that she was about to lose her patience with the reporter. It would be just like Sam to try to smooth things over, even if the woman *was* asking ridiculous questions. "We'll just wait and let the proper authorities do their jobs."

"Have you retained a lawyer?"

"Don't need one," Sam replied as he shot a glance in Phyllis's direction. "I haven't done anything wrong."

"He certainly hasn't," Phyllis said.

"Just a couple more questions . . ."

Phyllis felt like telling the reporter what she could do with her questions, but she reminded herself that Dorothy and Ben still had to live here and run a business here. She didn't want to do anything that would create enemies for them.

So somehow she managed to put a smile on her face and said, "Of course."

"This isn't the first suspicious death you've been involved with, is it, Mrs. Newsom?"

The question took Phyllis by surprise, and now it was Sam's turn to begin getting annoyed by the reporter.

"How'd you know about that?" he asked.

"They have this thing called the Internet." The woman gave him an insufferably smug smile, then turned to Phyllis again. "I Googled you, Mrs. Newsom."

Phyllis never had gotten used to the sound of that expression.

"I found out that you've stumbled over dead bodies on several occasions besides this one. You've even been given credit by the authorities for solving some murders."

There was no point in denying anything, Phyllis told herself, especially in this day and age when practically everything about a person's life was out there on the Internet for anyone to see. She said, "I'm sure you've read the stories from the Weatherford and Fort Worth newspapers. You know what happened at the Peach Festival."

"And the school carnival and the Christmas party. It's almost like you're some sort of jinx, Mrs. Newsom."

Sam said, "That's just crazy. I was at those places, too,

and so were a bunch of other people. Phyllis didn't have anything to do with those folks gettin' killed, and if it hadn't been for her, the cops might not've ever figured out who *did* kill them!"

She wished he hadn't said that. She had never tried to imply that she had solved those murders when the police couldn't. She couldn't blame him for being upset with the pushy reporter, though. She wasn't too happy with the woman herself.

"There's really no need to go into all of this," Phyllis said. "Mr. McKenna wasn't murdered. I'm sure the medical examiner will confirm that he died of natural causes. It's an unfortunate situation—"

"Especially for Mr. McKenna," the reporter put in.

"But it's nothing like those other times," Phyllis went on determinedly. "Now, if you have all you need . . ."

The woman shrugged. "For now." She didn't protest as Phyllis led her to the front door and closed it behind her . . . maybe, just maybe, a little harder than was absolutely necessary.

When she came back to the parlor, Sam was shaking his head. "I reckon we shouldn't get too upset with the lady," he said. "I don't imagine it's every day that a fella drops dead on a fishin' pier around here."

"I suppose not." Phyllis paused. "Thank you for defending me."

"Hey, you were stickin' up for me, too." He grinned. "We make a pretty good team."

"I think so," Phyllis agreed. She sighed. "I have to get back to thinking about my entry for the contest. It's only a few days away, you know."

"I know. I'm not likely to forget a dessert contest. Accordin' to the paper, they're having a gumbo cook-off, too. And funnel cakes." He licked his lips in anticipation and looked so gleeful that Phyllis had to laugh.

"I know, you're going to spend all weekend gorging yourself."

"Maybe not the *whole* weekend . . ."

*   *   *

When Consuela had finished cleaning up after lunch, Phyllis found herself in the kitchen pondering her choices for the competition. Cookies, cakes, or pies? Or something a little more unusual? As far as she could see, there wasn't any way to make her entry relate to the coast. A pie was a pie was a pie, no matter where it was baked. And while, say, peaches adapted well to baked goods, nothing about the sea did. You couldn't make crab cookies!

And a crab cake wasn't the sort of cake you entered in a dessert competition, either, she told herself, although she loved a good crab cake. Consuela had made some for supper the night before, in fact, that had been delicious. Maybe, Phyllis mused, she could make a different sort of crab cake: a cake decorated with crabs made out of frosting . . .

The sound of the doorbell drove those thoughts out of her head. Consuela and her daughters had gone home for the afternoon. Consuela would return to prepare supper, but the younger women were finished with their cleaning for the day. The Forrests and the Blaines were out somewhere; Nick and Kate were upstairs "napping"— and maybe they really were, Phyllis told herself; and Eve and Carolyn had gone to check out some of the art galleries, dragging Sam along with them.

At one time, given the romantic interest that Eve had shown in Sam for months after he moved into the house in Weatherford, Phyllis might not have been too comfortable about letting them wander around art galleries together. But since the past Christmas, when she and Sam had finally admitted the attraction they felt toward each other, Eve had backed off and started treating him as a friend, rather than a potential husband number four . . . or was it five?

"You'll enjoy it, dear," Eve had told him as she patted his grizzled cheek. "I'm sure at least one place will have paintings of John Wayne and Elvis on black velvet."

"I can't wait," Sam had said with mock enthusiasm.

That left Phyllis to answer the door again. She hoped that this time it wouldn't be someone as annoying as that reporter had been.

There wasn't one person waiting on the porch; there were three: two men and one woman. All of them were in their forties, and Phyllis was surprised to see that the two men were twins, short, stocky men with sharp faces and sleek dark hair. She wasn't sure why them being twins surprised her. She'd had numerous pairs of twins in her classes, and they had to grow up into adults.

The woman had dark hair, too, and she looked enough like the two men for Phyllis to realize that they were all siblings. Not triplets, though. The woman appeared to be several years older.

"We're looking for Phyllis Newsom," she said.

"I'm Mrs. Newsom," Phyllis told them. "Can I help you?"

"My name is Frances Heaton," the woman said. "I'm Edward McKenna's daughter."

"Oh, Ms. Heaton, I'm so sorry about what happened—"

"These are my brothers, Oscar and Oliver McKenna." Frances Heaton's voice was brusque and businesslike as she broke in on Phyllis's attempt to convey her sympathy.

Phyllis nodded politely anyway as she said, "I'm pleased to meet all of you. I just wish it were under better circumstances."

As she spoke she was thinking that Oscar and Oliver had probably been teased unmercifully about their names and about being twins when they were growing up. Both of them had that long-suffering look.

"Please come in," Phyllis went on as she stepped back, holding the door. She motioned for the visitors to enter the foyer. When they had done so, she closed the front door and led them into the parlor. "Have a seat. Can I get you anything? Something to drink?"

Frances Heaton shook her head as the three of them sat on the sofa, her in the middle and her brothers flanking her. "We're here to collect our father's things."

"Of course. I really am sorry. I suppose the police notified you?"

"That's right. We drove down from San Antonio right away."

They must have left immediately after the phone call bearing the bad news, Phyllis thought. There had been time for them to make the drive from San Antonio, but just barely.

She felt like she ought to say something else. "I didn't know your father for very long, but he seemed like a very nice man—"

"He was an idiot," one of the brothers said.

"He would have to be to trust *you* to run the company," the other brother said.

"Stop it," Frances said. "He never should have put either one of you in charge, and you know it."

Phyllis sat there during the sharp exchange, trying not to look flabbergasted. Obviously, the McKenna siblings didn't get along well, and they didn't bother hiding it even in the presence of strangers, when most people would at least try to put up a facade of cordiality. The resentment and dislike between them had to run pretty deep, and from the sound of it they hadn't cared all that much for their father, either.

Frances turned her attention back to Phyllis. "Have you already gathered my father's belongings?"

Before Phyllis could answer, the brother on Frances's left said, "He was our father, too, you know."

"You always say *my father*, like he wasn't even related to us," the other brother said.

Frances made a noise that was halfway between a laugh and an angry grunt. "Sometimes I wonder," she said.

"That's a terrible thing to say!"

"Can't you at least be civil, at a time like this?"

The three of them sat there glaring at one another, with Frances's head swiveling back and forth like she was watching a tennis match . . . a tennis match she found very annoying.

Their bickering made Phyllis uncomfortable. She didn't like it when families fought, and the hostility among these three was evidently of long standing. She started to get to her feet, saying, "I'll go get Mr. McKenna's things together—"

"Before you do," one of the brothers said, causing Phyllis to sink back into the armchair where she'd been sitting, "I for one would like to hear exactly what happened. All the chief of police said when he reached me at the office was that my father had passed away unexpectedly."

"Now who's calling him *my* father?" Frances asked.

"It's just a figure of speech."

"So it's all right for you but not for me?"

Phyllis fought down the impulse to tell all three of them to behave—and to use her teacher voice to do it, too. Instead, hoping that they would stop arguing if she told them what they wanted to know, she said, "It appears that your father had a heart attack, or possibly a stroke, while he was fishing out on the pier early this morning."

"Who found him?" Frances asked.

For once her brothers kept quiet and allowed Phyllis to answer the question. "My friend Mr. Fletcher and I were the ones who discovered that Mr. McKenna had passed away. We were walking out to the end of the pier, and as we passed your father, he fell into the water."

"You mean he had the heart attack at that exact moment?" asked either Oscar or Oliver. Phyllis wondered if there was any easy way to tell them apart. She had seldom seen twins so identical.

"Well, no," she admitted in answer to the question. "He must have . . . died . . . a few minutes earlier. We didn't realize that until Mr. Fletcher slapped him on the shoulder . . . you know, just a friendly greeting from one fisherman to another . . . and Mr. McKenna sort of . . . toppled over."

"My God!" the other brother said. "You mean this guy Fletcher knocked Dad into the water?"

"It was an accident," Phyllis said, "and it didn't really make any difference because I'm sure your father had already passed away—"

"You can't know that," Frances said, suddenly leaning forward like a hound scenting something interesting. "For all we know, the two of you contributed to his death."

"Sounds to me like negligence," the brother on her right said.

"And a wrongful-death suit," the brother on Frances's left said.

That was all Phyllis could stand. Without even realizing how she had gotten there, she found herself on her feet, and as she glared at the visitors, she said, "Good heavens, what's *wrong* with you people? Your father just died, and all you can do is snipe at one another and threaten innocent people with lawsuits?"

Frances's chin lifted. "There's no need to get unpleasant, Mrs. Newsom. We just came here to retrieve our father's personal effects."

"All right. I'll get them."

Phyllis stalked out of the parlor. She wished someone else were here so that she wouldn't have to leave the three of them alone. They were all dressed in expensive clothing, so she didn't really expect them to steal anything, but with people so—so *annoying*!—you couldn't really tell what they might do.

She got the master key from the office and went upstairs. She assumed that the door of the room Ed McKenna had occupied was locked, but she didn't know that for sure. As far as she knew, no one had even tried the door.

She grasped the knob and twisted it. Sure enough, it didn't turn. McKenna hadn't struck her as the sort of man who would go off and leave his room where just anybody could walk into it. She used the key and went inside.

He didn't have much other than fishing equipment. An old suitcase that showed marks of long use stood empty in the closet. Several pairs of khaki pants were hung up along with some plain, long-sleeved blue shirts and white shirts. She found strictly functional boxer shorts and socks in one of the dresser drawers. Fishing outfits, Phyllis thought. McKenna hadn't needed anything else because he didn't do anything else while he was here.

He hadn't been a poor man, though. He could afford to stay at the bed-and-breakfast when there were cheaper places in Rockport and Fulton, and even though Phyllis didn't know much about fishing gear, she thought the half-dozen rods and reels leaning in a corner looked expensive. Sitting on the dresser was a spare tackle box fully loaded with what appeared to be every variety of lure and hook ever made. A single-minded man, she thought. She had no idea what Ed McKenna had done the rest of the year—although the comments made by his children told Phyllis that he had owned some sort of company—but when he came to the coast he had only one thing in mind, only one goal: to fish as much as he could while he was here.

She put the suitcase on the bed and opened it, then gathered the clothes and placed them inside the suitcase. She would take it and the tackle box downstairs first, then return for the rods and reels. She wondered briefly what had happened to the gear Mr. McKenna had carried with him out onto the pier this morning. Maybe the police had taken it, she thought. That was none of her business, though, and it would be up to McKenna's children to recover it if they wanted it.

She closed the suitcase and fastened the latches, then

picked it up and hefted the tackle box in her other hand. As she left the room and went out into the hallway, she heard voices from downstairs and recognized Sam's deep, powerful rumble. He must have gotten back from his jaunt to the art galleries with Carolyn and Eve.

When Phyllis reached the bottom of the stairs, she could see into the parlor. Sam stood there with both of the McKenna twins on their feet, looking at him with angry expressions on their faces. Carolyn and Eve stood by, clearly worried, while Frances Heaton still sat on the sofa, wearing a smug smile now.

"I told you fellas I'm sorry for your loss," Sam was saying. "I don't know what else I can do."

"Get ready to defend yourself in a wrongful-death suit," one of the twins snapped. "That's what you can do."

"When our lawyers get through with you—" the other one began to threaten.

Sam held up a hand to stop him. "If you take me to court, you're gonna be mighty disappointed, boys. Even if you won, which I don't see how you can because I didn't have anything to do with your daddy dyin', I'm livin' on teacher retirement pay. You ever heard that old sayin' about gettin' blood from a stone?"

"We don't care. It's not about the money—"

Carolyn spoke up. "Whenever someone says it's not about the money . . . then it's *all* about the money."

"You stay out of it," Frances Heaton said. "This is none of your business."

"It most certainly is," Carolyn shot back, "whenever someone starts threatening a friend of mine!"

A year and a half earlier, Carolyn had been adamantly opposed to letting Sam—or any man—move into the house. Things had certainly changed since then, Phyllis thought as she came into the parlor carrying the suitcase and tackle box.

She was sorry that Sam had walked in and been ambushed by the McKennas like this. She said, "I have your father's things. If you'll take them I'll go back upstairs and get his fishing poles. That will finish our business."

The brothers both sneered at her. "You just wish that would finish things," one of them said.

Sam looked like he was getting fed up with them and ready to squash both of them like bugs. Phyllis moved between him and the twins and held out the suitcase and tackle box.

"Hold on a minute, Mrs. Newsom," a new voice said. Phyllis looked over her shoulder and saw Chief Dale Clifton standing in the foyer. He smiled and pointed a thumb at the door. "Hope you don't mind me barging in like this. The door was open, and I couldn't help over-hearing what you folks were talking about. Are those Mr. McKenna's personal belongings?"

"Some of them," Phyllis said. "I was just about to turn them over to his children here."

Clifton looked at Frances and her brothers and said, "You folks have already driven down from San Antonio, eh? That's good, since I need to talk to you anyway."

"What about?" Frances asked. "I thought everything was fairly cut-and-dried about our father's death."

"Except for the part that Fletcher here played in it," one of the twins added in a nasty tone of voice.

"Well, we sort of thought it was cut-and-dried, too," Clifton said as he came on into the parlor. "But that was before we got the preliminary report from the medical examiner." He reached for the suitcase and tackle box. "I'll need to be taking those with me."

"But why?" Phyllis asked.

"Because they may turn out to be evidence in a mur-der investigation."

With a thump, the suitcase hit the floor as it fell right out of Phyllis's hand.

Chapter 5

$\mathcal{S}$he managed to hang on to the tackle box, which was a good thing. If she had dropped it, it might have broken open and spilled lures, hooks, speck rigs, and assorted other bits of tackle all over the parlor rug.

"Did you say . . . murder?" she asked Chief Clifton.

"Not again!" Carolyn said.

That outburst brought a puzzled frown to the chief's face. "What does Mrs. Wilbarger mean by that?" he asked Phyllis.

She set the tackle box on the coffee table, afraid that she was too shaken to hold on to it any longer. "It's a long story," she said. "I've been involved in a few police cases up in Weatherford, where we all live."

"But not as a suspect," Sam pointed out. "Fact of the matter is, Phyllis has solved a few murders for the cops up there."

Clifton's bushy white eyebrows rose. "Is that so? Well, maybe I'll have to call on you as a consultant in this case, Mrs. Newsom."

Phyllis shook her head. "No, thanks. If it's all right with you, Chief, I'd just as soon stay as far away from any murders as I can."

"Unfortunately, that's not going to be possible here."

Clifton's tone of voice hardened a little as he went on. "You and Mr. Fletcher are involved because you discovered the victim's body."

Frances Heaton was on her feet now. She took a step closer to the chief and asked him, "You keep saying that our father was murdered. Do you have any proof of that?"

"The autopsy turned up evidence of poison in his stomach contents." Clifton grimaced. "Sorry to have to be so blunt about it, folks, but there it is."

Sam said, "The autopsy's already been performed? That's mighty fast, isn't it?"

"We don't have a lot of suspicious deaths in Aransas County. The medical examiner got to it right away. Anyway, the procedure is still going on, but the ME gave me a call as soon as he found the poison mixed in what appeared to be crab cakes." Clifton looked at Phyllis. "I assume he ate the crab cakes here?"

Carolyn said, "Who eats crab cakes for breakfast?"

One of the twins said, "Our father would eat crab cakes for every meal if he could."

"He loves them," the other brother said, adding with a slight catch in his voice, "Loved them, I should say."

Even that tiny display of emotion made the man go up a notch in Phyllis's estimation. Maybe Ed McKenna's death actually meant something to his children after all . . . at least to one of them. As she thought that, she recalled something that had happened the previous evening.

"We had crab cakes for supper last night," she said. "Consuela cooked them. They were delicious. But we *all* ate them. I don't see how they could have been poisoned."

Clifton shook his head. "It wouldn't have taken that long for the stuff to take effect. McKenna would have died within an hour or so of ingesting the poison."

Phyllis thought about it some more and then nodded. "There were some left over at supper. I remember now, Mr. McKenna asked Consuela if she would save them for him so he could eat them for breakfast this morning. He said he liked cold crab cakes for breakfast." A shudder went through her. That didn't sound good to her at all. But then, she had never been one to eat cold pizza for breakfast, either, and she knew there were plenty of people who did that. Sam, for one.

"Who was there when Mr. McKenna said that?" the chief asked.

"It was at the dinner table. We were all there, I suppose. I don't remember any of the guests missing supper last night. Even though Dorothy and Ben call this a bed-and-breakfast, they offer three meals a day, and nobody wants to miss out on Consuela's cooking."

Phyllis looked at Sam, Carolyn, and Eve to see if their memories differed from hers. Carolyn and Eve shook their heads, and Sam said, "The whole bunch was there, all right."

"So anybody could have heard him say he was going to eat the leftover crab cakes for breakfast," Clifton mused, "which means . . ."

His frown deepened as his voice trailed off. Phyllis finished the thought for him.

"Which means that anyone who's staying here could have poisoned those crab cakes, knowing that Mr. McKenna was the only one likely to eat them. Isn't that what you mean, Chief?"

"Well, I hate to say it . . . but that's the way it looks to me, Mrs. Newsom."

"That's ridiculous!" Carolyn burst out. "All of us barely knew the old sourpuss!"

"That's our father you're talking about," Frances Heaton said through gritted teeth.

"Well, I'm sorry," Carolyn said, without actually sounding very sorry at all. "Your father just fished all the time and barely said a word to anyone. Why, when he asked Consuela to save those crab cakes, that was probably the longest speech I ever heard him make. *And* the nicest."

"Carolyn's right about one thing," Phyllis said. "None of us would have any reason to harm Mr. McKenna. We never even met him until a few days ago."

"What about the other guests staying here?"

"You'd have to ask them ... although it's possible that the Blaines and the Forrests were acquainted with him, since they always come to the coast about this same time of year, and from what they told me, they always stay here."

"Dad always took his vacation at this time, too," one of the twins said. "It had to be one of those people who poisoned him, Chief. You should arrest all of them—"

Clifton held up a hand to forestall that suggestion. "Nobody's talking about arresting anybody just yet," he said. "We may be a small department, but we can mount a thorough investigation when we need to. We'll be looking into every angle of this case." He glanced down at the closed suitcase lying on the floor between his feet and Phyllis's. "That'll include taking custody of his belongings and going through them, as well as searching the room where he's been staying." He lifted his eyes to meet Phyllis's gaze. "Will we have to get a search warrant in order to do that?"

Phyllis thought about it and shook her head. "I don't see any reason why that should be necessary."

"Wait just a minute," Frances said. "If it's our father's belongings that you intend to search, then you most certainly *do* need a search warrant."

Her brothers nodded firmly in agreement.

Chief Clifton looked at them for a moment, then said, "You think your father might have something in his bags that he wouldn't want the police to see?"

"Not at all," Frances answered. "I think if you get a search warrant—and I know you'll probably be able to find a judge willing to sign one—I don't believe you'll find anything except some old clothes and a bunch of nasty old fishing gear."

"And maybe a couple of Western paperbacks," one

of the twins added. "Dad liked to read those Louis L'Amour books."

"It's just the principle of the thing," Frances went on. "You should follow proper procedure."

"And this will give us a chance to consult with our attorneys, too," the other twin said. His brother and sister shot him slitted glances, Phyllis noted, as if they wished he hadn't brought that up. She knew from talking to Mike that the police automatically grew more suspicious of someone who insisted on "lawyering up."

Chief Clifton looked like he wanted to sigh in weary exasperation, but he just nodded instead. "All right," he said. "I'm going to impound this suitcase and tackle box as possible evidence, but they won't be opened and searched until we have a warrant. Same thing holds true for your father's room upstairs."

"How did you know Mr. McKenna's room was upstairs?" Phyllis asked.

"I've been friends with Dorothy and Ben for quite a while," the chief told her with a smile. "This isn't the first time I've been in this house, and I know all the guest rooms are upstairs."

"That's true," Phyllis admitted.

"You mind coming up there with me so you can lock it up and I can seal it until we're ready to get in there?"

"Of course not."

"We'll be going now," Frances announced. "When will you be able to release our father's body?"

"That's hard to say," Clifton replied with a shake of his head. "What with the uncertain circumstances and all, and having to get search warrants . . . might be several days, I suppose."

Frances glared at him. "You're just trying to make things more difficult for us."

"No, ma'am," the chief said. "Just following proper procedure."

Her eyes narrowed even more, but she didn't say

anything else. She turned and marched out of the parlor with her brothers following her.

"When you get a place to stay, call the station and let us know where we can find you," Clifton called after them.

When the front door had slammed behind the McKenna siblings, Sam said, "I don't reckon those folks like you very much, Chief."

"The feeling's mutual, even though I just met them." Clifton turned to Phyllis. "Now, if you'll show me Mr. McKenna's room, Mrs. Newsom . . ."

"Of course. Come with me."

Sam followed them up the stairs. As the three of them went along the hall, Clifton said, "I wouldn't mind hearing more about those murder cases you've been mixed up in. I didn't know there was such a thing as an amateur detective in real life."

"Oh, goodness, don't call me a detective. I just kept my eyes open and made a few suggestions to the authorities—"

Sam snorted. "Don't let her fool you, Chief. She figured out who committed those murders, plain and simple. If that's not detecting, I don't know what you'd call it. Problem is, pokin' into those killin's nearly got Phyllis hurt a time or two."

"It did not," she argued. "I was never in any real danger."

"Well, if you have any suggestions to make to me, feel free," Chief Clifton said. "I'm just a small-town cop. Break up a few fights and haul in a few drunks on Saturday night, keep the college kids in line during spring break. That's my job. I don't remember the last time we had anybody poisoned on purpose around here."

"Say, you think maybe it was an accident?" Sam asked.

"Doubtful. The doc didn't give me all the details yet, but I don't think McKenna could've gotten that stuff in his stomach unless somebody meant for it to be there."

Phyllis paused in front of the door to McKenna's room. "What if it wasn't an accident? What if Mr. McKenna took the poison on purpose?"

Clifton shoved his hands in the pockets of his khaki uniform trousers and frowned. "Committed suicide, you mean? I suppose it's possible. Having kids like those three I met downstairs might drive a man to doing something like that. But poison's usually not the way a man kills himself, if you'll pardon my gender-stereotyping."

"No, I suppose not."

"Still, at this point we can't rule out anything." Clifton gestured toward the door. "If you'll do the honors . . ."

Phyllis took the master key from the pocket of her blue jeans and locked the door. The chief took a roll of yellow crime-scene tape from his pocket and ran a strip along the jamb from top to bottom, sealing the room.

"Keep an eye on it and make sure nobody messes with it, if you would," he told Phyllis. "Wouldn't want to give McKenna's kids any ammunition for a lawsuit. They seem like the type."

"They already threatened to slap me with one," Sam said. "Hey, if somebody poisoned McKenna, then for sure I didn't have anything to do with him dyin'."

"I probably shouldn't tell you this, but the doc said there was no water in his lungs. He was dead when he went in, all right."

Sam nodded. "That's a relief. I didn't think he could've drowned in the amount of time he was under, but still, I worried a little about it."

"You can ease your mind on that score . . . as long as you're not the one who slipped the poison into the crab cakes."

Phyllis shuddered. "Don't even joke about it."

"Oh," Chief Clifton said, "I wasn't."

When the chief was gone, Phyllis, Sam, Carolyn, and Eve gathered in the kitchen. All thoughts of the Just Desserts contest coming up in a few days had fled from Phyllis's mind. She couldn't believe that even here, hundreds of miles from home, murder had cropped up yet again.

Maybe that reporter was right. Maybe she *was* some sort of jinx.

The others were worried, too. As they sat around the kitchen table drinking coffee, Sam said, "You don't reckon the chief meant what he said about considerin' me a suspect in McKenna's murder, do you?"

Phyllis sighed. "He meant it, all right. He seems like a nice man, but I'm sure he considers *all* of us to be suspects until he finds some evidence indicating otherwise."

"You'd think that all he'd have to do is check our backgrounds," Carolyn said with an indignant snort. "We're retired schoolteachers, for goodness' sake! We don't go around poisoning people!"

Phyllis's shoulders rose and fell in a shrug. "Not normally, maybe, but murder never occurs in normal circumstances, does it?"

"So what are you going to do, dear?" Eve asked. "Are you going to investigate Mr. McKenna's death?"

"Chief Clifton pretty much gave her the go-ahead to do just that," Sam said.

Phyllis shook her head. "I don't believe he meant that. He was just being nice. No chief of police is really going to want some civilian poking around in a murder investigation."

"You never know," Sam mused. "Maybe this fella's different."

"Well, *someone* had better solve it, and quickly, too," Carolyn declared. "I don't like the idea of spending even one more night under the same roof as a murderer."

Phyllis thought about the guests staying at the bed-and-breakfast. It seemed impossible to her that any of them could have committed this crime. The Blaines and the Forrests seemed like such nice, normal couples, and Nick and Kate Thompson obviously weren't interested in anything except each other.

That left Consuela, and who would have had a better

opportunity to poison the leftover crab cakes? She was the one who wrapped them up and put them away, after all. She might have even served them to Ed McKenna that morning, although it was possible that McKenna had gotten them out of the refrigerator and helped himself.

Something else occurred to Phyllis then. Usually, Theresa and Bianca weren't at the house during the late afternoon and evening, but they had come by after supper the day before to pick up Consuela. Something about her car not starting at home, so they'd had to drop her off earlier, Phyllis recalled. So the girls had been here in the kitchen while the guests were eating supper. Either of them could have heard Mr. McKenna ask Consuela to save the crab cakes that hadn't been eaten . . .

Phyllis closed her eyes and rubbed her temples. Sam asked, "Are you all right?"

She nodded as she opened her eyes again. She didn't tell him that she had been trying to force those suspicions of Consuela and her daughters out of her mind. The Anselmo family had been working for Dorothy and Ben for years. It was beyond belief that any of them would have suddenly poisoned one of the guests.

But Phyllis had been involved with other murder cases where she would have said that the identity of the killer was beyond belief. Even though she firmly believed that some people were utterly incapable of harming another human being, no matter what, she had learned that under the right circumstances some people could be driven to kill when they never would have otherwise.

That thought didn't make her feel any better, but in answer to Sam's question she said, "I'm fine. Just shocked that such a thing could happen."

"Again," Carolyn added, which Phyllis didn't think was really necessary.

She nodded anyway and agreed. "Again."

The four friends were still sitting there around the table, brooding, when the back door opened and Consuela came in. Phyllis glanced at the clock on the wall and saw that it was time for Consuela to start preparing supper. What with the chief's visit and the unexpected and unwelcome news he had brought with him, Phyllis hadn't paid much attention to the passage of time. She could barely remember eating lunch, because that had happened before they found out that Ed McKenna had been murdered.

Consuela looked around at them and asked, "Why all the long faces? Are you still upset about poor Mr. McKenna?"

"Poor Mr. McKenna is right," Carolyn said. "The man was murdered."

Phyllis might have preferred that Carolyn not blurt out the news that way, but she supposed it didn't matter. Consuela had to find out sooner or later, and there was no way to sugarcoat murder.

Consuela's eyes widened, and her face paled despite her skin's normally dark tint. "Murdered?" she repeated. "But . . . but I thought he had a heart attack!"

Phyllis said, "That's what we all thought until Chief Clifton came by and told us that the autopsy found poison, along with those leftover crab cakes he ate for breakfast."

"*Madre de Dios!* My crab cakes never poisoned anyone! It's impossible!"

And then Consuela startled Phyllis even more by pulling out one of the empty chairs at the table, sitting down, covering her face with her hands, and bursting into tears.

Chapter 6

The other four people sitting at the table exchanged uncomfortable glances that said they were unsure what to do next. They had to do *something*, though, Phyllis thought. They couldn't just sit there and let Consuela go on bawling. It was such a strange sight, because Consuela had always seemed so unflappable during the time Phyllis and her friends had been here.

Finally, Phyllis stood up and moved around the table. Standing beside Consuela, she patted the woman on the shoulder and said, "There, there. It's all right. Nobody thinks you had anything to do with Mr. McKenna being poisoned."

Two things occurred to Phyllis as she spoke. She wondered why people always said *There, there* in a situation like this. It was a meaningless phrase.

And more important, the other thing was that what she had just said was a lie. She didn't know that nobody suspected Consuela of being involved in McKenna's murder. In fact, from the way Chief Clifton had acted, he considered everyone in this household a suspect.

"Yes, don't worry, dear," Eve said. "It won't be long before Phyllis has solved this murder, anyway."

Consuela looked up, wiping her eyes. "Señora Newsom? Why ... why would you solve a murder?"

"She does it at home all the time," Carolyn said.

Phyllis suppressed the feelings of exasperation that tried to well up inside her. "Mrs. Turner and Mrs. Wilbarger are exaggerating," she told Consuela. "I'm not a detective or anything like that." She paused. "But I am wondering why you're so upset. No offense, but you didn't seem all that fond of Mr. McKenna."

Consuela knuckled the rest of the tears from her eyes. "He was just one of the guests, that's all. Less trouble than some, so I guess I liked that about him. But he never left tips, either, for me or my girls, and he wasn't friendly to any of us. He acted like we weren't even there unless he wanted something from us, like saving those crab cakes for him. No, I'm upset because of ... because of what the police are going to think."

"Like I told you, no one is blaming you," Phyllis said.

"Begging your pardon, Mrs. Newsom, but I know how the law works. They always suspect the people who have been in trouble before."

Carolyn said, "But surely you haven't been in trouble with the law, Consuela. I just can't believe that, even though I've only known you for a few days."

Consuela shook her head. "Not me. My husband, Tom. He ... he was in prison years ago, when he was young."

"Not for murder, I hope." Carolyn frowned, and Phyllis knew what she was thinking. Tom Anselmo did a considerable amount of work around the bed-and-breakfast—taking care of the yard, painting and repair, plumbing, and all the other handyman jobs that came up. The idea that a man who was around so much could be a killer was disconcerting. Phyllis felt the same way.

Consuela was still shaking her head, though. "No, no, he never killed anybody," she said. "He wouldn't do that. He's a good man. But he grew up in a rough neighborhood in Corpus Christi. Even then there were gangs and drugs, and people had to do things they normally wouldn't to survive . . . He served five years in the penitentiary for selling heroin."

Phyllis noticed that Consuela didn't claim Tom had been innocent. In fact, just the opposite, because the woman went on. "He wanted to do his time. Afterward he said getting sent to prison was the best thing that could have happened to him, because he'd either get strong or he would die in there." A faint smile appeared on her face, and there was a note of pride in her voice as she continued. "He got strong. He came back and told me he'd never do anything to get sent to prison again. I was waiting for him. I'd promised to marry him. I did, and Tom's been a law-abiding man, a good man, ever since."

"I believe you," Phyllis said. "But does my cousin know about this?"

"Dorothy and Ben know all about it. We wouldn't lie to them, not after they've treated us so good." Consuela sounded a little offended by the very idea.

"Then why are you so upset?" Phyllis wanted to know.

"I told you. The police will blame him, even though he didn't have anything to do with what happened to Mr. McKenna."

"From what I saw of him, that doesn't seem like something Chief Clifton would do. Anyway, he acted like he's a friend of your family."

Consuela shrugged. "We've known him for a long time. He knows everybody around here, all the permanent residents, anyway. But it doesn't matter. He's still a policeman. He has to find somebody he can blame for what happened, and Tom's got a felony conviction on his record."

Sam clasped his hands together on the table and leaned forward. "Was your husband even home last night or this mornin'?" he asked. "I thought he works on a drillin' rig out in the Gulf."

She should have thought to ask that herself, Phyllis realized.

Consuela nodded. "He does. But he came home last night, and he doesn't have to go back until tomorrow night. He planned to come over here tomorrow during the day and do some yard work."

"But what possible motive for murder could he have?" Carolyn asked. "Did he and Mr. McKenna even know each other?"

"I guess. I don't know. Tom never had much to do with the guests. But Mr. McKenna has been coming here for several years. He and Tom probably talked a little now and then."

"It sounds to me like you don't need to worry," Phyllis told her. "Tom doesn't have any motive, and it's quite a stretch to even say that he had the opportunity to poison Mr. McKenna."

"Yeah, but it's all gonna come out anyway, the part about him being a drug dealer and being in prison. And then the girls . . . the girls will find out . . ."

"They don't know?" Phyllis asked.

Consuela shook her head. "That their *papi* is a jailbird? No."

It had been a long time since she had heard anybody use the expression "jailbird," Phyllis thought. No matter what you called it, though, it wasn't a good experience to have, especially when you'd been sent to prison for something as sordid as selling heroin. And it wasn't something that would make your children look up to you, either.

"Well, maybe it won't come out," Phyllis said. She knew it was a pretty weak thing to say, but those were the only words of consolation she could come up with.

Consuela looked up at her and shook her head. "Unless they find the killer right away, it will. When it's murder, *everything* comes out."

Thinking back to the other cases she'd been involved with, Phyllis knew just how true that was. Murder had a way of dragging everyone's secrets out into the light, no matter how ugly they were.

And she knew all too well that everyone had secrets ...

Consuela calmed down after a while. She had a meal to prepare, and her dedication to her job meant that she couldn't neglect that duty, no matter how upset she was. She summoned up a smile, even though Phyllis could tell that it was false, and shooed everyone out of the kitchen.

"We're having seafood quesadillas tonight," Consuela told them. "And I guarantee, no poison."

The weak attempt at levity fell flat, but after everything that had happened, no one paid much attention to the failed joke. Phyllis, Sam, Carolyn, and Eve went out into the parlor and left Consuela to her work.

Carolyn leaned close to Phyllis and asked in a half whisper, "Do you think it really is safe to eat the food now?"

"Of course it is," Phyllis answered without hesitation. She didn't believe for a second that Consuela was guilty, nor that her husband, Tom, or their daughters were involved with Ed McKenna's death.

But *someone* had poisoned those crab cakes, she reminded herself, and she had a hard time believing that anyone else who had been in the house could have done such a thing.

That was one of the problems with murder, she reflected. Somebody had to be guilty.

A short time later, the Blaines and the Forrests returned from wherever they had been all afternoon. The day had warmed up considerably, and they all looked a little heated. Even though it was autumn, the days could get quite warm, especially with the constant high levels of humidity factored in.

The guests were laughing among themselves as they came into the house, which bothered Phyllis a little. It was true that the four of them hadn't exactly been friends with Mr. McKenna, but they had sat down at the same table and shared meals with him. To Phyllis's way of thinking, a little more decorum on their part would have been nice, as a way of showing respect for the deceased.

She saw Sam frowning and asked quietly, "Does it bother you, too?"

"'Any man's death diminishes me,'" he quoted. "Hemingway, right?"

"I think he got it from John Donne."

Sam shrugged. "Works either way. You'd think it'd bother 'em at least a little that a fella they knew keeled over dead this mornin'. Of course, they don't know yet how come he died."

"That's right," Phyllis said as the unpleasant realization hit her.

Somebody was going to have to tell the guests that Ed McKenna had been murdered . . . and that the killer might still be under this very roof.

She called out to them as they started through the hall toward the stairs. "Excuse me. . . . I need to have a word with you folks."

Jessica Blaine and Raquel Forrest were each carrying several plastic bags. Loot from their day of shopping, Phyllis thought. They wore impatient looks as they turned toward her.

"What is it, Mrs. Newsom?" Leo asked. "We're all a little tired. Like to freshen up a bit before dinner."

"There's some news about Mr. McKenna that I need to share with you."

"What happened?" Leo smiled. "He didn't turn out to be alive after all, did he? A little resurrection?"

"Leo, stop it!" Jessica scolded. "I swear, you try to make a joke out of everything."

"A man died," Sheldon said. "It's not funny."

It was even more "not funny" than they knew. Phyllis said, "The chief of police came by here a while ago. The autopsy on Mr. McKenna wasn't complete at the time, but the medical examiner was already sure that he didn't die from a heart attack or a stroke."

"What else is there that'd kill a guy so sudden like that?" Leo asked, frowning now instead of grinning. "Some sort of embolism or aneurysm or something like that?"

"No," Phyllis said. "He was poisoned."

Leo's frown deepened. "I don't understand. How'd he get into poison around here?"

"Wait a minute," Sheldon said. "You don't mean he was . . ." His voice trailed off, as if he were unable to bring himself to say it.

Phyllis nodded. "That's right. The police are treating it as a homicide investigation now. Chief Clifton believes that Mr. McKenna was murdered."

She watched them all closely as she said it, looking for any sign that one of them already knew about it.

But instead, all four looked profoundly shocked, as if they couldn't believe what they had just heard.

Of course, one of them could have been acting. Phyllis had run into murderers before who had the ability to behave as if nothing had ever happened. It was a useful talent to have if you planned to go around killing people.

Still, she had a hard time believing it of any of these four, who seemed as normal and innocent as they could be. After that initial moment of surprised silence, they began bubbling over with questions. Phyllis let them yammer on for a few seconds, then raised her hands to call for silence, like she would have in her classroom.

"If you'll go in the parlor and sit down, I'll tell you what Chief Clifton told me."

Still carrying the packages from their shopping trip, the couples went into the parlor and sat down, the Blaines on the sofa, the Forrests in a couple of armchairs. Phyllis stood in the middle of the room, where she would be able to see all four of them.

As concisely as she could, she covered the news that

Chief Clifton had brought. The couples listened in silence, although Phyllis could tell that Leo, especially, was almost bursting with the desire to ask questions. He let her finish, though, before he said, "Is it possible that the crab cakes just . . . you know . . . went bad?"

Beside him, Jessica nodded. "That's right. I've heard of people dying from food poisoning before."

"If someone *put* the poison in the crab cakes," Sheldon said, "you could call that food poisoning, couldn't you?"

Raquel reached over and punched him lightly on the upper arm. "You're not funny," she said.

"I'm not trying to be funny," Sheldon insisted, and as a matter of fact, he did look serious. Deadly serious, Phyllis thought. "I'm just trying to point out that the terminology could apply to either case."

"Terminology, schmerminology," Leo said, and like "jailbird," Phyllis thought it had been a long time since she had heard anybody use an expression like that. Leo went on, "The guy was murdered, plain and simple. And some woman did it."

That bold declaration made Phyllis frown. She couldn't stop herself from asking, "How in the world do you know that?"

"Because if a guy wanted to kill somebody, he'd shoot 'em or stab 'em or take a baseball bat to their head. He wouldn't sneak around and slip poison into some frickin' crab cakes—pardon my language."

"You're nuts," Raquel said. "You can't just say that no guy would ever poison anybody."

"Leo's right about men being more violent overall, though," Sheldon pointed out. "It's something atavistic in us. However, I agree with Raquel that you can't automatically rule out all men as suspects just because the murderer employed poison as the means to his or her particular end."

"So you think a guy could have done it?" Leo said.

"Of course."

"Then you're the one who's nuts."

None of them seemed to take offense at anything the others were saying, and Phyllis supposed that was because they had all been friends for so long that they were accustomed to such good-natured wrangling. She said, "I don't think any of you are nuts, as you put it. I just wanted you to know what the situation was. I'm sure the police will be coming around to ask more questions about Mr. McKenna—"

"Oh, my God," Jessica interrupted as her eyes widened. "They don't consider us suspects, do they?"

Earlier Phyllis had tiptoed around that same question from Consuela. She didn't feel like tiptoeing anymore.

"I got the feeling that Chief Clifton considers everyone to be a possible suspect at this point."

Leo came to his feet as an angry expression darkened his broad face. "Well, that really *is* crazy! We barely knew Ed McKenna. None of us would have any reason to kill him."

"Didn't he usually stay here at the same time as the four of you?" Phyllis asked. She was just assuming that based on comments she had heard them make over the past few days, but it was something that could be easily checked by going over Dorothy's records. She was sure the police would get around to doing just that, probably sooner rather than later.

"It's true that our visits usually overlapped to a certain extent," Sheldon said. "They seldom dovetailed precisely."

"He was here when we got here," Raquel said.

"And he usually left before we did," Jessica said.

"We don't know anything about him except that he went fishing all the time," Leo added. "Hell, I don't even know where he's from."

"San Antonio," Phyllis said.

"See? Why would I kill a guy when I don't even know where he's from?"

Phyllis didn't think that made much sense, but Leo seemed to, and his wife nodded supportively.

"You know who had the best opportunity to poison somebody?" Raquel mused. "Consuela."

Jessica put a hand to her mouth. "That's right! She prepares all the food. She could have put anything in it, for all we know! We could all be poisoned right now!"

Leo turned toward her and shook his head. "You're not poisoned. None of us has been poisoned."

"How do you know that?"

"You feel okay, don't you?" He looked at Sheldon and Raquel. "You guys are all right, aren't you?"

"A little hot and sweaty, maybe," Raquel said, "but other than that, yeah, I guess I'm all right. How about you, Sheldon?"

"I feel fine," Sheldon declared.

"You see," Leo said to Jessica. "If Consuela had poisoned us this morning, we'd all be dead by now."

"Not necessarily," Sheldon said. "If she used a different type of poison on us, it might be considerably slower-acting. We might not die until later tonight, or even tomorrow."

"That's right," Jessica practically wailed. "We won't know until it's too late!"

Phyllis had listened to all of this she could stand. She said, "No one else has been poisoned, and none of you are going to die. Consuela didn't murder Mr. McKenna."

"You don't know that for sure," Sheldon pointed out. "The police haven't made any arrests yet, have they?"

"Well, no."

"And as you said yourself, the chief considers everyone a suspect at this point, and if he feels that way, I don't see how we can feel any differently."

"Well, I know one thing," Jessica said as she got to her feet. "I'm not going to stay in a house where people get poisoned. Come on, Leo, we have to pack. We're getting out of here!"

Chapter 7

"Wait a minute," Phyllis said. "You can't just leave. You have reservations here for the next ten days."

Leo shook his head. "That doesn't mean we have to stay. And don't think you can get away with threatening to keep our payment, either. In a case like this we ought to get a full refund!"

"Yes, I'd say that's warranted," Sheldon said. "And refusal would be the grounds for a rather nasty lawsuit. I'm sure the owners wouldn't want the whole thing dragged into court. That would mean a lot of bad publicity about how one of the guests died after eating poisoned food."

Raquel snorted. "That'd be the kiss of death for a bed-and-breakfast as far as I was concerned. I'd never stay there again, and I bet nobody else would, either."

Phyllis felt control of the situation slipping away from her ... as if she'd ever had it in the first place. She held up her hands and said, "Please, everyone, just slow down. We don't need to be talking about leaving, or refunds, or filing lawsuits—"

"You don't expect us to *stay* here after what's happened, do you?" Jessica asked. "It's just not safe."

"I'm convinced that it's perfectly safe—"

"Then you stay here and eat the food," Leo said. "As

for me, though, I'm going somewhere where they don't poison you."

Phyllis felt awful about what was happening, and yet she knew she couldn't have kept the truth about Ed McKenna's death from them. They would have found out by the next day, at the very latest, when the story about McKenna's murder appeared in the local newspaper.

Now Dorothy and Ben were faced with all the bad publicity, not to mention the possibility of legal action by their customers. Phyllis knew that none of this was her fault, but at the same time she couldn't help but feel that she was letting her cousin down.

She couldn't have prevented this mess ... but maybe she could put a stop to it before it got any worse.

But that would mean finding Mr. McKenna's killer. Playing detective again, as Carolyn and Eve would probably phrase it. She had no desire to do that.

And what if it turned out that Consuela really was the killer? That would truly finish the job of ruining all future business for the bed-and-breakfast.

One problem at a time, she told herself. She couldn't fix everything at once.

An idea occurred to her. She said, "Listen, if you'll stay here, I'll talk to Dorothy about giving you a reduced rate. That way we can refund some of your money."

She was going to have to call Dorothy, anyway, to tell her about Mr. McKenna. She should have done it before now, Phyllis knew. She'd been putting it off because it was bound to upset her cousin, and Phyllis hated to be the bearer of bad news for anyone.

"You expect us to risk our lives for a reduced rate?" Leo asked with a tone of amazement in his voice. "Forget it!" He grasped his wife's hand. "Come on, Jess, let's go."

Sam's familiar voice drawled from the doorway, "I reckon that'd be about the worst thing you could do, Mr. Blaine."

Phyllis hadn't heard him come up, but she was glad

to see him. Just having him around made her feel a little stronger. As usual, he looked very much at ease, leaning a shoulder against the side of the arched entrance between the parlor and the foyer.

Leo wheeled around to face Sam and thrust his jaw out belligerently. "You're not threatening me, are you, Fletcher?"

"Nope," Sam said. "Wouldn't think of it. But it seems to me there's somethin' you haven't thought of, either."

"And what might that be?"

"The cops're liable to take it to be a mite suspicious if anybody goes runnin' off so soon after Ed McKenna was murdered."

Sheldon said, "Are you saying that if we leave, the police will think that one of *us* poisoned that man?"

"That's crazy!" Leo said. "We've already been over that. None of us had any reason to kill the guy!"

Sam shrugged. "No reason that we know of. But if the cops start diggin' around, who knows what they might turn up. And they'll dig harder if they think somebody's actin' suspicious."

"That sounds like blackmail to me," Sheldon said with a frown.

"Yeah, I think it was a threat to start with, just like I said," Leo added. "If we leave, you'll tell the cops that I had a big fight with McKenna last night."

"Did you, Mr. Blaine?" Phyllis asked. "I didn't notice that."

"That's because it never happened! It's a big, fat lie. But that might not stop you from trying to get back at me any way you could."

With a frown, Jessica said, "I don't really think Mrs. Newsom would do that, Leo."

Leo waved a hand toward Sam. "Well, what about her boyfriend there?"

Sam straightened from his casual pose. "I'm not in the habit of lyin' to the police," he said. "Fact of the matter is, I try not to lie to anybody."

"You could've fooled me, all that talk about us being suspects if we leave—"

"You're already suspects," Phyllis broke in. "We all are. I told you that. So what Sam says just makes sense. The police won't want you to leave town while they're conducting their investigation, and if you try to, it'll make you look more guilty."

"Maybe we won't leave town," Sheldon said, "but we could spend the rest of our vacation somewhere else in Rockport or Fulton. That way we'd still be available for the police to question at their convenience, and yet we wouldn't be risking our lives by continuing to stay here in this . . . this murder house."

Phyllis almost lost her temper at that lurid description of the bed-and-breakfast. Oak Knoll wasn't a *murder house*, for goodness' sake. It was a perfectly respectable establishment, and it had been for years. She couldn't let this unfortunate incident ruin the place's reputation. She just couldn't.

But the Blaines and the Forrests weren't going to be persuaded to change their minds, either. Leo had hold of Jessica's hand and practically dragged her out of the parlor. He headed for the stairs, saying, "Come on, babe. Let's make some calls and see if we can find some other place to stay. Someplace where they don't murder their guests!"

Phyllis winced at that.

Sheldon and Raquel followed their friends. Raquel seemed to be the most sympathetic to Phyllis's plight. She cast a glance back and shrugged her shoulders, as if to ask *What can you do?* Leo had his mind made up, and he seemed determined to bulldoze the others into going along with him.

Sam looked at Phyllis and shrugged, too. "Sorry," he said. "I was tryin' to calm 'em down and help 'em see that they were makin' a mistake, but I reckon I just made things worse."

"You just told the truth," Phyllis assured him. "If they left and went home, it *would* look suspicious to Chief Clifton."

Something else was on her mind, something that she told herself was completely irrelevant, and yet it wouldn't let go of her thoughts.

Leo had called Sam her boyfriend. Was it so obvious that they had taken a romantic interest in each other? Phyllis believed that such things were best kept private, so she supposed she would have to start paying more attention to her words and her actions whenever Sam was around.

At her age, she certainly didn't want anybody thinking she was making calf eyes at him, not even Sam!

A few minutes later, Nick Thompson came downstairs. His steps had a little bounce in them, typical of the exuberance of youth. He found Phyllis and Sam talking in the parlor and used his thumb to point to the upstairs.

"Hey, who put the bug up Leo's, uh, backside, if you'll pardon the expression? We heard him going on about how they were gonna pack up and leave. He was talking so loud he woke up Kate and me. We were, uh, catching a little nap before supper."

Phyllis's spirits sank. Now she had to go through the whole thing again. She managed a weak smile and said, "You haven't heard the latest news, Mr. Thompson."

"Nick," he said. "Call me Nick."

Phyllis was more than happy to do that, since Nick was about her son's age and she had a hard time calling anyone that young *Mister*. She said, "Chief Clifton was here earlier."

"Yeah, I saw what looked like crime-scene tape on Mr. McKenna's door and figured the police must have been here. Why would they seal it off like that? It doesn't make sense. I mean, he died of natural causes, right? There weren't any signs of foul play . . ." Nick's eyes widened as his words trailed away. He swallowed and went on, "Wait a minute. Are you saying that there *was* foul play involved in Mr. McKenna's death?"

"He was poisoned," Phyllis said. "The preliminary findings from the autopsy were that someone poisoned the leftover crab cakes he ate for breakfast this morning."

"Son of a—! No way!"

Sam nodded and said solemnly, "Way."

Nick sank onto the edge of the sofa, disbelief still evident on his face. "But that means somebody in this house must've ... I mean, if the stuff was in the crab cakes, then it had to have been put there between supper last night and breakfast this morning, because nobody else died."

Phyllis nodded. "It seems to have been aimed solely at Mr. McKenna. He said at supper last night that he was going to eat the crab cakes for breakfast this morning."

"Yeah, but somebody else could have gotten into them, too. I might have decided to come downstairs and grab one for a midnight snack!"

"Good thing you didn't," Sam said. "I guess the killer didn't care all that much if he got somebody else by accident, as long as McKenna died."

"That's terrible!"

"Murder always is," Phyllis said.

Nick sat back and shook his head, not denying Phyllis's statement, just in awe at the situation. "So that's why the Blaines and the Forrests are leaving?" he asked. "They don't think it's safe to stay here?"

"You can't blame them for feeling that way," Phyllis admitted.

"Yeah, staying at a bed-and-breakfast where breakfast kills somebody isn't something most people would do. I guess I can understand why they were upset."

Phyllis didn't want to make things worse, but there was no point in delaying the inevitable.

"What about you and Kate, Nick?" she asked. "Will you be moving out, too?"

"I don't know. This is all so unexpected. I guess I'd better talk it over with Kate and find out what she thinks." He shook his head again. "If she's too scared, I couldn't really ask her to stay. I mean, I can't believe that anyone here would commit *murder*, for God's sake, but somebody had to put that poison in the crab cakes."

Phyllis nodded wearily. There was no getting around that fact.

Nick put his hands on his knees and pushed himself to his feet. He had lost a lot of his exuberance in the past few minutes.

"I'll let you know what we decide," he said. "We may *have* to stay here tonight. It's not going to be easy finding a vacancy this late in the day. But, uh, Kate may want to, uh, eat out somewhere . . ."

"I understand," Phyllis said.

And she did. If the situation had been different, *she* wouldn't have wanted to stay at a place where one of the guests had been fatally poisoned by something he ate there. She just wouldn't feel comfortable at all.

That discomfort on the part of the public could spell ruin for the bed-and-breakfast, she thought, unless the murder was solved quickly and it was obvious to everyone that negligence wasn't the cause of Ed McKenna's death. Of course, it might be just as bad if Consuela or a member of her family turned out to be the killer. The bed-and-breakfast would share in some guilt by association. There wasn't really a good solution, Phyllis thought . . .

Just as there was no good way to put off making that call to Dorothy any longer.

Dorothy was upset, of course. Phyllis wouldn't have expected any other reaction from her cousin.

"We'll drive back down there right away," Dorothy said after Phyllis had filled her in on everything. "First thing in the morning. Goodness, this is terrible! I just wish . . ."

"What is it, Dorothy?" Phyllis asked, sensing that more was going on than her cousin had told her.

"It's just that Wendy really needs me here, too. The baby has some medical problems. They may have to perform open-heart surgery."

"Oh, no!" Phyllis said. "You hadn't told me anything about that."

"I didn't want to worry you without any reason, in case things turned out all right. The doctors are still running tests, and they're not sure yet what they'll have to do."

"Listen to me," Phyllis said. "You and Ben stay right there and help Wendy and her family as much as you can. That's the most important thing right now."

"But Ed McKenna was murdered, you said!"

"Yes, which means it won't help him for you and Ben to rush back down here," Phyllis pointed out. "The police investigation will carry on whether you're here or not."

"Yes, I suppose that's true." On the other end of the phone line, Dorothy sighed. "That poor man. He's been coming to Oak Knoll for years now. Staying there and fishing was just about the only joy he got out of life."

"Do you know anything about him? He didn't talk much at all while we were here."

"I know he owns—or rather, owned—some sort of electronics company in San Antonio. They make components for radar equipment, I believe he said, and have a lot of military contracts. He's been trying to retire for several years now. He even put his sons in charge of the company for a while, but one of them made some sort of mistake on a contract and cost them quite a bit of money, so Ed turned everything over to the other son. That caused a lot of hard feelings, of course. I could have told him that it would. Mixing family and business never works out very well."

"Certainly not with *those* children." Phyllis knew it was a tacky thing to say, but she couldn't help herself, not after the unpleasant meeting with Frances Heaton and Oliver and Oscar McKenna earlier in the day.

"You've met them, have you?"

"They came by this afternoon. They drove down from San Antonio after Chief Clifton notified them of their father's death. That was before we found out it was murder. Actually, they were here when the chief stopped by."

"I've never met them," Dorothy said, "but from listening to Ed talk about them, I don't think I've missed much."

"You haven't," Phyllis agreed. "It sounds like Mr. McKenna talked a lot more to you than he did to us."

Despite the seriousness of the situation, Dorothy laughed. "It took years to find out that much about him, a little bit at a time. And now we'll never learn any more, the poor man."

The cousins shared a few seconds of silence, a bit of mutual mourning for a man neither of them had really known; then Phyllis said, "So, are you and Ben going to stay up there in Dallas and let me take care of things down here?"

"I really hate to dump this mess on you, Phyllis—"

"You didn't have anything to do with it. You were four hundred miles away when it happened, remember?"

"Yes, but Oak Knoll isn't your responsibility, and we should be there, sink or swim."

"Don't even consider it," Phyllis said. "Stay right where you are and do everything you can to help your daughter and grandbaby. That's the most important thing right now. Everything will be fine here."

"I don't see how that's possible."

To tell the truth, Phyllis didn't, either, but she wasn't going to say that to Dorothy. She made her tone as bright and optimistic as she could as she went on, "I'm sure by the time you get back down here the police will have solved the murder and the whole thing will have blown over."

"Oh, I hope so. Dale Clifton is a good chief of police, and to tell you the truth, I'm not sure but what his daughter, Abby, is even better at police work. The FBI tried to recruit her while she was in college, you know, but she wanted to come back home and work for her dad."

"From the sound of what you say, mixing family and business worked out there."

"It certainly did," Dorothy said. "I'm just going to tell myself that between the two of them, they'll find out who killed Ed, and people will see that no one at the bed-and-breakfast was to blame."

No one who worked there, anyway, Phyllis thought. But it still seemed likely to her that the killer must have *some* connection to Oak Knoll.

Phyllis and Dorothy said their good-byes, with Phyllis promising to let her cousin know about any new developments right away. She had just hung up the phone when heavy footsteps on the stairs announced the arrival of Leo Blaine and Sheldon Forrest. Neither man looked happy.

"We've been calling around," Leo said without preamble, "and there aren't any vacancies to be had this side of Victoria one way and Corpus the other."

"Every place around here is booked up because of the SeaFair," Sheldon said. "And the weekends are always busy all up and down the coast."

"Let me get this straight," Phyllis said. "You're telling me that you're not leaving after all?"

"You haven't already given away our rooms to someone else, have you?" Sheldon asked.

She might have, Phyllis thought, if anyone had called asking if they had any vacancies. But that hadn't happened.

She was still just angry enough not to answer Sheldon's question right away. Instead she asked, "Are you sure you really want to stay in a murder house?"

"Hey, we have every right to be upset," Leo said. "A

guy gets poisoned, and we don't know how it happened except that the stuff was probably in the crab cakes he ate here. What are we supposed to think?"

"You're right, of course," Phyllis admitted. "And I haven't given your rooms away to anyone else. You're welcome to stay here for as long as you have reservations."

And maybe for longer than that if they wanted to, as unlikely as that might be, she told herself. Once the news got around about Mr. McKenna's murder, people who had reservations for later in the fall might decide to cancel them.

But they would cross that bridge when they came to it, she thought. Maybe things would work out.

"Please tell your wives that I'm glad you'll be staying," Phyllis went on, "I'm sure everything will be just fine."

"We'll see," Leo said, but he didn't sound convinced. "Meanwhile, we won't be here for supper tonight. We're going down to the Big Fisherman."

Phyllis had already heard about the Big Fisherman, although she and her friends hadn't sampled the food there yet. It was one of the best-known restaurants in the area, located about halfway between Rockport and Aransas Pass. Famous for its chicken-fried steaks, it offered lunch specials that drew people from all over this part of the country.

"I understand," she said.

"We'll probably eat breakfast somewhere else in the morning, too," Sheldon added.

"Whatever you think is best." Phyllis squared her shoulders and lifted her chin. "But we'll be offering the best breakfast you'll find anywhere around here, whether you choose to eat it or not."

"Yeah, fine, whatever," Leo said with a shrug of his shoulders. He and Sheldon turned and started back up the stairs.

Phyllis watched them go, telling herself as she did so

that she shouldn't resent their attitude. Deep down, they were just scared, that was all. They didn't want to risk their lives or the lives of Jessica and Raquel, and she couldn't blame them for that.

But if everyone else felt that way, then the days were numbered for her cousin's business. Dorothy and Ben probably didn't actually need the money they made from the bed-and-breakfast to survive, but it had been their livelihood—their life—for a long time. If it failed and was disgraced and vilified in the process, that failure would haunt them for the rest of their lives.

So she would just have to do everything she could, Phyllis told herself, to make sure that didn't happen.

That was the thought going through her head when she happened to glance out the front window and see the police car coming to a stop in front of the house.

Chapter 8

This time it was Assistant Chief of Police Abby Clifton, rather than her father, Dale, who got out of the car and came along the walk toward the house. Phyllis opened the front door as Abby started up the steps to the porch. The young woman smiled and said, "You must have seen me coming, Mrs. Newsom."

"I was in the parlor and saw the car through the front window," Phyllis said. She pushed the screen back. "Please come in."

"Thank you."

"I hope you've come to tell us that you found out who murdered poor Mr. McKenna," Phyllis said as Abby stepped into the foyer.

Abby's smile disappeared. She shook her head and said, "I'm afraid not. But the autopsy is complete now and there's no doubt that Mr. McKenna was poisoned. There's still a faint possibility that he ingested the poison by accident, I suppose, but Chief Clifton and I don't believe that's what happened."

"Neither do I, to be honest."

Abby looked interested. "Oh? Why is that? Are you basing your opinion on your experience with those other murder cases you investigated?"

Her father must have told her what Sam had said earlier. Phyllis felt uncomfortable. It would be just fine with her if people would stop bringing up those other cases. She didn't expect that to happen anytime soon, though . . . especially not if she managed to keep on getting herself involved with more murders.

"I just don't see why there would be any poison around here for anyone to get into accidentally," she said. "Although, come to think of it, there might be some rat poison or something like that out in the toolshed in the backyard."

As soon as she said it, she wished she could recall the words. While Tom Anselmo wasn't the only one with a key to the shed, of course, he was the person who went in there most often because the lawn mower and the other tools for yard work were kept there. Pointing out that he might have easy access to rat poison would just make the police even more likely to suspect him, especially once they found out about his criminal history. Phyllis didn't know exactly what sort of poison had been used to kill Ed McKenna, but she didn't want to throw any unjustified suspicion on Tom Anselmo.

"We'll find out," Abby Clifton said. "Since Mr. McKenna's children insisted that we get warrants to search his room and his belongings, the chief decided to just get a single warrant and ask the judge to include everything on the premises. So we'll be taking a look in the toolshed, as well as everywhere else."

"Oh," Phyllis said. "Well, I suppose that makes sense."

"Is that all right with you, Mrs. Newsom?" Abby asked, and Phyllis thought the young woman was watching her a little more closely than was really necessary. Looking for any sign of guilt, perhaps?

"That's fine with me," Phyllis said with a firm nod to show Abby that she didn't have anything to hide.

Abby smiled again. "Good. Now, can you tell me which of the guests are here right now?"

"All of them, as far as I know. I'm pretty sure they're all upstairs."

"I'd like to speak to them, please, as well as everyone else who's staying here."

"That would be the three people who came down here with me from Weatherford," Phyllis said. "Why do you need to speak to them?"

Abby didn't answer the question. Instead she said, "It would be easier if I just explained it to everyone at once."

"All right," Phyllis said with a shrug. "I'll see if I can round them up." She paused on her way out of the parlor. "What about Consuela?"

"You might as well ask her to step in here, too," Abby said.

Phyllis found Carolyn in the kitchen with Consuela and asked them to step into the parlor. Consuela frowned and gestured toward the stove, where several pans sat on burners with tendrils of steam rising from them.

"I've got supper cooking," she said. "I can't just leave it."

"Assistant Chief Clifton was pretty insistent on talking to everyone," Phyllis explained. "I'm sure if you just take everything off the burners until she's finished, everything will be all right."

Consuela made a little noise, as if Phyllis should have known better, being a cook herself. And in truth, Phyllis *did* know better. Most things required a constant temperature for a certain amount of time. Most seafood required little cooking and too much would ruin it.

Carolyn didn't like it, either. "That policewoman's going to interrogate all of us," she declared. "You just wait and see."

"I don't think that's what she has in mind," Phyllis said, but in truth, she didn't really know what Abby wanted with them. Maybe she *was* going to give them the third degree, to use another old-fashioned term.

With a disapproving frown, Consuela turned off the burners on the stove, and she and Carolyn headed for the parlor while Phyllis went up the rear stairs.

She found Sam and Eve in their rooms and asked them to join the group gathering in the parlor. "Oh, dear, that sounds ominous," Eve said. "A gathering of the suspects, just like in an Agatha Christie novel."

"That's not it at all," Phyllis said, although, again, she didn't know that for sure.

Sam didn't object, just shrugged and headed for the stairs. Of all the people in the house, other than herself, Phyllis was certain that Sam was the one with the least amount of secrets to hide.

She knocked on the door of Nick and Kate Thompson's room next, hoping that they were decent. They must have been, because Nick opened the door just a couple of seconds after Phyllis knocked on it.

"Assistant Chief Clifton wants to speak to everyone downstairs, in the parlor," she told him. Over his shoulder she saw Kate standing in front of the mirror attached to the dresser, running a brush through her thick brown hair. Both of them were dressed casually in shorts and T-shirts.

"Sure," Nick said. "We were just about to go out, but it can wait for a little while. I assume this is about what happened to Mr. McKenna?"

"That's right. At least, I assume it is, too. She didn't really say." Phyllis paused, then resumed. "If you don't mind my asking . . . have you decided to stay here?"

Kate put the brush down on the dresser and came toward the door. "Of course we're staying," she said. "There's no reason to leave. What happened to Mr. McKenna was either a terrible accident, or someone was out to get him. Either way, it doesn't have anything to do with Nick and me."

"That's the way I feel, too," Nick added. "This is a charming place. Anyway," he went on with a smile, "I heard Leo and Sheldon complaining about how there aren't any other places around here with vacancies right now, so it wouldn't do any good to try to leave, would it?"

Phyllis returned the smile, though hers was a bit rueful. "I suppose not. But thank you anyway."

"You're welcome. We'll be right down."

Phyllis nodded and moved on to the rooms where the Blaines and the Forrests were staying. She knew they hadn't left yet to eat supper at the Big Fisherman, but they probably planned on going soon and she felt certain Leo would complain about being forced to stay here and listen to whatever Abby Clifton had to say.

If Abby tried to question them, Phyllis was even more certain that Leo would refuse to answer and would insist on a lawyer. That was his right, of course, but it would complicate things even more.

There was no way around it. She knocked on the door of the room where Leo and Jessica were staying.

To her surprise, Sheldon Forrest opened the door. He seemed a little surprised to see her, too, as he fastened the top button of his shirt. "What is it, Mrs. Newsom?" he asked.

"Assistant Chief of Police Clifton is here," Phyllis said. "She wants everyone to come down to the parlor so she can speak to the whole group."

"We were going to be leaving soon for supper . . ."

"I know. I hope this won't take very long."

"But you don't know that, do you?"

"No," Phyllis admitted, "I don't."

"Very well. There seems to be little choice in the matter."

Phyllis looked past Sheldon in an attempt to see if Leo was in the room. She didn't see him, though. All she saw was Jessica, who looked rather flushed and out of breath.

Oh, dear Lord, Phyllis thought.

"I, uh, need to find Mr. Blaine and Mrs. Forrest—" she began.

"Don't bother," Sheldon said. "We'll tell them. And if you'd be so kind as to inform the assistant chief that we'll be downstairs in just a few minutes ... ?"

"Of course. Thank you." Phyllis was glad when Sheldon closed the door and she could turn toward the stairs. She didn't want to think the thoughts that were going through her head and didn't want to have to see anything else that might support them.

Good Lord, she thought again.

By the time she reached the parlor, Sam, Carolyn, Eve, and Consuela were already gathered there, along with Nick and Kate Thompson. They were all sitting around while Abby Clifton stood near the front window. No one was talking, and the atmosphere in the room was rather strained and tense.

"The Blaines and the Forrests will be down in just a minute," she told Abby, who nodded and smiled, although Phyllis noted that the expression didn't dilute the alertness in the younger woman's eyes.

"Thank you," Abby said. "We'll wait for them, if that's all right."

"It pretty much has to be, doesn't it?" Carolyn said.

Her sharp tone didn't shake Abby's smile. "We appreciate the cooperation."

With a clatter of footsteps, the other two couples came down the stairs less than a minute later. Phyllis couldn't stop herself from looking at Leo and Raquel to see if there was any sign that the two of them had been together like Sheldon and Jessica were. Everything seemed perfectly normal, though, with Leo, as usual, blusteringly taking the lead.

"What's this all about?" he demanded as he came into the parlor with the other three trailing close behind him. "Do I need to call my lawyer in Houston?"

"Why would you need to call your lawyer, Mr. Blaine?" Abby asked.

"If you're planning on giving me the third degree, you're not gonna get away with it."

Phyllis tried not to wince, even though it bothered her that Leo had just unwittingly echoed the thought that had passed through her mind earlier.

"Nobody's giving anybody the third degree," Abby said with the pleasant but noncommittal smile still on her face. "At some point we're going to want all of you to come down to the police station and give us your official statements about what you did and saw this morning, but that's just routine. And we're going to start with Mrs. Newsom and Mr. Fletcher, since they're the ones who actually discovered that Mr. McKenna was dead." She looked at Phyllis and Sam. "If you could come by tomorrow morning, we'd appreciate it."

"All right," Phyllis said, and Sam nodded his agreement. Even though Abby had phrased it as a polite request, she had a feeling the police wouldn't take it kindly if they refused.

"I'm not signing any statement until my lawyer's looked it over," Leo insisted.

"Of course, that's entirely up to you," Abby told him.

There was no veiled threat in her voice that Phyllis could hear, but Leo seemed to take it that way. "Hey, I don't sign *anything* until my lawyer's checked it out," he said. "Ask anybody who's done business with me. I'm careful that way."

"We can do that," Abby said without hesitation, which made Leo's frown deepen. Jessica touched his arm, as if she sensed that he was digging himself into a hole with his attitude, but he ignored her.

"If you're not gonna question us, then what's this meeting all about?" he demanded.

"I just came by to make sure that all of you were still here and hadn't tried to leave town."

"We would have moved to different accommodations," Sheldon said, "if any had been available. But we weren't going to leave town."

"Yes, it gets pretty crowded around here during the

week leading up to the SeaFair," Abby said, "and, of course, the weekend itself will be really hectic. It would probably simplify matters for everybody if you folks could just stay here."

Leo grunted. "Bed-and-breakfast, and no extra charge for murder. Well, if you don't mind, we're gonna be eating our meals somewhere else for the duration."

Consuela looked daggers at him for that, Phyllis noted, but also as usual with him, Leo was oblivious to the effect his rude comments had on other people.

"We plan on wrapping up the investigation as quickly as possible," Abby said, "so with any luck you won't have to stay here for very long unless you just want to. But I can tell you, Oak Knoll is one of the best bed-and-breakfasts in the area."

"We always thought so," Jessica said somewhat forlornly. "Until this terrible business with Mr. McKenna happened, that is."

"My wife and I will be around anytime you need to talk to us," Nick told Abby. "We're willing to do anything we can to help." Kate nodded in agreement with what he'd said.

"Thank you, Mr. Thompson. Citizen cooperation always makes our job easier."

Abby wasn't looking at Leo as she said that, but he reacted anyway. "Hey, I got a right to a lawyer."

"No one said you didn't, Mr. Blaine." Abby started toward the door, saying, "I'll let you people go on about your business now. Thank you for your patience."

Leo wasn't ready to let it go. He pointed at Consuela and said, "You didn't tell *her* not to leave town."

"I don't think Consuela's going anywhere," Abby said. "She and her family have lived here for a long time."

"That's right," Consuela said. "And we got nothing to hide, either. Me and my girls will talk to you anytime."

"Thanks." Abby gave them all a nod as she left the parlor. "Good evening, everyone."

As soon as the front door had closed behind her, Leo

said, "Of all the blasted . . . I'm gonna call Roger right now!" He reached in the pocket of his trousers to dig out his cell phone.

Phyllis supposed that Roger was his lawyer.

Jessica said to her husband, "He's probably left the office by now—"

"I'll call him at home! I'm not gonna put up with harassment like this!"

Phyllis thought that Abby Clifton had gone out of her way *not* to say or do anything that smacked of harassment, but obviously Leo saw things differently. What was that old line . . . ? Oh, yes.

What color is the sky in your world?

Evidently in Leo Blaine's world, the sky was, say, a deep, angry purple, Phyllis thought.

"I thought we were going to eat supper," Sheldon said.

"Yes," Jessica said as she tugged at Leo's sleeve. "Let's go have a nice, peaceful supper. This has been a stressful day, and I just want to relax for a little while."

Leo had his cell phone open in his hand now. "I want to call Roger—"

Jessica reached out and closed the phone, surprising Phyllis by standing up to Leo that way. "You can call him later," she said. "*After* we eat."

"All right, all right," Leo grumbled as he slipped the phone back in his pocket. "But if that lady cop thinks she can railroad me, she's got another think comin'!"

The four of them filed out of the parlor and left the house. After they were gone, Nick Thompson looked at Consuela and said, "You've worked here for a while. Is he *always* like that?"

Consuela shrugged and said, "Mr. Blaine has always been loud. And he likes to complain. But this business with Mr. McKenna has made him worse. I think he's scared but just doesn't want to admit it."

Sam spoke up, saying, "That's what I figure, too. All that bellerin' is just to cover up how nervous he is."

"We're all nervous," Carolyn pointed out. "That doesn't give anybody an excuse to be obnoxious."

Nick leaned toward his wife and whispered something in her ear. He had to stretch up a little to do so, since she was taller than him. She looked at him, shrugged, and nodded.

Nick turned back toward Consuela and smiled. "We've decided that we're going to eat here tonight after all. That is, if there's enough food for everyone."

"Plenty to go around," Consuela assured him. "And you won't be sorry, Mr. Thompson. My seafood quesadillas are the best you've ever had."

Nick chuckled. "Well, I don't think we've ever had seafood quesadillas before, so I'm sure they will be."

"But they would be even if we ate them all the time," Kate added.

The talk of food reminded Phyllis that she still had to decide what she was going to make for the Just Desserts competition. Despite Ed McKenna being murdered, the SeaFair would go on as scheduled, and so would the dessert contest. Life for the rest of the world didn't grind to a halt just because one cantankerous old man had been poisoned.

People wanted their pies and cakes and cookies, no matter who was dead!

Chapter 9

The seafood quesadillas were every bit as good as Consuela claimed they would be. Stuffed with cheese, shrimp, crabmeat, and other things that Phyllis couldn't identify, they were delicious, she thought. It was a perfect blend of flavors and it went nicely with the tossed salad and sliced cantaloupe Consuela served.

But even so, she had to admit deep down, doubt nagged at her mind every time she took a bite. Consuela would have to be a lunatic to think that she could poison everyone at the bed-and-breakfast and get away with it, but such things happened sometimes. That was why the insanity defense existed. Some people just didn't know they were doing anything wrong, no matter how heinous their crime.

Not Consuela, though, Phyllis told herself. The woman was a hard worker, a loving mother to her daughters, a good wife to her husband. She couldn't be a killer.

The forced smiles on the faces of the others at the dinner table, as well as the slightly hollow sound of their conversation, told Phyllis that they were all trying to convince themselves of the same thing.

They all made a valiant effort to behave normally, though. Everyone avoided the subject of Ed McKenna's death and the very real possibility that he had been murdered. Instead they talked about the upcoming SeaFair and the other things going on in the Rockport/Fulton area.

"Me, I'm lookin' forward to the gumbo cook-off," Sam said. "It's been a while since I've had real good gumbo. Used to get some down in Louisiana."

"When were you in Louisiana?" Phyllis asked.

"Did my army basic trainin' there at Fort Polk, back in the sixties."

"I never knew you were in the army," Eve said.

Sam grinned. "Well, it wasn't exactly my idea, if you get my drift."

"You were drafted," Carolyn said.

"Yep. Tramped around the Louisiana swamps for six weeks, then spent the next eighteen months trampin' around the swamps of Vietnam."

"How terrible!"

"It was no picnic," Sam acknowledged. "But I made it through with a whole skin and made some friendships that lasted a long time. I reckon it was what you call a valuable experience. One I'd just as soon not have had, though."

Phyllis was surprised by what he'd said. All this time she had known him, and she had no idea until now that he had been in Vietnam.

That brought back memories of how she and Kenny had worried that he would be drafted, back in the days when they were first married. Fortunately, his student deferment had kept him out of the service. They had both been finishing up their college education at the time, getting ready to go out into the world and become teachers. Molders of young minds. They had both been so young, so filled with visions of being part of a noble calling.

And teaching *was* a noble profession, at its core. She still believed that. It was just accompanied by a lot of truly hard work that beginners never knew about until they were actually doing it. If people really knew . . .

She pushed those thoughts out of her head and put her attention back on the conversation going on around the dinner table. Nick was asking, "How in the world do you get a crab to race?"

"Same way people get jumping frogs to race, I guess," Sam said. "Put it down on the course and holler as loud as you can and hope it goes the right way."

Phyllis knew they were talking about the crab race, another SeaFair attraction . . . although watching a bunch of crabs scuttle around didn't sound all that interesting to her.

"I'm looking forward to the arts and crafts exhibitions, myself," Eve said. "I've heard that artists from all over the state come here to show their work."

Nick nodded. "It's an artsy area, all right. You can tell that from all the galleries downtown. That artistic atmosphere is just one more reason people want to live here. The place is already booming, and the market here is just going to get stronger."

"The market?" Phyllis asked.

"The real estate market." Nick waved a hand. "Sorry. I guess you didn't know I'm a real estate consultant in the real world. Something I don't want to have anything to do with while I'm on vacation, thank you very much."

"To tell you the truth," Phyllis admitted, "I don't know what any of the guests do for a living."

Maybe that was something she ought to look into, she thought. It was possible there was some sort of business connection between one of them and Ed McKenna that had led to McKenna's death. She wondered if the information would be in Dorothy's files. She wasn't sure she had any right to go poking around in there, but she didn't think Dorothy would mind, given the fact that she wanted to help the police solve the murder so that the good name of the bed-and-breakfast could be cleared.

There. She had finally admitted it to herself in so many words. She wanted to solve the murder. That was the only thing she could do to help Dorothy and Ben, who had more than enough trouble already on their plate with their grandchild's medical problems.

It wasn't going to be easy, though. Figuring out the identity of a killer never was, and this would be even more difficult than in the past because here she didn't have Mike to help her. Her deputy sheriff son had often provided her with vital information that wasn't available to the general public. She knew he risked getting in trouble every time he did that, but he always insisted that she shouldn't worry about him.

She supposed she had gotten used to having that advantage, because she thought about how helpful it would be if Abby Clifton were to drop by and bring her up to date on the progress of the investigation. That wasn't going to happen, though, no matter how much Abby and her father talked about being open to any suggestions from Phyllis. That was just talk. She knew they considered her a suspect in Ed McKenna's death just like everyone else in the house. Not an overly serious suspect, perhaps... but she would have bet that they hadn't ruled her out.

"I don't know about the Blaines and the Forrests," Nick was saying, "but Kate here is a financial whiz. She's a vice president in a real estate development company. That's how she and I met."

Kate pushed her hair back from her face and smiled. "Don't make it sound more impressive than it is, honey. You didn't mention that my father owns the company. I'm a living, breathing case of nepotism."

"Are you kidding? Your father would fire you in a minute if you weren't doing the job to suit him."

"Anyway, I know what Sheldon Forrest does," Kate said. "His wife told me one day while we were talking. He's an aerospace engineer. He has something to do with NASA there in Houston where they live."

"That's interesting," Phyllis said. "Leo Blaine doesn't strike me as an engineer. Of course, maybe he's not. He and Sheldon may not be friends from work."

"Maybe they go to the same church," Sam suggested.

Phyllis doubted that. If the sort of hanky-panky she suspected was going on among the Blaines and the Forrests was really taking place, then they weren't the churchgoing type, either.

"Anyway, about the SeaFair," Nick went on, "what do they have besides a gumbo cook-off and crab races and arts and crafts?"

"A dessert competition," Phyllis and Carolyn said simultaneously.

Nick looked back and forth between them for a second before a sly smile broke out on his face. "Ah, ladies! Do I sense a bit of rivalry?"

"Don't get them started," Eve advised with a laugh. "They've been trying to outdo each other at cooking contests for years now."

"Oh, for heaven's sake!" Carolyn said. "It's not that bad. We just enjoy baking, isn't that right, Phyllis?"

"Of course," Phyllis said. And Carolyn enjoyed winning all the contests she had won, too. Of course, Phyllis reminded herself, she would be less than honest if she didn't admit that she relished her occasional victories, too.

"So you're both entering the dessert contest at the SeaFair?" Kate asked.

"I suppose so," Phyllis said. "That's one reason we came down here."

"What are your recipes going to be?"

Phyllis and Carolyn looked at each other, but neither said a word.

Nick hooted with laughter. "I think you hit a sore spot there, sweetheart. There's a little culinary intrigue going on, maybe."

"I prefer to keep my recipe to myself until the actual contest," Carolyn said rather stiffly. She unbent a little as she went on, "But you can read it later, because I think they publish the winning entries in the newspaper after the contest. That's the way these competitions usually operate."

"Well, I'll, uh, have to keep an eye out for that," Kate said as she glanced at Phyllis. She knew as well as everyone else around the table that Carolyn had just staked her claim on having the winning entry.

Phyllis didn't rise to the bait. For one thing, there were different divisions within the contest, and as long as each of them kept her recipe secret, they wouldn't know which division the other was entering. It might turn out that they weren't even competing directly against each other.

So Carolyn's implied boast didn't bother Phyllis. She had known her old friend for way too many years to let such a thing get under her skin. She just said, "I'm sure all the recipes will be good ones. There are bound to be a lot of fine cooks around here."

"But I reckon the best ones still come from Weatherford," Sam said.

Nick laughed and picked up his glass of iced tea. "I'll drink to that," he said. "A gallant sentiment, Sam."

"Like Walter Brennan used to say, 'No brag, just fact.'"

"Who?" Kate asked.

At least the discussion about the SeaFair and its assorted attractions had gotten everyone's mind off poison for a while, Phyllis thought later as she settled herself in front of the computer in Dorothy's small office nestled behind the kitchen. She didn't even mind the slight awkwardness that had come up concerning her long-running rivalry with Carolyn. That was a small price to pay for making the situation more comfortable for everyone else.

Now, though, everyone had scattered throughout the house. Nick and Kate were in their room. The Blaines and the Forrests had returned from supper and gone to their rooms, too, and Lord knew what *they* were doing up there, Phyllis thought. The Lord could know, but she certainly didn't want to. Consuela had finished cleaning up after supper and had gone home. Sam was in the parlor watching TV; Phyllis could hear it through the office door, which was open a couple of inches. Eve and Carolyn were around somewhere, although she didn't know exactly where.

And she was at the computer, about to go poking around in things that technically were none of her business.

Dorothy had told her enough about the software program the bed-and-breakfast used to keep track of its guests so that Phyllis was able to open it without any trouble. She wasn't the most naturally computer-savvy person in the world, but she had learned enough to navigate her way around most common programs. She didn't have any trouble locating the files that contained information about Leo and Jessica Blaine and Sheldon and Raquel Forrest.

It was pretty basic stuff, she saw as she scanned through the pages. Names, addresses, phone numbers, credit card numbers and expiration dates, scans of everyone's driver's license. There was a space for employment information, and Phyllis saw that Sheldon listed his employer as the National Aeronautics and Space Administration, just as Kate had said. Leo's employer was listed as the Jefferson-Bartell Group, whatever that was.

That was all she found in Dorothy's files, so Phyllis began surfing the Internet. She did a search for Sheldon's name first and found that he was the author of a number of articles about mass propulsion and overcoming inertial drag, all of which had been published in various technical and physics journals. Some of them were available online, and Phyllis called up one to look at it.

She had done reasonably well in all the science

courses when she was in school herself, including physics, but Sheldon's article was just so much gobbledygook to her. It might as well have been written in a foreign language. From the looks of the comments accompanying the article, though, Sheldon seemed to be a well-respected member of his profession.

She didn't find anything personal about him online, only the work-related articles. She moved on to Leo.

The search on his name brought up a lot more hits. Some of them were links to newspaper stories. Phyllis began checking them and found that most were from the society pages of the Houston newspaper. They included photos taken at various charity events and fund-raisers, and Leo and Jessica were in most of them. Smiling and dressed in a tuxedo, Leo didn't appear nearly as unpleasant as he did when he was blustering and stomping around here. In a low-cut evening gown and with her hair artfully done, Jessica Blaine was positively gorgeous, Phyllis discovered, not at all the perky, wholesome little housewife Phyllis had first taken her for.

The real surprise was seeing Raquel in some of the photos with the Blaines. She looked equally glamorous. The captions identified her as Raquel Jefferson Forrest.

There was the link between the couples, Phyllis thought as she typed swiftly. She did a search for the Jefferson-Bartell Group.

It took only a few moments for her to discover through numerous newspaper and business magazine articles that the company specialized in designing high-tech electronic guidance systems, with much of its work being done for NASA. Phyllis leaned forward as excitement gripped her. Ed McKenna's company in San Antonio manufactured electronic components. Maybe one of its contracts was with the Jefferson-Bartell Group.

The next fifteen minutes were frustrating as Phyllis continued navigating the tricky waters of the Internet. She found quite a few mentions of the prosaically named McKenna Electronics, but nothing that connected the company to Jefferson-Bartell. She read a story about Ed McKenna stepping down as CEO but remaining as president while his sons, Oliver and Oscar, handled the day-to-day duties of running the operation. She found another article from the business section of the San Antonio paper about Oscar McKenna being reassigned to the research division of the company while his brother, Oliver, remained as CEO. Phyllis had already heard about that, but this was confirmation of Oscar's demotion. The newspaper story gave no reason for the action, but she knew it had to do with some mistake Oscar had made that cost the company a considerable amount of money.

She didn't find anything about Frances Heaton. Frances must keep a pretty low profile, Phyllis thought. It was unusual in this day and age to run into anyone who didn't have at least a few pages on the Internet that mentioned them.

Engrossed in what she was doing, she went back to looking up everything she could about the Jefferson-Bartell Group. Founded by Charles Jefferson and Mitchell Bartell in the early eighties, it had ridden the crest of that decade's high-tech boom and survived the bust of the nineties, remaining a viable player in the electronics arena with lucrative connections to the aerospace, oil and gas, and communications industries. Mitchell Bartell was dead, having succumbed to pancreatic cancer in 1997, but Charles Jefferson remained alive and in control of the company, aided by his son-in-law and vice president, Leo Blaine.

So Leo was a wealthy businessman and Sheldon was just a humble engineer, Phyllis mused, but Sheldon also happened to be married to the daughter of Leo's boss. That was typical of the complex relationships, both business and personal, that grew up among people all the time, Phyllis thought.

But learning about it hadn't brought her any closer to seeing a connection between the Blaines and the Forrests and Ed McKenna, other than the fact that they were all staying at the same bed-and-breakfast on the Gulf Coast. And if there was no other connection, then there couldn't be any motive for any of them to be involved in McKenna's murder, unless it had to do with something that had happened here at Oak Knoll . . .

Consuela hadn't mentioned any problems between McKenna and the two couples from Houston, but Phyllis decided it might be a good idea to ask Theresa and Bianca about that. Even though she carried the title of head housekeeper, Consuela spent most of her time in the kitchen. What cleaning she did was there and in the other downstairs rooms. As far as Phyllis could tell from what she had seen so far, the two younger women were responsible for taking care of the guest rooms upstairs. That meant they might have seen things that their mother hadn't.

"Never knew you to stay chained to the computer for this long," Sam drawled from the doorway of the small office.

Phyllis looked up from the monitor, taken a little by surprise. She had been so wrapped up in her thoughts that she hadn't heard him come down the hall from the parlor. "I'm just doing a little Internet surfing," she told him.

"I don't reckon that's as dangerous as the other kind."

Phyllis smiled. "No, I never saw the appeal of standing on a little board on top of a big wave, either."

"Maybe we're just not the adventurous types. At least, not most of the time."

Phyllis wondered if he was talking about the time when a killer had tried to stab him. She still regretted that she had put his life in jeopardy that day, although he had passed it off lightly as just a bit of excitement. It was easy to get caught up in the mental challenge of trying to solve a murder, Phyllis thought, but at the same time there was always real danger involved.

Because a person who had been driven to kill once usually wouldn't hesitate to kill again to keep his or her crime a secret.

"I'd just as soon have my adventures vicariously," Phyllis said.

"Speakin' of which . . ." Sam jerked a thumb toward the parlor. "There's a John Wayne movie fixin' to come on, if you'd care to join me."

Sam was just about the world's biggest John Wayne fan, and Phyllis didn't mind watching the Duke. It had been a long day that had gotten off to an early, highly unpleasant start with Ed McKenna's death, and ever since then Phyllis's mind had been full to bursting with the convoluted possibilities that accompanied any murder. Sitting on the sofa next to Sam and watching John Wayne put things right for a couple of hours might be just the thing she needed in order to relax before turning in.

With a smile, she logged off of Dorothy's computer and said, "That sounds just fine to me, pilgrim."

Chapter 10

$\mathcal{P}$hyllis's sleep was restful, instead of haunted by dreams of Ed McKenna's death as she had feared it might be. No answers came to her as she slept, though, so when she woke up just before dawn the next morning she was no closer to knowing who the murderer was than when she went to sleep.

As she went downstairs, the delicious aromas of coffee brewing, bacon frying, and biscuits baking greeted her and told her that Consuela was already on the job. Phyllis went into the kitchen and saw that Consuela was preparing the usual full breakfast, including *huevos rancheros* and *migas*.

"Good morning," Consuela said. She smiled as she nodded toward the various pots and pans on the stove. "They may not eat it, but I'm going to fix it anyway. That way the choice is up to them."

Phyllis knew who Consuela was talking about: the guests who were still sleeping upstairs. Phyllis admired Consuela's determination and said, "If those wonderful aromas don't make them change their minds, then I don't know what in the world could. Everything smells delicious."

"*Muchas gracias, Señora Newsom.*"

The decanter on the coffeemaker was full. Phyllis poured herself a cup and asked, "Am I the first one up?"

"You're the only one I've seen so far." Consuela paused, then asked with a worried frown, "You and Mr. Fletcher have to go to the police station this morning, right?"

"I suppose so." Phyllis sipped her coffee. "I hope by the time we get there they'll have solved Mr. McKenna's murder ... or decided that it was an accident after all, even though I don't hold out much hope for that."

"I know they're gonna call Tom in," Consuela said with a sigh. "I'm surprised they haven't already done it, since Chief Clifton knows about him doing time in Huntsville."

"Maybe Chief Clifton has already decided that Tom couldn't be guilty. I suppose you've told him about it?"

"Tom?" Consuela nodded. "I told him right away, so he'd know to expect trouble."

"But he hasn't even been here at the house since he got back in from the oil rig this time, has he?" Phyllis asked. "You said he was going to do the yard work today."

Consuela didn't answer, just stood there slowly stirring something that was simmering in a pot.

Phyllis frowned. "Wait a minute. Are you telling me that Tom *has* been here since he got back?"

Consuela grimaced, clearly not wanting to answer Phyllis's question and yet unwilling to lie about it. "Night before last," she finally said. "I went off and forgot my purse, so I sent him back over here to get it. I told him to just let himself in the back door, get the purse out of the cabinet, and not to bother anybody."

"I never even knew he was here," Phyllis said.

"Well, he probably didn't turn on any lights. He knows his way around this house pretty good."

He ought to, Phyllis thought, since he handled all the maintenance work on the place. What Consuela was telling her now meant that Tom Anselmo had had the opportunity to poison those leftover crab cakes.

But he'd had absolutely no reason to do anything like that, as far as Phyllis could see. Tom probably remembered Ed McKenna from McKenna's past visits, but Tom hadn't even been in town for the first part of McKenna's stay this time.

Unless Tom had been waiting to commit murder ever since McKenna's visit the previous year, and that seemed too far-fetched for Phyllis to give the idea any credence at all.

Would the police believe that it was equally far-fetched, though? Or would they think that given Tom's criminal history, his presence on the scene automatically made him the strongest suspect?

"You won't tell the cops what I just told you, will you, Mrs. Newsom?" Consuela asked.

Phyllis didn't know what to say, and her silence was all the answer Consuela needed. The woman's shoulders slumped.

"Ah, *Dios mio*," she said. "How could I even ask such a thing of you? Of course you have to tell the police the truth. Anyway, it's not gonna matter. They'll ask Tom himself as soon as they get around to questioning him, and he'll tell them. He's too proud to lie. I'm betting that'll be sooner rather than later."

"I'm sure everything will work out all right, Consuela," Phyllis said, trying to make her tone as comforting as possible. "We just have to wait and see what happens."

Consuela nodded. After a moment of silence, Phyllis went on. "I'm going to step out onto the porch and watch the sun rise."

"Breakfast will be ready soon."

"I won't be gone long."

Pink streamers of clouds floated low over the water as Phyllis went out onto the porch carrying her coffee. The sun was still below the horizon, though it would be peeping into view any minute now. Sunrise was close enough so that a vast pink-and-gold arch had already formed in the sky, heralding its arrival. Just like the day before, nature was rewarding early risers with a glimpse of breathtaking beauty.

But not everything was like it had been the day before, Phyllis reflected.

Yesterday at this time, Ed McKenna had still been alive, even though the poison was already working in his body.

Life drew sharp dividing lines. The birth of a child, the death of a loved one ... any birth and any death, really ... and nothing was ever exactly the same afterward as it had been before. What was, could never be again. Sometimes the change was for the better, but even in those instances, Phyllis reflected, for every gain there was a loss, and that was sad somehow.

There ought to be a way to go back, if only for a moment, and reach out to touch the past. To feel her husband's hand in hers, to hear the sound of her son's laugh when he was a baby and feel the warmth of his breath on her cheek. Memories were all well and good ... in the end they were all anyone had, after all, and they had to suffice ... but as the days of her life grew shorter, what Phyllis would have given to be able to hold all the things that were gone. If she could only do that, she might not ever let them go.

She wasn't aware that her shoulders were shaking with sobs until Sam's hands rested on them lightly. She turned, coffee sloshing out of the cup and splashing on the porch as she did so, and went into his arms. She pressed her face against his chest.

"Whoa there," he said. She felt him take the cup out of her hand; then he put both arms around her and held her. "I don't know what's wrong, Phyllis, but there's no need to cry. Everything's gonna be all right."

"You ... you don't *know* that."

"Well ... no, I reckon I don't. But I can hope." He

kept his left arm around her and lifted his right hand to the back of her head. He stroked her hair and went on, "I've already had more luck than I ever figured I would again. I hate to think what my life would've been like if Dolly Williamson hadn't told me about that room you had for rent. I never would've met you and Carolyn and Eve, never would've had all the good times we've had—"

"They haven't all been good."

"Maybe not. But a heck of a lot more good than bad, I'd say. And the bad times ... well, the way I look at it, they're just the price we've got to pay for the good ones."

Phyllis shook her head. "No. The price for life is death." She looked up at him. "My God, Sam, you and I both know that as well as anyone. You lost your wife. I lost my husband. Those McKennas, as horrible as they seemed to us, they lost their father. Nothing will ever be the same for them again."

"Maybe that's the way one of 'em wanted it," Sam said, his jaw tightening. "Sounded like they had some grudges against the old man."

"But surely they wouldn't have ... wouldn't have killed him." Even after all the things she had seen in her life, Phyllis could barely conceive of such a thing. "Anyway, they couldn't have poisoned those crab cakes. They were in San Antonio."

"They said they were, anyway."

Phyllis used the back of her hand to wipe away the tears that lingered on her face. Sam had a point there, and she was grateful to him for distracting her from the gloomy mood that had seized her for a moment.

All three of the McKenna siblings had been in San Antonio yesterday morning, because they had driven down here together after the police notified them of their father's death. But Alamo City was close enough so that any of them could have driven to Fulton the night before, gotten into the bed-and-breakfast somehow, and poisoned the crab cakes, then driven home to wait for the fateful call from the police the next morning.

That was crazy, Phyllis told herself as soon as those thoughts went through her head. The idea had so many holes in it, it wasn't even funny. For one of the McKenna siblings to be the killer, he or she would have had to get in and out of the house without leaving any sign and would have had to know that the crab cakes would be wrapped up and sitting in the refrigerator, waiting for Ed McKenna to have them for breakfast. Phyllis just couldn't make herself believe it.

But she couldn't ignore the theory entirely, she realized. She didn't know what Oscar, Oliver, and Frances were capable of. Maybe one of them knew how to pick locks. Maybe Ed McKenna had talked to one of his children on the phone that night and mentioned the crab cakes he planned to eat the next morning. As nutty as it seemed to Phyllis, things *could* have happened that way.

And one thing was certain, at least according to statistics: You were a lot more likely to be murdered by a family member than by a stranger, and while Tom and Consuela and their girls weren't exactly strangers to Ed McKenna, they weren't nearly as close to him as his children were. None of the Anselmos had a motive, but Oscar McKenna might hate his father for giving him power in the company and then snatching it away. Oliver and Frances might have equally powerful reasons for wanting their father dead. The more Phyllis thought it, the more intrigued she was by the idea.

Feeling better now, she picked up the coffee cup from the porch railing where Sam had put it. She used her other hand to squeeze his arm and said, "Let's go have some breakfast. We have to talk to the police this morning, so we should probably have a good meal first."

"In case they lock us up and put us on bread and water?" he asked with a grin.

"Don't even joke about it," Phyllis said. Food was serious business.

Not as serious as murder, of course . . .

They had brought Phyllis's Lincoln and Sam's pickup on the trip down from Weatherford, loading most of their bags in the back of the pickup. They took the pickup this morning, Sam following Fulton Beach Road as it twisted its way along the shore of the bay. As was true the overwhelming majority of the time, a wind was blowing in from the water, keeping the humidity high but maintaining pleasant temperatures as well. That near-constant wind was what had caused the trees along the shore to grow in bizarre shapes that leaned sharply inland.

Though Rockport and Fulton had a thriving fishing industry, both towns relied heavily on tourism as well. As they drove along the beach road, Phyllis and Sam passed numerous places for tourists to stay, ranging from small, independently owned motels and cabins to old-fashioned motor courts that dated from the forties to fancy, sprawling resorts that looked like they had been built within the past few years. The resorts catered to a very wealthy clientele, judging by the luxury vehicles in the parking lots.

"If this is the slow time of year, the folks who own these places must be makin' money hand over fist durin' the summer," Sam commented.

"That's the way Nick made it sound," Phyllis agreed. "This is one of the biggest growth areas along the coast. Maybe *the* biggest."

"I'll bet the folks who live here year-round miss it bein' the way it used to be. They can't be happy about all the traffic and the crowds." Sam rasped a thumbnail along his jaw. "Reckon they're probably pretty happy about all the money the tourists bring in, though."

"I'd say you're right about that."

They reached the municipal complex a few minutes later and found a parking place without any trouble.

The rest of Rockport and Fulton might be crowded, but the police station, fire station, and city hall weren't. When Phyllis and Sam went inside, the dispatcher on duty directed them to the office of Assistant Chief Abby Clifton.

"I think she's waitin' for y'all, honey," the woman said. "Just knock and go right on in. We don't stand much on ceremony around here."

Phyllis had spent enough time in the police station and sheriff's office in Weatherford in recent years so that she wasn't as uncomfortable about being here as some civilians might have been. The same was true of Sam, she supposed, or maybe it was just the fact that he was one of those men who was comfortable wherever he happened to be.

They went down the hall to Abby Clifton's office and found the young woman sitting in front of her computer. The monitor was turned so that Phyllis couldn't see the screen, and even though she was curious, she didn't think Abby would appreciate it if she leaned over the desk to take a look.

Abby smiled at them and said, "Mrs. Newsom, Mr. Fletcher. Please have a seat and I'll be right with you." She clicked the mouse a couple of times as Phyllis and Sam sat down, then turned away from the computer. "Thank you for coming in like this."

"We're glad to help," Phyllis said. "I want this matter cleared up as quickly as possible."

Abby nodded. "So that it doesn't damage the reputation of your cousin's business too much, I'd expect."

"That's right."

"Having guests drop dead can't be very good for a bed-and-breakfast. That's one reason right there to think that you didn't have anything to do with Mr. McKenna's death."

That was pretty blunt of her, Phyllis thought, but undoubtedly true.

Abby went on, "Then there's the fact that you and

your friends didn't even know Ed McKenna until you got here a few days ago. I suppose a motive for murder could have developed in that amount of time, but it seems unlikely."

"We appreciate you givin' us the benefit of the doubt," Sam said.

"Just trying to be reasonable about things," Abby said. She opened a desk drawer, reached inside, and took out a small digital recorder. As she placed it on the desk, she continued. "What I'd like for the two of you to do is simply tell me in your own words what happened yesterday morning. Include everything that you can remember, up until the time that the police arrived on the scene. I'm going to record your statements, and then they'll be transcribed so that you can sign them. Does that sound agreeable to both of you?"

"Fine by me," Sam said.

"Do you want one of us to step outside while the other gives their statement?" Phyllis asked.

Abby smiled again. "Oh, I don't really think that's necessary. For one thing, I don't think either of you are going to lie, and for another, if you wanted to tell some phony story, you've already had plenty of time to work it out between you, haven't you?"

"I guess that's true," Phyllis admitted. If there was anything she and Sam wanted to conceal about Ed McKenna's death, they could have agreed to it in the time they'd waited for the police to arrive the previous morning and solidified all the details in the more than twenty-four hours since then.

Abby poised a slender, graceful finger over the recorder. "Ready?"

Phyllis and Sam both nodded.

Abby turned the recorder on and said, "This is Assistant Chief of Police Abby Clifton." She gave the date and time. "These statements are being given by Mrs. Phyllis Newsom and Mr. Sam Fletcher. Mrs. Newsom and Mr. Fletcher, will you each give me your name and place of residence?"

They did so, Phyllis fighting the temptation to lean forward and raise her voice. She knew those little recorders were sensitive enough to pick up her words just fine if she sat normally and spoke in her usual tone.

"Thank you," Abby said. "Now, I'm going to advise you of your rights and ask you if you understand those rights." At the look of surprise on Phyllis's face, Abby clicked the recorder off and added, "This is just a formality. Don't worry."

"It's just that I thought you only had to advise people of their rights if you were arresting them," Phyllis said.

"No, we do it every time we take a statement from someone, too, just to cover all the bases."

The bases weren't what they were trying to cover, Phyllis thought, but she didn't say it. She just nodded and said, "All right."

Abby turned the recorder on again and Mirandized them, reading the rights from a laminated card she picked up from her desk. When she was done, Phyllis and Sam both stated that they understood and were giving their statements of their own free will.

It didn't take long. Phyllis went first, telling about their brief, earlier encounter with Ed McKenna as he was leaving the bed-and-breakfast with his fishing gear, then explaining how shocked she was when he fell in the water. She explained how Sam had jumped in, brought McKenna to the surface, and then towed him to shore, where Phyllis had helped pull him out of the water.

"I knew he was dead when I got a good look at his face," she said. "It was horrible. Then I went back across the road to the house, where I ran into Nick and Kate Thompson, two of the guests who are staying at the bed-and-breakfast. Kate took me in the house while Nick called 911 and went to wait with Sam until the police and the ambulance arrived."

Abby nodded and looked at Sam. "Mr. Fletcher?"

"Well, it all happened just the way Phyllis said it did."

"In your own words, please, Mr. Fletcher."

Sam went through the story, too, adding a few things from his point of view that Phyllis couldn't have known, such as his reaction when he saw Ed McKenna topple face-first into the water.

"It surprised the heck out of me," Sam said. "My first thought was that I'd knocked him in, but I knew good and well I hadn't hit him hard enough to do that. I didn't really hit him at all, just slapped his shoulder friendly-like, you know. When I got underwater and started feelin' around for him, it took me a minute to find him. When I did, I could tell by the way he felt that it wasn't good. There's a reason they call it deadweight. I got him to shore as fast as I could, and me and Phyllis hauled him out. But I knew it was too late."

"Did you think that he had drowned?" Abby asked.

Sam shook his head. "I knew he wasn't under long enough for that. That's why I thought right away that he might've had a heart attack or a stroke."

Abby looked at Phyllis again. "Mrs. Newsom, you mentioned earlier that Mr. McKenna said something about not feeling well when you and Mr. Fletcher spoke to him?"

"That's right." Phyllis thought back to the conversation. "He said he hoped getting out in the sun might make him feel better. Poor man. I suppose it was already too late by then for anything to help him."

Abby nodded. "I'm no doctor, but I'd say so." She turned off the recorder and went on, "If you don't mind waiting, I'll have this transcribed and then you can sign the statements. It'll only take about fifteen minutes or so."

"That's fine," Phyllis said. She didn't think it would hurt anything to ask, so she continued. "Did the rest of the autopsy turn up anything else?"

Abby looked a little surprised by the question, but she said, "Oh, yes, I'd forgotten that you're used to doing a little detective work of your own. But I'm afraid I really can't discuss any details of the case."

"Of course. I understand."

The young woman picked up the recorder and said, "I'll be right back."

She left Phyllis and Sam alone in her office. Phyllis eyed the computer. She was willing to bet that the autopsy report was on there somewhere. She was also sure that she wasn't just about to start poking around in the assistant chief of police's computer. That would be a good way to get thrown in the slammer, as Sam might say.

"Reckon we convinced her that we're not guilty?" he asked.

"I don't think she believes that we are. She's just trying to be thorough. I'm glad she didn't ask me about—"

She stopped short and looked around. There was no two-way mirror in the office, no mirror of any sort, in fact. But the room could be bugged, she supposed. She was glad she hadn't said anything about Tom Anselmo, as she had been about to do.

What she had said, though, might be enough to arouse suspicion in Abby Clifton if she had indeed been listening in on their conversation.

Phyllis worried about that while Abby was gone, but when the assistant chief came back, she didn't seem any more suspicious than she had been when she left. She was carrying the transcribed statements. She handed them to Phyllis and Sam and said, "If you'd just look these over and make sure that they're correct . . ."

When they had done so and agreed that the statements were accurate, they signed where their names were supposed to go and Abby collected the papers, reminding Phyllis a little of when she had taken up tests in her eighth-grade history class.

"Thank you so much," Abby said. "That's all we need

from you right now. We'll be in touch if we need you to come in again. In the meantime, I'm sure I'll be seeing you when my father and I come over later to serve that search warrant."

"You'll be there today?" Phyllis asked.

Abby nodded. "Dad's seeing the judge right now."

They stood up to leave, and Abby showed them out. When they were back in Sam's pickup, heading away from the police station, he said, "That wasn't so bad. That gal seems friendly enough."

"Yes, she's very nice," Phyllis agreed. "But that won't keep her from doing everything she can to find the murderer."

"Nope. I expect it won't."

On the way back they drove past Rockport Beach and the large, parklike area where the SeaFair would take place in a couple of days. Big tents with brightly colored stripes on them were already being set up, and there were signs along the road announcing the SeaFair and pointing toward parking areas. A carnival with a Ferris wheel and midway rides had already arrived, although everything was still packed onto the trucks parked near the boat basin. When the SeaFair actually began, throngs of people would be everywhere, Phyllis thought.

And she was running out of time to come up with a good recipe for the Just Desserts contest. Already it was too late for her to do much experimentation.

Sam veered off onto Fulton Beach Road, and a few minutes later they approached the bed-and-breakfast. As they came around one of the bends in the road as it followed the water, Phyllis spotted a couple of police cars parked up ahead. She put a hand on the pickup's dashboard and leaned forward as she asked, "Are those police cars at the bed-and-breakfast?"

"Looks like they are," Sam said. "I reckon the assistant chief didn't know for sure what her daddy was doin' after all. I think he's already here servin' that search warrant."

"Or maybe she did know and lied to us," Phyllis said. "I have a bad feeling about this."

Her worries were confirmed a moment later when Sam parked the pickup behind the police cars and they got out. Phyllis heard loud, angry voices coming from inside the house.

It sounded like quite a crowd had gathered . . . and all of them were unhappy.

Chapter 11

Phyllis hurried up the walk with Sam close behind her. Not surprisingly, she was able to pick out Leo Blaine's booming tones as he gave voice to a litany of complaints. He wasn't the only one, though. Everybody sounded mad.

"Hell's a poppin'," Sam said as they reached the porch.

"And then some," Phyllis agreed.

They went inside to find more than a dozen people gathered in the parlor. The Blaines, the Forrests, and the Thompsons were all there, along with Carolyn, Eve, Consuela, Theresa, and Bianca. A medium-sized man with graying hair and a narrow mustache stood next to Consuela with his arm around her shoulders. Phyllis hadn't met him yet, but she was confident he had to be Tom Anselmo. In other words, all the guests and staff of the Oak Knoll Bed-'n'-Breakfast.

In addition, Frances Heaton and her brothers, Oscar and Oliver McKenna, were there. Frances had her arms crossed and wore a pinched expression on her face as the toe of one shoe tapped angrily on the floor. The twins were red-faced and competing with Leo Blaine in complaining. The man at whom those complaints were directed rounded out the gathering in the parlor.

Chief Dale Clifton stood in the center of the room with his hands in the pockets of his uniform trousers and a placid expression on his weathered face. Obviously he had plenty of experience at letting complaints from angry citizens roll right off his back. Phyllis could tell that he wasn't going to let them get in the way of him doing his job.

She didn't see anyone else, but she didn't have to wonder where the other officers from those police cruisers were. She knew they were probably spread out through the house and over the rest of the property, conducting the thorough search that Chief Clifton had promised.

The chief turned, smiled, and nodded to Phyllis and Sam as they came into the parlor. "Hello," he said. "I wondered when you folks would get back."

"We've been at the police station giving our statements to your daughter," Phyllis said. She felt rather irritated herself. She didn't like being lied to. "She did a good job of delaying us until after you got here."

A slight frown creased Clifton's forehead. "Now, why in the world would she do that?"

"I don't know, but she told us you'd be here later to search the place. She said you were getting the judge to sign the warrant this morning."

"That's what I did." Clifton shrugged. "Once I had it, I didn't see any reason to wait. Abby didn't know I was coming straight here." He chuckled. "When she finds out, she's liable to be a little put out with me herself. She expected to be here for the search."

Leo said, "But you just couldn't wait to bust in with your gestapo tactics—"

Clifton shook his head. "Now, I don't take kindly to that comparison, Mr. Blaine. I'm old enough to remember the real thing. You're not."

Phyllis doubted that Chief Clifton was old enough to

have firsthand memories of World War II, although he might have been a child then.

"You don't have any right to search our stuff—"

Again, Clifton didn't let Leo finish. "That warrant I showed all of you says different."

"My lawyer will be here later today. He's driving from Houston. You're gonna be sorry you tried to bulldoze me, mister. You're about to have the biggest law firm in Houston on your ass."

Frances Heaton said, "My brothers and I have spoken to our attorneys, too. They think we may have grounds for a harassment suit. You're violating our civil rights."

Those were empty threats, and Phyllis knew it. As long as Chief Clifton had a proper warrant, he could conduct the search when and how he saw fit, and no judge was going to find fault with that. A jury might, but any lawsuit like the one Frances was threatening would be tossed out of court before it ever got that far. They would all be better off just to sit down, be quiet, and let the police get on with their work, which was what was happening anyway despite all the bluster.

While Leo and the McKennas continued complaining and Chief Clifton continued ignoring them for the most part—except to shake his head and smile at some of their more outrageous threats—Phyllis and Sam moved around the room to join Carolyn and Eve.

"Are you two all right?" Phyllis asked them quietly.

"Of course we're all right," Carolyn answered. "I may not like having a bunch of small-town cops pawing through my things, but I have nothing to hide."

"Neither do I," Eve said. "Although considering how handsome the chief is, I might not mind if they found something that would justify him interrogating me."

Carolyn blew out her breath in an exasperated sigh. "Do you really enjoy being a living, breathing stereotype?"

"I enjoy almost everything about my life, dear. It's my

nature. You can look for the joy in life, or you can look for the disappointments. I choose to look for the joy."

That was about the most profound thing Phyllis had ever heard Eve say, and it took her a little by surprise. Thinking back on the numerous husbands Eve had lost through either death or divorce, it was obvious that she had had her share of disappointments. No wonder she tried to concentrate on the things that gave her pleasure.

Phyllis slipped on over next to Consuela. She held out her hand to the man who stood with the cook and housekeeper. "Hello, I'm Phyllis Newsom. I don't believe we've met."

"Tom Anselmo," he introduced himself as he shook hands with Phyllis. "I'm glad to meet you, ma'am. I just wish it was under better circumstances."

She smiled. "That goes for me, too, Mr. Anselmo."

"Please, call me Tom. We've always been sort of like family around here with Dorothy and Ben."

Phyllis nodded, feeling an instinctive liking for this man. He didn't look like someone who had once done time in the penitentiary for selling heroin. That had been almost a quarter of a century earlier, she reminded herself, and people could change dramatically in that time, especially when their criminal behavior had been caused at least in part by the hellish situations in which they found themselves.

While she had a hard time believing that Tom could have poisoned Ed McKenna, she wished she could ask him about his late-night visit to the house a couple of evenings earlier. He might have seen something while he was there, something that had seemed innocent at the moment but might take on new importance now.

That would have to wait for another time, though. Phyllis certainly didn't want to bring up the fact that Tom had been there right in front of Chief Clifton.

When Phyllis listened closely, she could hear footsteps upstairs and knew they belonged to the officers who were searching through the bedrooms. While they waited, a khaki-uniformed policeman came into the parlor and reported to Clifton, "I've been through the office, Chief, and copied the files on the computer." He held up a little USB drive. "You want me to pull the hard drive itself?"

"Are you sure you got everything?" Clifton asked.

"If there's anything else on there, it's so well hidden and encrypted that whoever put it there ought to be working for the NSA."

"I don't think Dorothy's that much of a computer whiz, and I happen to know that Ben can barely turn the machine on." Clifton smiled. "No, you can leave it intact, Ted."

"Gotcha, Chief. I have the victim's laptop, too, so I can go through the files on it at the station."

A moment later another officer came from the kitchen. "Nothing out there except plenty of food, canned goods, cooking utensils, pots and pans . . . just what you'd expect."

"Did you put everything back the way you found it?" Clifton asked.

"Yes, sir, Chief, just like you ordered."

That made the natural resentment Phyllis felt toward the chief ease slightly. Clifton wasn't being as hard-nosed about this as he could have been. He could have confiscated Dorothy's computer or at least the hard drive, and he could have had his men tear the place apart and leave it that way so that someone else would have to clean up the mess. Phyllis was sure the officers were conducting a thorough search, but at least the chief had instructed them not to cause too much havoc.

"Have you already searched in here?" she asked him when the second officer was through talking to him.

He turned toward her and nodded. "Yes, ma'am, we did that first, so there would be a place for everyone to come while the rest of the search is being carried out."

"Did you find anything?"

"You don't really expect me to answer that, do you?" Clifton paused. "Or maybe you do. From the sound of the newspaper stories I read about you, Mrs. Newsom, you're practically an unofficial member of the sheriff's department up there where you come from."

"I think you're exaggerating, Chief."

"Maybe a little. But reading between the lines, I figure your son provided you with a lot of information in those other cases. If his boss wants to let him get away with that, fine, it's none of my business. But that's not the way we operate down here."

Sam moved up alongside Phyllis's shoulder. "I don't reckon the lady was askin' for any special favors," he said, and now his voice was tight with anger.

Phyllis appreciated the way he sprang to her defense, in the face of even a mild rebuke from the chief. But she could fight her own battles, and this little confrontation wasn't even worthy of the name.

"I believe that if you take anything away from here as evidence, you're supposed to inform the owner of the items in question," she said. "Aren't we supposed to sign a form acknowledging that?"

For a second Chief Clifton looked like he wanted to smile, but he managed to keep his expression serious. "That's true," he admitted. "And if we impound any evidence, we'll let you know."

"Damned right you will," Leo said, horning into the conversation. "Try any high-handed tricks and I'll see to it that you lose your badge."

"No tricks," Clifton said, and now his eyes glittered with anger. He was getting tired of Leo trying to browbeat him, Phyllis thought.

A short time later she heard the back door open and close, and another officer came into the parlor carrying a large plastic bag with a cylindrical plastic container in it. The container reminded Phyllis of the sort of thing coffee came in. This one had a large black skull-and-crossbones symbol on it, though.

"I found this rat poison in the toolshed out back, Chief," the officer announced.

"Of course there's rat poison in there," Tom Anselmo said. "Sometimes we have rats. I hardly ever use it, though. I'd rather use traps." He gestured toward the container. "Go ahead and look inside it. You'll see that barely any of it has been used."

Working through the clear plastic bag, Clifton opened the plastic lid and looked inside. "You're right, Tom," he said. "There's not much gone."

He didn't say anything else as he snapped the lid back down, but the unspoken implication was clear, at least to Phyllis.

It didn't take much poison to kill a man.

Clifton handed the bag to his officer and said, "Tag it."

Jessica spoke up for the first time since Phyllis and Sam had gotten back, asking the chief, "Do you have those special lights that make blood glow like on TV?"

Leo turned toward her and snapped, "Why are you asking him a stupid question like that?"

"I'm just curious," Jessica said. She looked a little like a dog that had just been kicked. "I'm sorry, Leo."

"That's quite all right, ma'am," Clifton told her. "And to answer your question, we don't have a lot of that fancy equipment, but we can call on the forensics and crime-scene teams from the county sheriff's department anytime we need to." He smiled. "Anyway, a lot of that stuff you see on TV is pure science fiction, just as much as *Star Trek* was."

Leo took hold of Jessica's arm and led her over to one of the chairs. "Sit down and don't say anything else," he ordered. "We're not gonna talk anymore to this Andy Taylor wannabe until Roger gets here." He glanced at Clifton. "Then you'll see some fireworks."

Clifton didn't seem worried about the possibility of pyrotechnics. He just waited patiently for his other officers to report in from their parts of the search.

One by one, they did so, but none of them had found anything as possibly incriminating as the rat poison in the shed. However, a couple of the officers called Clifton out into the hall and talked to him in voices quiet enough so that Phyllis couldn't hear the words. They seemed to be showing things to the chief as well, but Clifton stood so that his body concealed whatever it was from the people gathered in the parlor.

That air of secrecy didn't bode well, Phyllis thought.

Clifton came back into the parlor. "We're going to be confiscating a digital camera that was found in your room, Mr. Blaine."

"What!" Leo's face started to turn purple. "You can't do that! You've got no right! Anything up there was private—"

"We'll give you a receipt for the evidence."

"It's not evidence, I tell you! You can't just go into a guy's room and take his stuff—"

"Mr. Blaine." Chief Clifton didn't raise his voice, but his voice was hard enough and sharp enough to cut right through Leo's bellowing. "If you'd like for me to go into detail about the photographs on that camera right here in front of everyone, so you'll know why we're impounding it, I can do that."

Leo paled, and he said, "No . . . no, you don't have to do that."

Jessica was on her feet again. "Leo, what's he talking about? What photographs?"

"They're still on the digital camera, ma'am," Clifton told her. "They haven't been printed out yet."

"That's enough!" Leo said. "Damn it, I'll sign whatever you want me to sign. Just don't—"

"Leo," Jessica said.

Bianca Anselmo put her hands over her face, let out a choked sob, and ran out of the room. "Bianca!" Consuela called after her, clearly startled by her daughter's sudden flight.

Clifton didn't make a move to stop her, and neither

did anyone else. Phyllis could only look on in shocked surprise. She could think of only one reason why the discussion of photos on Leo Blaine's digital camera would upset Bianca so much. She already disliked Leo because of his obnoxious bluster, and she had been offended by the way he had told Jessica to sit down and shut up. The potential sordidness of this new revelation involving Bianca just made her despise Leo even more.

Phyllis wasn't the only one who had come to the same conclusion. Jessica got in front of her husband and demanded, "Leo, what the hell is going on here? What's that girl got to do with any pictures?"

Tom Anselmo surged forward, pulling away from Consuela's hand on his arm. "I want to know the same thing, Mr. Blaine," he said. His hands closed into fists. Leo outweighed him by fifty or sixty pounds, but right now Tom clearly didn't care about that.

Leo ignored Jessica and Tom and glared at Chief Clifton. "You're gonna be sorry you pulled this stunt," he said. "By the time my lawyer gets through with you—"

"Maybe your lawyer will be more worried about the possible implications of what we've found here today, Mr. Blaine," Clifton cut in. "It seems to me that those pictures just might be a motive for murder."

Leo took a step back like somebody had just punched him in the face ... which Tom Anselmo still wanted to do, judging by his expression and stance. "Murder!" Leo said. "I didn't murder anybody! How ... how could those pictures have anything to do with Ed McKenna getting poisoned?"

"Maybe he found out what you'd been up to," Clifton suggested. "Maybe he threatened to tell your wife, or Bianca's parents. You might've decided to shut him up before he could do it."

"That's crazy! The old man didn't know ..."

"Didn't know what, Leo?" Jessica asked through gritted teeth in the silence that followed Leo's voice as it trailed off.

"Damn it, it was her idea!" Leo burst out. "She offered to pose for me if I'd pay her, and you've seen her. For God's sake, she's beautiful! But that's all I did, I swear. I took pictures of her, but I never touched the little hustler—"

"Tom, no!" Consuela cried, but the plea fell on deaf ears. Tom had already heard all he was going to listen to. He leaped at Leo and swung a hard punch into the middle of the bigger man's face. Leo grunted in pain and staggered back as blood spurted from his nose.

Phyllis had a feeling that Chief Clifton could have gotten between Tom and Leo and stopped that punch if he really wanted to, but the chief hadn't budged. He stepped in, though, as Tom swung again, catching hold of his arm and saying, "That's enough, Tom."

"You heard him!" Tom said, the rage he felt making him pant a little as he spoke. "You heard the filthy things he was saying about my Bianca."

"You saw him, Chief!" Leo said, his voice muffled a little by the hand he held to his bleeding nose. "You saw him assault me! I want him arrested, damn it!"

"He's the one you should arrest," Tom said. "Taking advantage of an innocent young girl—"

"Innocent, my ass! She offered to do plenty more if I paid her enough!"

This time it was Consuela who came after him, flailing at him as her anger poured out of her in swift, furious Spanish. Clifton couldn't let go of Tom to stop Consuela without risking that Tom would attack Leo again.

Jessica got into the act as well, joining Consuela in whaling on Leo, who threw his arms over his head to protect himself from the angry women and howled in dismay. Clifton yelled for his officers to come help him.

"Reckon I ought to give the chief a hand?" Sam asked Phyllis.

"I'd stay out of it if I were you," she advised him. "Anyway, I think Leo's got it coming."

"Can't argue with that," Sam replied with a shake of his head.

Several officers rushed into the parlor, summoned by Clifton's shouts, and grabbed Jessica and Consuela to pull them away from the hapless Leo, whose face was smeared with the blood that had leaked from his nose. He wiped some of it away and shouted, "What the hell is wrong with all you people?"

Nobody answered him, but a new voice asked sharply, "What's going on here? Leo, what sort of mess have you gotten yourself into this time?"

Everyone turned to look as a tall, silver-haired man in an expensive suit strode into the parlor. Phyllis hadn't heard him arrive. He must have opened the door and marched right in. He carried himself with the imperious air of a man who believed it was perfectly fine to do that because of who he was. The newcomer had to be Leo's lawyer, Phyllis thought.

But she was wrong, because a wide-eyed Raquel Forrest looked at the man and said, "Daddy!"

Chapter 12

$\mathcal{S}$o this was Charles Jefferson, cofounder of the Jefferson-Bartell Group, Phyllis thought. Leo's boss and Raquel's father. A very rich, powerful man whose expensive suit and arrogant bearing confirmed his status. Phyllis didn't know what he was doing here, but she figured that if they all waited, Jefferson would tell them.

He was followed into the room by a smaller, mostly bald man who carried a briefcase. That would be Leo's lawyer, Phyllis told herself. She wondered if he or his firm represented Jefferson-Bartell, too. That would explain how Charles Jefferson knew that Leo might be in some sort of trouble. The lawyer would have run to Jefferson as soon as Leo called him.

"Charles!" Leo said. "What are you doing here?"

"Roger told me there was a problem," Jefferson replied. "I thought I had better come down here and see what I needed to do to straighten it out."

Every silver hair on his head was in place. His face was tight and unlined. He didn't really look old enough to have a daughter Raquel's age, and Phyllis figured that he'd had some help from cosmetic surgeons to look that way. Vanity oozed from every dermabraded and avocado-scrubbed pore. Instinct made her dislike him, just as it had prompted her to like the much more down-to-earth Tom Anselmo.

"There's no problem—" Leo began.

"You told Roger there'd been a murder," Jefferson interrupted. "I come in to find you being pummeled by a couple of women, including your own wife, as well as being surrounded by the local police."

"These cops are crazy! They come in here with some Mickey Mouse search warrant and start pawing through our stuff and throwing around accusations—"

Jefferson turned his head and said, "Roger."

The bald-headed lawyer stepped forward. "Don't say another word, Leo," he ordered. He turned to Chief Clifton. "Have you interrogated my client without the benefit of counsel, Chief? If you have, I can promise that you'll be sorry."

Clifton didn't look overly impressed by either Jefferson or the lawyer. He said, "I haven't interrogated anybody yet. All we've done is execute a search warrant."

Roger frowned. "Highly questionable tactics. I should have been here to protect my client's best interests before any search was carried out."

"You can look at the warrant if you'd like," Clifton offered. "You'll find that all the t's are crossed and all the i's are dotted." His voice hardened slightly. "We're not quite the yokels that you seem to think we are, Counselor."

"I certainly do intend to examine the warrant, and nothing should be removed from the premises until I've done so."

"Fine by me," the chief said with a shrug. "I've got plenty of time to waste if you do."

Leo said, "Don't let him take my camera, Roger. You've got to stop him."

"Camera? Camera? What's this about a camera?"

"It belongs to your client," Clifton said. "And it's got nude pictures of a young woman on it. I happen to know she's of legal age . . . but not by much."

"Leo, for God's sake!" Charles Jefferson said with contempt in his voice.

"It's not what you think, Charles," Leo hurried to say. "It's not as bad as it sounds."

Jessica slugged him on the arm, hard enough to make him yelp in pain.

Raquel sidled up to Jefferson. "Hello, Daddy."

"Sweetheart."

Despite the endearment, Jefferson's tone was a little chilly and he barely glanced at his daughter. Not much love lost between those two, Phyllis thought, at least on Jefferson's part.

"I want to see this camera," Roger said to Chief Clifton.

The chief nodded to one of his men, who held up a clear plastic evidence bag with a tag attached to it. "That's it," Clifton said.

"I'd like to examine it to make sure that it hasn't been tampered with."

Clifton shook his head. "Request denied, Counselor. You'll have a chance to take a look at it later, if you want."

"After you've manipulated the images on its memory card?" It was Roger's turn to shake his head. "A competent trial judge would throw out any such images that you tried to introduce into evidence."

"Who said anything about a trial? At this point, we're just trying to figure out what happened." Clifton paused. "Unless you're assuming that your client's going to be charged with something . . . ?"

"No, no, of course not. Leo's innocent of any wrongdoing. Aren't you, Leo?"

"Of course I'm innocent," Leo said, gingerly touching his nose as if he were the only injured party in the room.

"What about what he did to my daughter?" Tom demanded.

"I never touched the girl!" Leo insisted. "And she's

not underage. That hick cop admitted that himself. I didn't do anything wrong." He turned to Jessica and added hastily, "Legally, of course. Morally, I shouldn't have ever listened to her when she started trying to tempt me—"

Clifton moved a little to get between Leo and Tom again, and Jessica said in disgust, "Just shut up, Leo. You're only making yourself look more foolish."

Jefferson put his hands in his pockets—being careful not to spoil the line of his trousers, Phyllis noted—and said, "I'd like for someone to tell me exactly what's going on here. Who was murdered?"

"And I'd like to know who you are and what your connection with this case is," Clifton shot back.

Jefferson smiled. "Of course. I haven't actually introduced myself, have I?" Clearly, he was accustomed to everyone he came in contact with just knowing who he was. "My name is Charles Jefferson. I'm the president and CEO of the Jefferson-Bartell Group, headquartered in Houston. Leo works for me. And so does Roger Fadiman here, of course."

"And he's my father," Raquel said.

"Yes, that's true," Jefferson said. "Now, Chief, if you'd be so kind as to tell me what's going on here . . ."

Clifton's answer was blunt. "A murder investigation. One of the guests staying here was poisoned sometime yesterday morning or late the night before."

"Who was the victim?"

"A man named Ed McKenna."

"McKenna!" For the first time, Jefferson's air of perfectly coiffed and dressed composure appeared to be shaken. "Of McKenna Electronics in San Antonio?"

Roger practically sprang forward. "Don't say anything else, Charles! Not a word!"

Anger flared in Jefferson's eyes, probably at the notion that one of his employees would speak to him in that tone of voice, Phyllis thought, but he followed Roger's orders and didn't say any more.

Frances Heaton did, though. She stepped forward and demanded of Jefferson, "How do you know our father?" When Jefferson just gave her a stony stare in return, Frances turned to her brothers. "What do the two of you know about this? Have you been keeping secrets from me about the company?"

"I'm the CEO of McKenna Electronics," Oliver told her. "I don't have to answer to you, Frances."

"He doesn't know anything," Oscar scoffed. "He never knew anything except what Dad told him. He's always been content just to be a figurehead and a yes man. I wasn't, and that's why Dad canned me."

"That's a damned lie!" Oliver said. "You don't know anything about it, Oscar."

"I know you've never been anywhere near as smart as you think you are."

The twins clenched their fists and glared at each other. Phyllis wondered if they were about to start throwing punches. It wouldn't have surprised her a bit. With all the tension and anger in this room, she was sure that chaos would have ensued by now if not for the presence of Chief Clifton and the other officers.

Clifton acted to make sure that didn't happen by saying, "All right, everybody settle down. We came here to conduct a search, not to referee a free-for-all." He glanced at Charles Jefferson. "Although I *am* mighty curious about your connection with Ed McKenna."

"Don't say anything, Charles," Roger Fadiman warned. "Not a word."

Jefferson lifted his chin defiantly but followed his attorney's advice, keeping his mouth shut.

Clifton looked around the room. "I'll be talking to all of you later," he said. "If you'd like to have a lawyer present, of course that's fine. We'll be in touch."

"You can't take any potential evidence with you until I've seen that warrant," Roger reminded him.

Clifton took a folded document out of his pocket and handed it over to the lawyer. Roger studied it for sev-

eral minutes with a frown on his face, flipping through
the several pages. Finally, with a grimace, he handed it
back.

"Everything appears to be in order," he said, sounding disappointed.

"Just like I said." Chief Clifton put the search warrant
away and motioned for the other officers to leave the
room. They filed out, taking the evidence bags with them,
and Clifton brought up the rear of the procession.

He paused in the foyer and looked back at the group
gathered in the parlor. "I really don't want to be called
back here to break up a riot," he told them. "Keep that
in mind."

He went on out, heading for one of the cruisers parked
in front of the bed-and-breakfast. The search was over.

But the case was far from concluded, Phyllis told
herself.

And a moment later, that riot Chief Clifton had
warned against seemed to be on the verge of breaking
out, as seemingly everyone in the parlor began talking
loudly and angrily at once.

Not all of them were arguing, though. Consuela left
the room, heading toward the kitchen, and Phyllis went
after her.

Bianca had gone in that direction when she fled the
parlor, and Phyllis found mother and daughter in the
kitchen. Bianca was dry-eyed now, but the streaks left
behind by the tears she had shed were still visible on
her cheeks and she was obviously shaken and upset.
Consuela was speaking to her in rapid Spanish. Phyllis
caught only a few words, but they were enough to indicate to her that Consuela was demanding to know what
in the world Bianca had been thinking by posing in the
nude for Leo Blaine.

"He was lying, Mama," Bianca insisted when her
mother let her get a word in. "I never offered to pose for
him. It was all his idea."

"It doesn't matter whose idea it was! You should have

told him no! You should have told me what he asked you to do!"

Bianca looked like she might start crying again. "But you would have told *Papi*, and then he would have hit Mr. Blaine and there would have been a lot of trouble—"

"You think there's not a lot of trouble now?" Consuela asked with a disgusted snort. "What were you thinking?" she asked again, in English this time.

Bianca began to sob again and didn't answer.

Consuela shook her head and turned to Phyllis. "I'm so sorry, Señora Newsom. We'll all quit and leave this house. We've brought shame on Oak Knoll—"

Phyllis didn't let her go on. "Don't say that," she said. "You haven't done anything wrong, Consuela, and I'm sure that if Dorothy were here she'd tell you the same thing. She certainly wouldn't want you to leave. Any of you."

"The shame is that I raised my daughter to be a *puta*."

"Mama!" Bianca cried. "That's not true. I didn't do anything with Mr. Blaine. I swear it!"

"You let him take those pictures of you!"

"For the money! I didn't think it would do any harm. I didn't think anybody would ever find out about it."

Phyllis said, "Did Mr. McKenna find out about it, Bianca?"

The young woman blinked teary eyes in confusion. "Mr. McKenna? The old man who died?"

"Chief Clifton thinks that if Mr. McKenna knew about the pictures Mr. Blaine took of you, he might have threatened to tell Mr. Blaine's wife, or your parents."

Bianca shook her head. "He didn't know about it. Nobody knew about it except me and Mr. Blaine. Unless . . . I guess he could have found out somehow. Maybe Mr. Blaine told him."

Leo wouldn't have done that, Phyllis knew. Leo wanted the whole thing kept secret, and for good reason.

"He didn't accidentally come in while Mr. Blaine was taking pictures of you or anything like that?"

"No, ma'am."

Phyllis believed that Bianca was telling the truth . . . as far as she knew it. But it was still possible that Ed McKenna could have stumbled over Leo's little photography session and threatened to expose him. Considering what was going on between Leo and Jessica, and Sheldon and Raquel, some people might think that Jessica didn't have any right to be upset with Leo over a few pictures, but from the way she had attacked him downstairs, clearly she had been. Leo must have known that she would be.

It was a motive for murder, and Phyllis had learned that the question of whether a motive was good enough could be answered only by the person who committed the murder. Whatever the motive, it had been good enough for him or her to lace Ed McKenna's leftover crab cakes with poison, that was certain.

"How many times?" Consuela said.

Bianca blinked up at her. "Mama?"

"How many times did this happen? How many times did you degrade yourself for that man?"

"Just the once, I swear. I . . . I was too ashamed to do it again, even though Mr. Blaine wanted me to. That's the truth, Mama."

"Where was Mrs. Blaine when it happened?" Phyllis asked.

"She had gone shopping with their friends, Mr. and Mrs. Forrest. It was one morning when Mr. Blaine told them he didn't feel good. I came in to clean and he was still in the room. I told him I would come back later, but he said it was all right. He had his computer open on the table, but I didn't pay any attention to what was on it until he . . . he showed me. There were pictures of women . . . and he said he would pay me if I would let him take pictures like that . . ." Bianca took a deep, ragged breath. "I started to run out of the room—"

"You should have," Consuela said.

"But then I thought of the money ... and he promised he wouldn't hurt me, and that nobody would ever find out ... and I thought maybe it would be okay—"

"You thought wrong," Consuela said.

"I know that now, Mama. But then I didn't. So I said I'd do it. It didn't take long, and then ... and then I put my clothes on and left. That was all. I swear it on the Blessed Virgin."

Consuela crossed herself, then glared down at her daughter. "You're gonna be grounded for so long—"

"Mama, I'm eighteen! You can't ground me."

Consuela snorted again. "You don't think so? You just watch!"

Phyllis wanted to stay out of this part. She had come to the kitchen to make sure that Bianca was all right, as well as to ask a few questions of her own. Now that she was satisfied she had learned all she could from the young woman, at least for now, she would leave the rest of it to Consuela.

She gave Consuela a sympathetic pat on the shoulder and then left the room, returning to the parlor. The Blaines and the Forrests were nowhere in sight, and Frances Heaton and her brothers were gone, too, as were Charles Jefferson and Roger Fadiman. Nick and Kate Thompson were still sitting there with Sam, Carolyn, and Eve, though, and Tom Anselmo paced back and forth across the rug, pausing occasionally to smack his right fist lightly into his left palm.

Theresa met Phyllis just inside the door. "How's Bianca?" she asked.

"Well, she's upset, of course—" Phyllis began.

"Of course she's upset," Tom said. "She acted like a slut."

Theresa rounded on him. "*Papi!* Don't talk like that. You know better. You know Bianca is a good girl."

"Good girls don't do what she did," her father said with a stubborn shake of his head.

"They do if they make a mistake. I know Bianca. I know she didn't think it would hurt anything. And really, what *did* it hurt?"

"She shamed herself and her family!"

"The shame is in your eyes," Theresa said.

"The shame is in the eyes of anybody who's decent," Tom insisted. He flung his hands in the air. "Ah, I'm not gonna argue about this! I'll go mow the grass. I got to have something to do!"

He stomped out of the room, and Theresa headed for the kitchen to join her mother and sister.

Nick Thompson looked around and said, "Boy, lot of fireworks today, huh?"

"Don't make fun of it," his wife scolded. "Those people are really upset."

"I'm not making fun of it," Nick said. "It's just that murder really brings out everybody's dirty laundry, doesn't it?"

"I never thought that Mr. Blaine would have done such a sleazy thing," Kate said.

"I'm not a bit surprised," Carolyn said. "I didn't like him right from the start. I could tell that he was a terrible man."

And Carolyn didn't even know everything that was going on, Phyllis thought.

"That Charles Jefferson was certainly a handsome, well-dressed man, though," Eve put in.

"Oh, don't start," Carolyn said. "Anyway, I'm sure he has a wife. A trophy wife, more than likely, some nipped and tucked and silicone-enhanced twenty-five-year-old."

"I don't think they use silicone implants anymore, dear. They turned out not to be safe. Of course, *I* never needed anything to attract a man other than what the Good Lord gave me."

Carolyn rolled her eyes. Phyllis sat down and forestalled any more bickering between the two of them by saying, "Jefferson certainly had heard of Ed McKenna before. That was a surprise."

"McKenna was in the same business as Jefferson, right?" Sam asked.

"A related business. Jefferson's company designs guidance systems for the aeronautics industry. McKenna's company actually manufactures electronic components."

Carolyn frowned at Phyllis. "You've been studying up on these people, haven't you? I knew you were going to try to solve the murder."

"I just want everything cleared up before it ruins things for Dorothy and Ben," Phyllis said. "If Chief Clifton or somebody else—anybody else!—solves the murder, that's just fine with me."

"With your competitive nature? That's a laugh."

Eve leaned toward Sam and laughed. "Pot, meet Kettle."

"I heard that," Carolyn snapped.

Nick said, "You know, if there *is* some sort of connection between Jefferson and McKenna, then maybe *he* had something to do with the murder. Maybe McKenna was standing in the way of some business plans Jefferson has, and he decided to get rid of the old guy."

"I don't know," Kate said. "He didn't look like the kind of man who would break into somebody's house and poison some crab cakes."

"Well, he probably wouldn't do it himself, of course. But he could hire somebody to do it. Or get somebody who already works for him to do it."

"Like Leo Blaine?" Phyllis asked.

Nick nodded. "That's what I was thinking."

"Or maybe Mrs. Forrest," Kate suggested. "She's Mr. Jefferson's daughter, after all. And did you see the pathetic way she kept trying to get his attention? He must not have ever paid any attention to her when she was a kid. I'm sure she'd do anything to try to please him."

"Maybe, maybe," Nick agreed, sitting forward in his chair. "Hey, we're really getting into the spirit of this detective stuff, aren't we? Maybe *we* could solve this murder, honey."

"Oh, no. This is a vacation, remember? At least, it was supposed to be before poor Mr. McKenna dropped dead."

"Yeah, but people go on mystery cruises and things like that, where there's a murder for them to solve."

"A *fake* murder," Kate said. "This is the real thing."

Nick looked a little ashamed of himself. "Yeah, that's true. McKenna's really dead. It's not a game, is it?"

It wasn't a game at all, Phyllis thought. It was real, deadly real.

But Nick had definitely been right about one thing.

Murder brought out everyone's dirty laundry . . . and Phyllis had a feeling that there was plenty of dirt that hadn't even seen the light of day yet.

Chapter 13

It was a subdued lunch. The Blaines and the Forrests didn't come down to eat and didn't go out, either. They remained in their rooms. Phyllis kept an ear out for the sound of things being thrown. She would have to intercede if Jessica started heaving things at Leo. She couldn't allow them to bust up Dorothy's furnishings.

Everything was quiet, though ... almost ominously so.

Nick and Kate shared lunch with Phyllis, Sam, Carolyn, and Eve. They seemed to have forgotten about worrying over whether the food might be poisoned. They hadn't forgotten the murder, though, and were still discussing various possibilities.

"I think this guy Jefferson is the key to the whole thing, myself," Nick said. "He's rich, and where you've got a lot of money in play, you've got a motive for murder."

"And we all saw the way he reacted when he heard Mr. McKenna's name," Kate added. "There's definitely some sort of connection there."

Phyllis said, "I'm sure the police will look into that. Chief Clifton and his daughter both strike me as competent investigators."

"But you're better, Mrs. Newsom," Nick said. "Heck,

from what I've heard about you, I'll bet you've solved more murders than those cops have. How often do they have unsolved murders in a place like this?"

"I don't know," Phyllis admitted. "Probably not that often."

"So Mr. Thompson's right," Carolyn said. "You're better qualified to investigate what happened."

Phyllis shook her head. "You're forgetting that I have no official standing to question anybody."

Carolyn snorted and said, "That never stopped you before, did it?"

Phyllis knew there was no point in being irritated with her old friend's attitude. And she supposed that Carolyn had a point. She had poked into things in the past without any official standing. She could do it again. She *wanted* to do it again.

"I'll think about it," she said.

"I'd start with Oliver McKenna, if I were you," Nick suggested. "It seemed to me like he knew something about the connection between his father and Jefferson."

That had seemed possible to Phyllis, too. She nodded but didn't commit herself to anything.

After lunch was over, she went out into the kitchen, where Consuela was cleaning up. The woman's face still bore lines of strain from the confrontation with her daughter earlier that day, but she was going about her work with her usual enthusiasm.

"Let me give you a hand," Phyllis offered.

"That's not necessary, Mrs. Newsom," Consuela said. "I just have to finish putting a few things in the dishwasher and get it started; then I can go home for a little while. I already have everything on hand I'll need for supper, so I don't have to go to the store."

"Is Bianca still here?"

Consuela's face turned stonier. "No, I sent her home. It's not fair to Theresa, making her do some of her sister's work that way, but I wanted to get some distance between Bianca and Tom." She nodded toward the kitchen window. Phyllis heard the lawn mower still running outside. Tom had already had time to cut all the grass. He had to be going back over it again, distracting himself with work from what his daughter had done.

"You know," Phyllis said, "it's really none of my business . . . and I admit that I have a son, rather than daughters, and I guess it really is different whether it ought to be or not . . . but I don't believe that Bianca meant any harm. She just made a decision without thinking it through. Eighteen-year-olds do that all the time. I've read that it has to do with how some portions of their brains haven't developed as much at that age."

"I raised both my daughters to be good girls," Consuela insisted. "Bianca knew it was wrong, what that man wanted her to do." She closed her eyes for a moment and made the sign of the cross. "Thank the Blessed Virgin that she was smart enough not to do anything else."

"Well, like I said, it's really none of my business. But from what I've seen, Bianca really is a good girl, despite making a mistake, so I hope you won't be too hard on her."

"All I know is, it won't happen again. When Dorothy hears about it, she'll fire Bianca. She may fire all of us."

"Oh, no," Phyllis said. "I can't see that happening. Dorothy's very understanding."

Consuela shrugged. "She won't have any choice. When word gets around about what happened, it'll hurt business. She'll have to let us go."

"I'll talk to her," Phyllis promised. "I'll make sure she understands that what happened wasn't Bianca's fault, and you and Tom and Theresa certainly weren't to blame. As far as I'm concerned, it would be very unfair to dismiss any of you."

"I appreciate that, Mrs. Newsom," Consuela said, but the tone of dull resignation in her voice made it clear that she didn't think Phyllis's efforts would do any good.

"Anyway," Phyllis added, "I'd think that Mr. McKenna being murdered would have a much worse effect on business than . . . what Bianca did."

"Maybe so." Consuela smiled humorlessly. "Be thankful for small favors, eh?"

"That's not what I meant," Phyllis began, then stopped as she realized that of course Consuela knew that. After a moment she went on, "But speaking of the murder, do you recall if Mr. McKenna received any mail while he was here, or any unusual phone calls?"

Consuela shrugged. "I don't think he got any mail, and I don't remember him ever getting any phone calls while I was around. Of course, in this day and age when everybody's got a cell phone, anybody who wanted to get in touch with him would have called him directly. They wouldn't have called the bed-and-breakfast."

"That's probably true," Phyllis said with a nod. "I just wondered what the connection was between Mr. McKenna and Charles Jefferson."

"You mean Mrs. Forrest's papa? The rich guy who was here earlier?"

"And he's Leo Blaine's employer, too," Phyllis pointed out.

Consuela's face hardened again at the mention of Leo's name. "I wouldn't know. I never saw Mr. Jefferson before today."

"You don't recall ever hearing Mr. McKenna mention him?"

Consuela thought about it, then shook her head. "No. But it's kind of funny, isn't it, the way all those people seem to be tied up to each other somehow?"

Phyllis nodded. "Yes," she said. "Funny."

But not in a ha-ha way, she thought. It wasn't that sort of funny at all, whenever murder was involved.

Oliver and Oscar McKenna and their sister, Frances Heaton, had to be staying somewhere in the area. Chief Clifton had asked them to keep themselves available, and Phyllis didn't think they would leave as long as the question of their father's murder was still up in the air, anyway. So she set out that afternoon to find out where they were.

In the old days she would have had to hunt up a phone book and start calling all the places to stay around Rockport and Fulton. Now she used the computer in Dorothy's office to search for upper-end resorts in the area, figuring that the McKenna siblings wouldn't be staying in run-down tourist cabins that had been built in the forties, or even in some of the newer motels.

Once she had done that, though, and compiled a list of numbers, she still had to call each one. Each time she asked to be connected to Oliver McKenna's room. At the first half-dozen places, she was told that no one by that name was registered there, and asking for Frances Heaton turned up blanks, too.

But on the seventh call, which was to a very new-looking resort Phyllis recalled seeing on Fulton Beach Road near the boat basin, the operator said, "One moment, please," when she asked for Oliver McKenna.

The phone rang a couple of times before it was picked up and Phyllis heard Oliver McKenna's somewhat surly tones on the other end. "Yes, what is it?"

"Mr. McKenna?"

"That's right. Who's this?"

"Phyllis Newsom, Mr. McKenna. From the Oak Knoll Bed-'n'-Breakfast."

"I know who you are, Mrs. Newsom," Oliver said. "It hasn't been that long since my brother and sister and I were there. What do you want?"

He wasn't going to be pleasant about this, Phyllis thought, which came as no surprise.

"I was wondering if I could come by there and see you for a few minutes," she said.

"What for? How'd you know where we're staying, anyway?"

"I heard your sister mention it," Phyllis said. That

wasn't true, of course, but she had gotten used to stretching the truth a little in a good cause. Right now she couldn't think of a better cause than finding out who killed Ed McKenna and saving the bed-and-breakfast from ruin. "You were lucky. Most places are booked up. They must have had a cancellation."

"I don't know that I have anything to say to you. For all I know, you had something to do with my father's death."

"You don't really believe that, Mr. McKenna. I never even met your father until a few days ago. I didn't have any reason to harm him. I'm very sorry about what happened, and I want to do whatever I can to make things right."

"You can't. My father's dead. You can't fix that."

"I know. I'm sorry. I shouldn't have said it that way. I just want to know if there's anything I can do to help."

"I don't know what it would be," Oliver said in a hard, flat voice. "Good-bye, Mrs. Newsom."

"Wait," Phyllis said quickly. "I have something here that the police didn't find during their search. Something I think your father would want you to have."

Now that was an outright lie, not just a stretching of the truth.

But it kept Oliver from hanging up, and that was what Phyllis wanted. "What are you talking about?" he demanded.

Phyllis could only make a guess. "Some business documents," she said. "I had them with me when the police showed up to execute their search warrant, and they never checked my purse."

That was a plausible story, she thought, especially considering that she had just made it up off the top of her head. But her instincts had served her well, she realized when she thought about it for a second. All Ed McKenna and Charles Jefferson had in common was their connection to the electronics industry. It stood to reason that whatever their relationship—if indeed there *was* such a relationship—it would have something to do with the business both of them were in.

The silence on the other end of the phone told her that Oliver wasn't dismissing her claim out of hand, another indication that there might be something to it. Finally he asked in a tense voice, "What do you want?"

"Just to talk to you for a few minutes, face-to-face."

"By God, this smacks of blackmail."

Phyllis's anger was real as she said, "I never blackmailed anyone in my life, and I don't appreciate being accused of it."

"All right, all right, calm down." Now it was Oliver trying to keep her on the phone instead of the other way around, which told Phyllis yet again that she was on the right trail, even though getting there had been something of an accident. He sighed and went on, "I'll talk to you, but I don't want my brother and sister to know about it. They're not aware of everything that's going on. I'll meet you somewhere privately."

Phyllis felt a tingle of apprehension. At this point she had no real reason to suspect that Oliver McKenna was to blame for his father's death, but as far as she was concerned he was a suspect. The last thing she wanted to do was meet somewhere in private with a possible murderer, especially after hinting to him that she might have some evidence against him.

"I think it would be better if we spoke somewhere in public," she said, hoping that wouldn't scare him off. "But your brother and sister don't have to know anything about it."

He seemed to be thinking it over. Then he said, "Where?"

"What about the fishing pier at the Copano Bay Causeway?"

"Where's that?"

"Go north up Fulton Beach Road," she told him. "When you come to the end of it, turn right on the highway, and that will take you to the causeway. They've turned the old causeway into a fishing pier, right beside the one that crosses the bay now." She had read up on the area before coming down here and recalled that bit of history. Although the old causeway no longer completely spanned the bay, it ran a long way out into the water on each side and now operated as a private fishing pier. There would be plenty of people around, so that Oliver couldn't try to throw her in the bay, and yet the pier was long enough so that they could get out of earshot of the nearest fishermen and have some privacy.

"I don't much like the idea, but I suppose it'll do," Oliver said. "Half an hour from now?"

"That's fine," Phyllis said as she checked her watch. She hoped she could get Sam to go with her, but if not, she wasn't worried about meeting Oliver in broad daylight on a public fishing pier.

Well, not *too* worried, anyway . . .

He said a curt "good-bye" and hung up. Phyllis hung up as well and went to find Sam.

He was sitting in one of the rocking chairs on the front porch, rocking slightly as he looked out at the water. Phyllis took the chair beside him, and for a moment they sat there in a familiar, comfortable silence, the only sound the faint squeaking of their chairs. Across the road, a pelican swooped over the water in a stately glide. No fish made the fatal mistake of venturing too close to the surface, so the pelican flew on in search of a snack elsewhere.

"Another exciting day in paradise," Sam observed dryly.

"I don't want any excitement," Phyllis said. "I'd just as soon it had left us alone."

"Life's not in the habit of doin' that."

"I know." Phyllis paused, then went on, "I'm supposed to meet Oliver McKenna on the causeway fishing pier in a little less than half an hour."

Sam looked over at her, frowning in surprise. "Say again?"

"I'm meeting Oliver at the causeway. We're going to

discuss the connection between his father and Charles Jefferson."

"How in the world did you get him to agree to that?"

"I made him think that I had some sort of secret documents belonging to Ed McKenna that the police didn't find."

A grin began to stretch across Sam's rugged face. "In other words, you told him a bald-faced lie."

Phyllis didn't see any point in denying it. She nodded and said, "That's right."

Sam chuckled. "And now you want me to go with you so Oliver won't try to pitch you into the drink."

"Something like that." Phyllis smiled. "You know me too well, Sam Fletcher."

"I know that you're the brains in this partnership and I'm the brawn."

His choice of words took her aback. "Are we a partnership now, Sam?"

"Well... when it comes to crime-solvin', anyway. We'll have to talk about the other, one of these days."

"All right. So you'll come with me?"

"Sure." He got to his feet. "I'm ready when you are."

She went inside and got her purse, then joined him at his pickup. They drove north on Fulton Beach Road, the same route she had told Oliver McKenna to take, and turned toward the causeway.

She didn't know what vehicle he was driving, so she couldn't tell from the cars and trucks and SUVs parked at the fishing pier if he was already there. Sam parked, and as they approached the booth at the beginning of the pier where an attendant collected the fees, Phyllis reached for her purse.

The man working there waved them on past. "I can tell you folks are just sight-seein'," he said. "We charge accordin' to the pole, and you don't have any."

"How's the fishin' here?" Sam asked. "I might want to come back and get my line wet."

"Pretty good most of the time. Takes a good hand, though, to work a fish all the way up before it flops off the hook, since we're sort of high off the water."

Sam nodded. "I can see that it would." He lifted a hand in farewell as he and Phyllis started out onto the pier.

"You fit right in down here," Phyllis commented.

Sam shrugged. "How could a fella keep from fittin' in? Folks are about as friendly as any I've ever run across, and you sure can't complain about the weather. I'm not sure I'd want to live somewhere you'd have to worry about hurricanes, though."

"There are barrier islands offshore that keep them from hitting full force along here. The storm surges aren't as bad as they are in other places along the coast. That's why there are quite a few houses around here that are a hundred years old or more, like the Fulton Mansion."

"Been readin' up, I see."

She laughed. "I was a history teacher for a long time. Those things interest me."

In spite of the pleasant conversation, she was keeping her eyes open for Oliver McKenna. They passed numerous fishermen as they strolled along the old causeway. Even though it made for a high fishing pier, Phyllis imagined that driving over it in the old days must have been a little nerve-racking. In a car it would have seemed like you were barely above the surface of the bay, which was at least a mile wide at this part. Phyllis had never cared much for bridges, especially long ones.

She hadn't seen any sign of Oliver so far, but there were people along the edges of the old causeway all the way out to its end, so she and Sam had to keep going. She checked her watch. A little more than half an hour had passed since her conversation with Oliver. He should have been here by now.

"Quite a hike all the way out to the end," Sam said.

"And back," Phyllis said, because they were close

enough now that she could see the rest of the people on the causeway and none of them was Oliver McKenna. "We can turn around now. He's not out here."

"Maybe we'll run into him on the way back in."

"Maybe," Phyllis said.

She was beginning to think that Oliver had stood her up. They were almost back to the shore when she spotted him coming toward them. "There he is," she told Sam, and they stopped and let Oliver come the rest of the way out to where they were. No fishermen were lined up along the railings at this point, so it would be a good place to talk. The constant humid wind pushed Phyllis's hair in front of her face for a second. She pulled it back and wished she had thought to pin it down. You always had to take the wind into account down here.

"I didn't know you were going to bring your boyfriend with you," Oliver said with a frown as he came up to them.

"Anything you can discuss with me, you can talk about in front of Sam."

"I don't want to discuss anything." Oliver thrust his hand out. "I want those papers. You don't have any right to them. They belonged to my father."

"So now they would belong to you and your brother and sister," Phyllis said. "At least, that's the way it seems to me."

"They're business documents, and I'm the CEO of McKenna Electronics. Hand them over."

Sam moved forward a little and said, "Maybe you could be a little more polite, mister."

"And maybe you could butt out," Oliver said. "What I ought to do is call the police and have you and your girlfriend arrested for blackmail or extortion or whatever you want to call it. That's exactly what I'm going to do if I don't get those documents right now."

The confrontation had turned tense in a hurry, and Phyllis was glad she had brought Sam along. The way Oliver McKenna looked, she wasn't sure that he wouldn't have tried to take those nonexistent documents by force if she had been alone.

"I think we should all just settle down," she said. "I don't know that the papers should go to you or not, Mr. McKenna. Maybe I should just hand them over to the police myself."

A new voice said, "I think that would be a terrible mistake, Mrs. Newsom."

Over the sound of the wind and the waves lapping against the pilings below, Phyllis hadn't heard anyone else approaching, and she and Sam and Oliver had all been concentrating on one another, not the other people on the pier.

She turned now and saw Charles Jefferson standing there, along with the lawyer Roger Fadiman. Suddenly she began to feel surrounded.

And it was indeed a long way down to the water, she thought as she glanced past the wooden railing at the choppy surface of the bay.

Chapter 14

Jefferson must have seen the sudden apprehension on Phyllis's face, because he lifted both hands, palms out, and went on, "I didn't mean that to sound threatening. I just meant that you might cause considerable trouble for some innocent people without even intending to."

"By innocent people, do you mean you and Mr. McKenna here?" Phyllis asked.

Jefferson shook his head. "No, I'm talking about the stockholders in both of our companies."

"Be careful, Charles," Fadiman advised. "We can't be sure how much she knows."

Jefferson frowned and snapped, "For God's sake, Roger, if she's got those documents, she must have read them. She knows that Jefferson-Bartell was about to take over McKenna Electronics, or else she wouldn't have called Oliver and tried to blackmail him in the first place."

Phyllis was beginning to lose her patience. "I'm not trying to blackmail anybody!"

"Nonsense," Jefferson said as he turned back to her. "How much do you want? If the news of the takeover leaks prematurely, McKenna's value could plummet and it might even have an effect on Jefferson-Bartell stock.

It's well worth a tidy chunk of change to me in order to keep things quiet until we're ready to finalize the deal. Say, twenty thousand dollars?"

Fadiman closed his eyes, shook his head, and backed away as if he were washing his hands of this discussion.

"You'd better not be expecting me to contribute to that payoff," Oliver said. "I don't have that sort of money."

"Of course you don't, Oliver," Jefferson said, "otherwise you wouldn't be selling your father's beloved company to me even though he hated the idea."

"Wait a minute," Phyllis said. "Ed McKenna didn't want you to buy his company?"

"Not at all. The deal was struck between Oliver and myself. But we had enough leverage to make Ed go along with it, although it would have been better if he hadn't found out until the deal was done."

"Talking too much," Fadiman said through gritted teeth.

"*Will* you be quiet," Jefferson said. "You know how I do business. Straight ahead."

"And damn the torpedoes," Sam said.

Jefferson jerked his head in a curt nod. "Exactly. No bullshit, if you'll pardon my language. I want McKenna Electronics, and I don't want anything to interfere with the acquisition." He held out his hand. "So if you'll give those documents, Mrs. Newsom, I'll be glad to write you a check for twenty-five thousand dollars."

"You said twenty thousand a minute ago."

Jefferson made a face and shook his head. "Five thousand here, five thousand there, what does it matter? You want fifty? I'll give you fifty." His voice hardened. "But I want those papers."

Phyllis's brain was working as fast as it possibly could. "Ed McKenna found out about the deal you and Oliver were working on and brought the documents he discovered with him when he came down here."

"That's right. Who knew the old geezer would be capable of hacking into Oliver's e-mail account and swiping the file with the merger agreement in it? Who knew he would even suspect such a thing?"

"He wouldn't have," Oliver said. A pained expression suddenly appeared on his face. He slapped himself on the forehead.

Sam glanced over at Phyllis and said, "People actually do that when they think of somethin'?"

Oliver ignored them. "Son of a—Oscar! It had to be Oscar. Dad could barely retrieve his own e-mail. I had to show him how to get the program back up after the screen saver came on, for God's sake! But Oscar could have done it. He found out about the deal and ran straight to Dad with it."

"I thought he couldn't stand your father," Jefferson said.

"Oh, he hated Dad for booting him out of being co-CEO with me," Oliver said. "But he could have thought that stabbing me in the back would get him back in Dad's good graces and out of the research department. I'm sure Dad came down here to try to think of some way to ruin the whole thing for us, just the way Oscar intended."

Roger Fadiman couldn't stand it anymore. He said, "Will you just *stop talking*? All you're doing is telling these people that you both had reason to want Ed McKenna dead!"

"They're not cops," Jefferson said with a negligent shrug of his shoulders, "and anything they tell the cops will be nothing but hearsay. Our hands are clean, Roger, and for good reason: I had nothing to do with Ed McKenna's death." He looked calmly over at Oliver. "I'm not sure everyone here can say the same thing."

Oliver's face reddened. "That's slander!"

"Not really," Fadiman said. "This isn't a public forum. No one heard what Charles just said except us. Also, he made no specific claims or accusations—"

"Shut up, you . . . you *lawyer*." Oliver turned to Phyllis. "I can't offer to pay you off, but I can promise you this: Turn those papers over to me and I'll see to it that my brother and sister and I won't file any sort of lawsuit against the bed-and-breakfast over my father's death."

"There's no grounds for a lawsuit anyway," Phyllis insisted. "No one who's connected with Oak Knoll had anything to do with what happened to poor Mr. McKenna."

"You don't know that," Oliver pointed out. "The police are still investigating his death. What if that cook is to blame? She had more opportunity to poison Dad than anyone else."

Phyllis knew that wasn't strictly true. Quite a few people in the bed-and-breakfast had had just as much opportunity as Consuela to slip the poison into those leftover crab cakes. But admitting as much wouldn't do anything to help her position, so she kept quiet about that.

"We can ruin your cousin's business," Oliver went on. "We can drag things out in court until she's bankrupt."

"Don't be too sure of that," Charles Jefferson said with oily glee. "I'm not sure but what the bed-and-breakfast is in a stronger position financially than McKenna Electronics is. You might be cutting your own throat if you get involved in a lengthy, expensive lawsuit, Oliver." He looked at Phyllis again. "My offer is still on the table, Mrs. Newsom. Fifty thousand dollars for the documents."

"What does it matter which one of you has them," Phyllis asked, "as long as they're not made public?"

"It really doesn't matter, I suppose," Jefferson replied with a shrug. "But considering the lack of security on Oliver's part that put us in this precarious position to start with, I'd prefer to have the papers in my possession, just so I'll be sure that they don't leak out." He thought for a moment and added, "For that matter, here's an alternative proposal: Take the documents out of your purse right now and throw them in the bay. I'll still pay you the fifty thousand dollars."

"But you'd want to examine them first, to make sure of what they were."

"Of course. A pig in a poke, and all that."

Oliver said, "I don't care anymore. I'm sick of the whole thing."

"You'll care when your company goes under without Jefferson-Bartell to bail you out," Jefferson predicted.

"You're not bailing us out. You're taking advantage of our bad luck to gobble us up. You're nothing but a damned shark!"

"I've been called worse," Jefferson said with a smile. "A shark is a very efficient killing machine."

He and Oliver both turned toward Phyllis and waited to see what she would do.

After a moment she said, "You don't believe I'd be foolish enough to bring the documents here with me, do you?"

"Where are they?" Jefferson asked in a soft, apparently casual manner.

Phyllis shook her head. "A very safe place, with someone who'll go straight to the police if anything suspicious happens to me."

"Ooh, you saw that in a movie, didn't you?" Jefferson asked.

Sam said, "Mister, I sure don't like your attitude."

"Well, I don't care for that beachcomber look of yours, either." Jefferson ignored the angry glare on Sam's face and went on, "All right, we're getting nowhere here. You know where I stand on all this, Mrs. Newsom. I've made my position very plain. I'm going to put my trust in you. You have no reason to try to damage my business, so I'm going to assume that you won't. If you cooperate, you should come out ahead in the long run. That's all I have to say." He jerked his head at Fadiman. "Let's go, Roger."

As they turned to walk away, Phyllis thought that she ought to just let them go. Somehow, she had managed to bluff her way through this and find out quite a bit of potentially valuable information in the process.

But she couldn't stop herself from saying, "You're forgetting one thing, Mr. Jefferson."

He stopped and looked back at her, wearing an apparently amused smile. His eyes were chilly and unamused, though, as he asked, "What have I forgotten?"

"The police took Mr. McKenna's computer. What if the documents were on there? The police may already have them."

"I suppose that's possible. Ed always struck me as being aggressively old-fashioned, though. A printout sort of fellow, if you will. Anyway, if Oliver's right and his fool of a brother is the one who tipped off Ed, Oscar probably just gave him the printouts of the e-mails, not the files themselves."

"You'd risk fifty thousand dollars on that chance?"

"I've risked more than that on longer odds. That fifty grand was just to increase the odds on my side."

Having never earned more than a teacher's salary, Phyllis couldn't understand that cavalier attitude toward money. She supposed that to a man who dealt regularly in millions, fifty thousand dollars really didn't amount to much.

Jefferson and Fadiman walked toward the shore. Oliver McKenna lingered on the pier for a minute, saying, "Do the right thing, Mrs. Newsom. It's not going to help you to ruin everything for me. And I can promise you, it'll be better for your cousin if you don't make an enemy of me."

"Just don't blame me if the police find out about the deal anyway . . . or already know about it."

"For everyone's sake, let's hope that doesn't happen."

He stalked off then, too, casting occasional hostile glances back over his shoulder at Phyllis and Sam almost until he reached the shore.

"Folks around here sure are fond of makin' veiled threats," Sam said. "And some of 'em aren't so veiled, at that." He looked at Phyllis and shook his head in admiration. "You were runnin' a bluff that whole time, just standin' there and lettin' those two compete to see who could spill his guts the fastest."

"The possibility that a retired schoolteacher might be outsmarting them would never even occur to men like that," Phyllis said. "We know now that Oliver was trying to go behind his father's back to let Jefferson-Bartell take over their company. But Mr. McKenna found out about it and might have tried to stop it."

"Meanin' that Oliver is Suspect Number One now. That makes a lot more sense than thinkin' that his murder was tied in somehow with the hanky-panky Leo Blaine had goin' on."

Phyllis nodded. "The problem is that Oliver would have had to come down here from San Antonio, get into the house, poison the crab cakes, and get back out again without anyone knowing about it. Either that, or pay someone to do it for him."

Sam nodded. "Either way sounds a mite far-fetched, all right. If he couldn't raise twenty thousand dollars, I wouldn't think he could afford to hire a killer. He doesn't seem to have enough spine to do the deed himself. Not impossible, but it just doesn't seem likely to me."

"But Leo was already right there in the house."

"Yeah, but we don't know for sure that McKenna knew about those naughty pictures of Bianca. Dang, it just goes around and around, doesn't it? In some ways it looks like Oliver's guilty, and in other ways it seems like Leo ought to be the killer."

"I'd rather see either of them turn out to be guilty than Consuela or Tom or one of their girls."

"Yeah, me, too. Can't forget Jefferson, either. He's just about the slimiest one o' the bunch."

Phyllis nodded as she pushed her hair back again. "I guess we might as well go back to Oak Knoll. We're not going to accomplish anything else out here."

"Not without a rod an' reel," Sam said with a smile.

*   *   *

Phyllis asked Sam to drive on down into Rockport and stop at the Wal-Mart there. Even with everything else that was going on, she hadn't forgotten that the Just Desserts competition was coming up, and it had occurred to her as she and Sam were walking in from the long pier that it was actually less than forty-eight hours until the judging. She needed to make up her mind what she was going to bake. She had already downloaded the entry form off the Internet, filled it in, and would send it back as soon as she decided on her entry. She also needed to remind Carolyn that today was the deadline.

Ever since the previous Christmas, she'd had a cookie recipe in mind that she wanted to try. It was one she had considered for the Christmas cookie contest sponsored by the local newspaper, but in the end she had decided to go with something more festive that tied in with the holiday itself. That decision had worked out all right, since her recipe had received an honorable mention in the paper. Carolyn's recipe had won, but that didn't really bother Phyllis. Not nearly as much as the murder that had taken place next door . . .

She put those bad memories out of her mind and turned her thoughts back to the cookies she was considering making for *this* contest. Oatmeal Delights . . . the name just popped into her head. It described the cookies very well. They were oatmeal cookies with pecans, coconut, and vanilla chips. She had made them several times at home and everyone liked them. Since she knew they were good, she wouldn't have to experiment with them before the contest, as she sometimes did with the recipes she entered.

With that in mind, she needed to gather up the ingredients. And, of course, once she was in Wal-Mart she thought of other things she needed, so for the next half hour she and Sam walked around the sprawling store, Sam traipsing along just behind her like a dutiful husband. That thought made Phyllis's face flush warmly, and she was glad that he couldn't see how pink she must be. By the time she brought the basket to a stop again, she had told herself to stop being silly and was back to normal.

"Why don't you go look at the books or something?" she suggested. "There's no reason for you to have to tag along with me."

"I like taggin' along with you," he said with a smile. "Anyway, I got myself a whole sack of paperback Westerns the other day at that big used bookstore on the edge of town. I've got plenty to read."

"Well, all right. I just don't want you to get bored."

"Not much chance of that," Sam said, and darned if she didn't blush again. "What's all this stuff for, anyway? Your entry in the dessert contest?"

"That's right. I've decided to make those oatmeal cookies you liked so much the last time we had them."

"The ones with the vanilla chips in 'em?" A grin spread across Sam's face. "Oh, man, those are good. Carolyn won't stand a chance."

"I wouldn't count on that. She nearly always manages to find a way to top me. But I don't even know what her entry is going to be. She might bake a cake or a pie."

"Maybe so, but whatever it is, it won't be as good as those cookies of yours."

Hearing that pleased her, too, although she might not have admitted it . . . even to herself.

By the time they got back to the bed-and-breakfast, Ed McKenna's death had crept into her thoughts again, but she was no closer to figuring out who had killed him than she was before. Today's revelations had increased the number of suspects, but none of them stood out above the others.

She was puzzled, too, by the fact that Leo Blaine hadn't seemed to know anything about a connection between Jefferson-Bartell and McKenna Electronics. Since Leo was a vice president of the company, shouldn't he have known about the impending takeover deal?

Unless for some reason Jefferson didn't trust him

and had been keeping the deal a secret from him for a reason.

Everything just got murkier and murkier, like the sea after it had been stirred up by a storm.

Consuela was already back, Phyllis noted as she saw the woman's car parked behind the house next to the garage and the toolshed. Since the front of the house was right on the street, the people who were staying there, both the full-time residents and the guests, all parked in a large area in back, paved with gravel and crushed seashells. Phyllis had been surprised when she first saw the crushed shells mixed in with the gravel until she thought about it and realized just how plentiful that material was around here. The bottoms of the bays were covered in many places with shells. All you had to do was scoop them up.

The entrance to the parking area was a lane from the next street inland. Sam drove along it and parked next to Consuela's car. They got out and carried the bags from Wal-Mart into the house through the back door.

Consuela had what smelled like chili simmering on the stove in a big pot as they came into the kitchen. Not surprisingly, she still looked upset, but she wasn't letting that interfere with her work. The chili smelled delicious. Phyllis smiled and told Consuela as much.

That brought a tiny smile to Consuela's face as well. "It's one of my favorite dishes—tamale soup—it's like a dressed-up chili," she said. "The guests always like it." Her expression grew more solemn. "Not that I expect them to eat tonight. They still don't trust me, except for Mr. and Mrs. Thompson." The look on her face hardened even more. "And I don't care if that Mr. Blaine ever eats any of my cooking again. If anybody deserved to be poisoned, it was him, not Mr. McKenna."

Phyllis figured it would be a good time to change the subject. "I hope you don't mind sharing the kitchen tomorrow. I have to bake some cookies."

"For the Just Desserts contest?" Consuela's expression brightened a little again. "Of course not. I'm looking forward to it. To tell you the truth, I thought about entering my coconut cake."

"Oh, you ought to," Phyllis urged. "You fixed it the first night we were here, and it was delicious."

"No, that's all right. Nobody would want to eat it." Consuela gave a bitter laugh. "After what happened to Mr. McKenna, everybody would think it might be poisoned."

"I'm sure no one would believe that," Phyllis said.

But she wasn't sure at all. With the cloud of suspicion hanging over Consuela, it would only be human nature for people to wonder.

"No, I won't be entering any contests. There'll already be your cookies and Mrs. Wilbarger's pie from Oak Knoll—"

Consuela stopped short, her eyes widening. "*Dios mio*," she went on. "She told me not to tell—"

"It's all right, Consuela," Phyllis assured her. "We didn't hear a thing, did we, Sam?"

"Not a thing," Sam said, lazily closing one eye in a conspiratorial wink.

Inside, though, Phyllis was glad. With Carolyn baking a pie, that meant the two of them would be competing in different categories. She could honestly root for Carolyn to win for a change.

"Where is everyone?" Phyllis asked as she began putting away the items she and Sam had brought in.

Consuela shook her head. "I don't know. Everything's been quiet since I came in a little while ago. I haven't seen any of the guests."

Phyllis wondered if she might be able to pry a little information out of Leo about the Jefferson-Bartell takeover deal. If she "accidentally" let it slip to him that she knew about it, his reaction might confirm or deny that he had been aware of it. If he hadn't known, if Charles Jefferson had been keeping it from him, there had to be a reason, and Phyllis wanted to know what it was.

When she had finished putting away the groceries, she went into the hallway with Sam and said quietly so that Consuela wouldn't overhear, "I want to talk to Leo again. Do you feel like coming with me, or have I taken up enough of your time today?"

"Hey, I'm on vacation," Sam said with a grin. "I got no place to be and nothin' to do. I'm glad to lend a helpin' hand."

"Come on, then." Phyllis started up the stairs.

They had just reached the second-floor landing when the door of one of the rooms down the hall was jerked open. Raquel Forrest stumbled out, her eyes wide and glazed-looking. Phyllis and Sam came to an abrupt halt, both of them shocked by the horrified expression on Raquel's face.

"He . . . he's dead," she said. She held out her hands toward Phyllis and Sam, as if she were displaying the crimson stains on them. Phyllis felt sick because she knew what those stains had to be.

What she didn't know was who she was going to find in that room. As she rushed past the stunned Raquel, she remembered the distasteful hanky-panky she believed was going on between the two couples, and she halfway expected to see Leo Blaine's body inside the room.

But instead it was Sheldon Forrest, Raquel's husband, who lay sprawled on his back on the rug beside the bed, the handle of what appeared to be a steak knife protruding from his chest. Feeling sick, Phyllis put a hand over her mouth, and she was glad that Sam had hurried into the room behind her and put his hands on her shoulders to steady her. All the life was gone from Sheldon's wide, staring eyes.

Outside in the hall, Raquel finally began to scream.

Chapter 15

"I didn't expect to be back here this soon investigating another murder," Abby Clifton said.

"Believe me," Phyllis said, "I wish you didn't have to."

Abby was in the parlor downstairs with her and Sam. Upstairs, crime-scene technicians were going over the room and the body of Sheldon Forrest. As the first officer on the scene and the assistant chief, Abby had called for assistance from the county sheriff's office this time. Chief Clifton hadn't arrived yet, but according to Abby, he was on his way.

"Tell me again what happened."

Phyllis sighed. She and Sam had been over this with Abby a couple of times so far, and none of the details of their stories had changed. Phyllis knew from talking to Mike that sometimes a rigidly consistent story was an indication of false testimony, since people seldom remembered all the details of an incident exactly the same every time they told it, even a very recent incident.

But in the case of her and Sam, both of them had had enough unwelcome experience in this sort of thing so that they tended to be more observant than most people. Phyllis wondered if she ought to point that out to Abby Clifton. She certainly wasn't going to make up inconsistent details just to make her testimony sound more believable.

For the moment, she settled for telling Abby once again about how she and Sam had gone upstairs—omitting the part about how she intended to question Leo Blaine about the impending takeover of McKenna Electronics by the Jefferson-Bartell Group—only to see Raquel Forrest come out of the room with blood on her hands.

Raquel had been too hysterical to be questioned right away. One of the ambulance attendants, who were standing by to take Sheldon's body away once the crime-scene techs were through with it, had given her a sedative, and she was lying down in one of the empty guest rooms with a uniformed officer on duty just outside the door.

Sam seemed to have picked up immediately on the fact that Phyllis wasn't telling Abby about the business intrigue involving the two companies, because he didn't mention it, either, when he repeated his version of the story when Phyllis was done. They might be letting themselves in for some trouble by keeping quiet about that, she thought, but they could honestly state that they had answered Abby's questions truthfully. Abby hadn't asked anything about McKenna Electronics or the Jefferson-Bartell Group. She mentioned Sheldon's work, but Phyllis had said honestly, "He's some sort of engineer for NASA. I don't really know what he does there."

Finally Abby said, "Can you account for the whereabouts of the other people staying here during the afternoon?"

Phyllis wanted to provide alibis for Carolyn, Eve, and Consuela, but she couldn't do that since she and Sam had been gone. "I'm afraid not," she said. "Sam and I were out most of the afternoon."

"Out where?" Abby asked.

Phyllis suppressed a surge of impatience. Like everything else, this had already been asked and answered.
"We drove up to the Copano Bay Causeway and walked
out onto the fishing pier," she said. It was possible that
Abby might come up with witnesses who had seen them
there, and she didn't want to be caught in a lie.

"Did you do any fishing?"

"No, just sightseeing. Looking at the bay." Phyllis
smiled. "I'm not much of a fisherman."

"What about you, Mr. Fletcher?"

Sam said, "Oh, I like to get my hook wet. I've mostly
fished in freshwater until now, though. I'm still gettin'
used to this saltwater fishin'."

"I mean, did you do any fishing from the causeway
pier?"

"Oh. Nope, didn't even take my tackle with us today."

"Did you talk to anyone while you were there?"

"The fella you have to pay if you're goin' to fish,"
Sam said. "And we shot the breeze a little with folks on
the pier. I swear, people down here are just about the
friendliest I've ever run into."

Abby smiled. "We pride ourselves on being friendly
in the Coastal Bend." She looked at Phyllis again. "So
you don't know where any of the guests were?"

"No, I'm afraid not," Phyllis said.

"What about Consuela Anselmo?"

"She goes home for a while between lunch and supper," Phyllis explained. "I suppose that's where she was."

"But you don't *know* that she left."

Phyllis shook her head. "I suppose not."

"And she was here when you and Mr. Fletcher got
back a little while ago."

"That's right," Phyllis admitted. "She was preparing
supper. Tamale soup." Knowing that it was irrelevant
but unable to stop herself, she added, "It's one of her
specialties, and it smelled delicious."

"All right," Abby said with a nod. "Did you see her
husband or either of their daughters?"

"No. Tom was doing yard work earlier, but I didn't see him when we came in this time. And I suppose the girls were finished with their work for the day and had gone home."

"My dad told me about all the uproar during the search this morning. It's fair to say that Consuela was very upset with Leo Blaine, isn't it?"

"She was upset with Leo," Phyllis admitted, knowing there was no point in denying that. "But as far as I know she hadn't had any trouble at all with Sheldon. He never bothered anyone."

Unless Leo hadn't known that Sheldon was fooling around with his wife. *That* might have bothered him, Phyllis realized. She had assumed that the carrying-on had been mutual with both couples, but maybe it hadn't. And if it hadn't, and Raquel had found out— or Leo—then either of them might have been angry enough to plunge a knife into Sheldon's chest . . .

Yet another complication, Phyllis thought, and a whole new motive for murder that might not have anything to do with Ed McKenna's death.

"I suppose that's all I need right now," Abby was saying. "You and Mr. Fletcher won't be leaving town anytime soon, will you?"

"We plan to stay until my cousin and her husband can come back down here to take over the business again," Phyllis said. That reminded her that she would have to call Dorothy and break the bad news of yet another murder. She hoped that at least the grandchild's medical condition was improving.

"You may have to stay longer than that," Abby warned, "depending on how the investigation goes. Right now, though, you're free to go on about whatever you need to do, as long as you don't leave town."

"Thank you," Phyllis said, and she couldn't completely eliminate the tone of stiff reserve from her voice. She didn't like what was going on, didn't like being on the outside of the investigation looking in.

Phyllis and Sam went out to the kitchen and found Nick and Kate Thompson there along with Consuela. "Is it true?" Nick asked. "Is Sheldon Forrest really dead?"

"How did you know it was Sheldon?" Phyllis asked.

Nick shrugged. "We saw Raquel on her knees out in the hall, screaming her head off and waving her bloody hands around. It seemed like a logical conclusion."

Phyllis nodded and said, "Yes, Sheldon is dead."

"Murdered?"

"Stabbed in the chest. I suppose that technically it *could* be suicide . . ."

"Did his wife do it?" Kate asked.

"I have no idea," Phyllis answered honestly. "If you saw Raquel, then you know as much as we do."

Consuela shook her head. "He could be an annoying man, but he really wasn't that bad. Not like his friend Mr. Blaine."

"Did either of you see or hear anything unusual this afternoon?" Phyllis asked Nick and Kate.

"Not until Mrs. Forrest started screaming," Nick said.

"Of course, we were asleep part of the time," Kate said. "There must be something in the air down here. I swear, I could take five naps a day. Couldn't you, Nick?"

"At least," he said. "It started as soon as we got here, too. Like Kate says, something in the air, I guess."

"Do you know where the Blaines are?"

"No clue," Nick said. "I know Mrs. Wilbarger and Mrs. Turner went shopping earlier, though. Are they back yet?"

"I haven't seen them," Phyllis said. Inside, she heaved a sigh of relief. She hoped Carolyn and Eve were still poking around shell shops and art galleries. The police wouldn't have any reason to suspect them of being involved in Sheldon Forrest's murder, but it would be even better if they weren't anywhere around when he was killed.

Turning to Consuela, Phyllis went on, "Did Tom finally stop mowing the grass and go home?"

Consuela nodded. "That's right. He left when I did, when I finished cleaning up after lunch." She drew in a sharp breath. "Wait a minute. You don't think Tom had anything to do with Mr. Forrest's death, do you, Mrs. Newsom?"

"Of course not. But the police are going to want to know where everyone was."

"Hey, Kate and I were here," Nick said with a worried frown, "and we don't have any alibi except each other."

"Don't be silly," Kate said. "We never even met any of these people until we came down here on vacation." Despite that, however, she looked a little worried, too. That was a natural reaction, Phyllis thought. Nobody liked being mixed up with murder, even as an rocent bystander.

"What about your girls?" Phyllis asked Consuela.

A stony expression came over the woman's face. "I'm not sure I want to say anything more to you, Mrs. Newsom," she said. "You act like *you* think we're all suspects, that it's not just the cops who feel that way."

"Not at all," Phyllis insisted. "I've never believed that any of you had anything to do with Ed McKenna's death, and I certainly don't think you had any reason to hurt Sheldon Forrest. I'm just trying to get everything straightened out in my own mind."

That seemed to mollify Consuela a little. She said, "Theresa and Bianca have gone home. Bianca's grounded indefinitely, and I asked Theresa to stay there, too, and make sure that her sister didn't go out before I get home this evening."

"What about Tom?"

Consuela shrugged. "I suppose he's there, too. He wasn't planning to go anywhere, as far as I know."

But what it came down to, Phyllis thought, was that Consuela couldn't positively account for the whereabouts of any of her family over the past couple of hours. None of them could have come in through the kitchen while Consuela was here cooking, but any of them could have slipped in the front, gone upstairs, and stabbed Sheldon Forrest, although for the life of her, Phyllis couldn't see any reason why Tom or Theresa or Bianca would have done so.

Unless there was something going on between Bianca and Sheldon, as there had been between her and Leo Blaine? On the surface, that idea seemed ridiculous to Phyllis. For goodness' sake, Sheldon should have had his hands full with the earthy, voluptuous Raquel, not to mention whatever he had been doing with Jessica Blaine.

Phyllis's previous investigations had taught her that almost nothing was too far-fetched to be impossible, though, when it came to murder.

Before she could ask Consuela about anything else, she heard the front door open; then Carolyn's loud, distinctive voice said, "Oh, dear Lord. Not another one?"

Phyllis and Sam hurried out of the kitchen and along the hall to the foyer, where they found Carolyn and Eve standing with their hands full of bags from a couple of souvenir and shell shops. Abby Clifton had emerged from the parlor and stood there, too.

"What do you mean by 'another one,' Mrs. Wilbarger?" the assistant chief asked.

"Why, another murder, of course," Carolyn answered without hesitation. "We come back here to find police cars and sheriff's department vans parked along the road and the assistant chief of police waiting in the parlor, what are we supposed to think?"

Abby didn't answer the question. Instead, she asked another of her own. "Where have you ladies been this afternoon?"

Carolyn held up the plastic bags that were decorated with the logos of various stores. "Isn't that obvious?"

"Are we playing Questions Only?" Eve asked.

Both Carolyn and Abby looked at her and said, "What?"

"Both of you keep asking questions but not answering them," Eve explained. "I thought you might be playing that improv game, Questions Only."

Phyllis knew good and well Eve hadn't really thought that. She was just trying to get on Carolyn's nerves, as she sometimes did.

Abby didn't seem to see the humor in it. She said, "I'll ask the questions, and I'd appreciate some straight answers."

"Eve and I have been shopping all afternoon," Carolyn said. "Is that straight enough for you, Officer?"

Abby didn't correct her, but Phyllis noticed that the assistant chief's jaw tightened a little. "Thank you," she said. "I'm sure plenty of people saw you?"

"Of course. And we have cash register receipts that may well have the time printed on them. I haven't bothered to look." Carolyn added pointedly, "I didn't know that we might be called upon to produce an alibi. Who's dead?"

Abby glanced at Phyllis and Sam, and Phyllis knew what she was thinking. As soon as Carolyn and Eve got a moment alone with them, they would tell the two newcomers what was going on. So there was no point in keeping it a secret.

"Mr. Forrest was killed this afternoon," Abby said.

"That nerd?" Eve said. "I mean, that engineer from NASA?"

Abby nodded. "That's right."

"Who'd want to kill him?" Carolyn asked. "I never saw anyone who seemed quite so harmless."

"Don't worry," Abby said. "We'll find out."

"Like you found out who murdered Mr. McKenna?"

Phyllis thought she ought to step in before Carolyn's blunt nature got her in trouble. She took Carolyn's arm and suggested, "Let's go out to the kitchen." She glanced at Abby Clifton. "That is, if it's all right . . . ?"

Abby nodded. "Go ahead. There's no need to question Mrs. Wilbarger and Mrs. Turner any further . . . right now."

Phyllis tried not to see that statement as being ominous. She and Sam headed for the kitchen with Carolyn and Eve. Consuela, Nick, and Kate were still waiting there.

"All right," Carolyn said when they were all gathered around the big table in the center of the room. "Tell us what's going on here."

"It appears to be the murder *du jour*," Eve said.

Phyllis winced. Unfortunately, Eve was right. Two days, two mysterious deaths . . . not a good pattern.

She told Carolyn and Eve everything she knew about Sheldon's death, which unfortunately wasn't much. However, she didn't say anything about the meeting she and Sam had had on the pier with Oliver McKenna, Charles Jefferson, and Roger Fadiman. She was going to keep that between the two of them for now. While she was convinced that Ed McKenna's death was tied somehow to the corporate intrigue going on, she didn't see any connection with Sheldon's murder other than the fact that he was Charles Jefferson's son-in-law.

But maybe there *was* something to that, she thought. Raquel could have found out about the takeover and told Sheldon, or he might have heard about it through his contacts at NASA, since both of the companies involved did some work for the space program. She would have to think that through, Phyllis told herself.

The front door opened again, and this time Phyllis heard the deep, powerful tones of Chief of Police Dale Clifton, though she couldn't make out any of the actual words. She supposed that Dale had gone into the parlor so that his daughter could fill him in on the developments in the case so far. To be honest, Phyllis didn't know if there had been any developments beyond the discovery of Sheldon's body. It was possible that the crime-scene techs hadn't found any evidence, although it seemed unlikely that the killer could leave the scene completely clean . . . at least, not according to TV.

A worried silence descended over the kitchen table as everyone waited to see what Chief Clifton would do. They heard heavy footsteps going up the stairs. Time stretched out uncomfortably. Finally, the footsteps came back down. A few minutes after that, Phyllis heard a bumping noise. It took her a moment to realize that the noise was caused by the gurney the ambulance attendants were taking up the stairs.

The bumps coming back down a few minutes later were louder, because now the gurney carried a weight on it, Phyllis thought. A deadweight. She steeled herself not to wince every time the wheels thumped down another riser.

At last the gurney rolled out the front door, taking its grisly burden with it. It was a small relief knowing that the bloody corpse was no longer upstairs, but the relief was short-lived because Dale Clifton appeared in the kitchen doorway with Abby behind him. A grim expression was etched into the chief's weathered face.

"Hello, folks," he said with a nod, but there was no friendly warmth in his voice. "Sorry to have to intrude on you like this again so soon." He paused and sniffed the air in the kitchen. "Chili?"

Consuela shook her head, then nodded toward the big pot still simmering on the stove. "That's tamale soup, Chief. It's almost ready. All it has to do is simmer a while longer. Then the frozen sliced tamales need to be added for the last few minutes."

"That's good. I'm sure one of these ladies can finish it," Clifton said, "because you're going to have to come with me, Consuela."

The woman stiffened in her chair. "Why? What have I done?"

"That's what we're going to find out," Clifton said. "I'm sorry, but I'm taking you in for questioning in the murder of Sheldon Forrest."

Chapter 16

$\mathcal{E}$veryone in the kitchen stared in shock at him for a long moment before Consuela said in a shaky voice, "I didn't do it. I swear to you, Chief, I didn't do it."

"She had no reason to kill Sheldon!" Phyllis burst out. "That's just impossible."

Clifton shook his head. "I'm sorry. Consuela, you know that I've known you and your family for a long time. Believe me, I wouldn't be doing this if I had any choice in the matter. But I've got to proceed as I see fit according to the evidence."

"There can't be any evidence," Consuela insisted. "I didn't do it."

Abby moved around her father and came into the kitchen. "Will you cooperate and come along with us, Consuela?" she asked. "You know it'll be better that way."

Even though she looked stunned, Consuela started to scrape her chair back. "I . . . I guess I can . . . ," she began.

"Hold on just a minute!" Carolyn said. "You can't railroad this poor woman! She's got a right to have a lawyer."

"She'll get to make a phone call after she's booked," Abby said.

"So you aren't just taking her in for questioning," Phyllis said. "You're actually arresting her?"

Chief Clifton sighed. "If you want to put it like that . . . yes."

"How else is there to put it?" Carolyn said with a disgusted snort. "I've seen the way the police sometimes try to railroad an innocent person. That's what you're doing here. You have no idea who killed Sheldon Forrest, or Ed McKenna for that matter, so you're just latching on to the most convenient suspect."

"No, if I was doing that I'd be arresting her husband, who already has a felony conviction on his record," Clifton said. "I don't want to be inhospitable to a visitor to our area, Mrs. Wilbarger, but I'd appreciate it if you'd stop trying to interfere with us carrying out our duties."

Carolyn came to her feet, ignoring the way both Phyllis and Eve plucked at the sleeves of her dress. "Or what?" she demanded. "You'll arrest me, too?"

"We just might," Abby said.

Phyllis stopped tugging, took hold of Carolyn's arm, and hauled her back down into her seat. "Blast it, Carolyn, sit down!" she said. "You're not helping things."

She knew that once the police had made up their minds to arrest someone, they wouldn't be argued out of it. Instead of wasting her time with that, Phyllis turned to Consuela and went on. "What would you like us to do? Should I call Tom and tell him what's happening, or do you want me to find a lawyer for you?"

Consuela still seemed so shocked that for a moment she acted like she didn't comprehend what Phyllis was asking her. Then, slowly, she shook her head.

"We have a family lawyer, but I don't know if he'd want to handle something like this," she said. "I'll call him. You call Tom. But tell him *not to come down there.* Tell him to stay with the girls."

Phyllis nodded, although she felt strongly that Tom Anselmo would ignore his wife's wishes and head for the police department just as fast as he could.

Abby moved in beside Consuela and took hold of her arm, firmly but not roughly. In fact, she seemed to be trying to handle the prisoner—because that's what Consuela now was—as carefully and gently as possible. They left the kitchen.

Dale Clifton lingered for a moment. He said, "You folks may not believe it, but I hate doing this as much as I've ever hated anything in this job. I know the Anselmos are good people . . . but sometimes even good people make bad mistakes."

Then he followed Abby and Consuela out of the house, leaving the people in the kitchen to sit there in stunned, angry silence.

That silence didn't last long. Carolyn glared at Phyllis and said, "You shouldn't have grabbed me like that. That so-called chief deserved getting a piece of my mind!"

"But that wouldn't have changed anything, dear," Eve pointed out. "Chances are that you would've just made him mad. That wouldn't help Consuela."

Sam said, "I don't reckon any of us can be much help to Consuela now. What she needs is a good lawyer. I hope that if the fella she's gonna call doesn't want to take the case, he can recommend somebody good to her."

Phyllis nodded. "I'm sure he will. In the meantime, I need to call Tom."

The number of the Anselmos' home phone was written on a dry-erase note board next to the back door. The wooden frame around the note board had a carved, painted fisherman on top of it, with a wooden "line" running down one side to the fish that formed the bottom of the frame. It was as cute as it could be, if a little kitschy, but at the moment Phyllis was in no mood to appreciate anything's cuteness.

She picked up the phone and dialed the number, listened to it ring a couple of times before a young woman answered. "Bianca?" she asked.

"No, this is Theresa," the older daughter replied. "Bianca's grounded and can't use the phone. Who's this?"

"Phyllis Newsom from the bed-and-breakfast."

"Oh, hi, Mrs. Newsom. I never talked to you on the phone before. Sorry I didn't recognize your voice."

"That's all right," Phyllis told her. "Is your father there?"

"No, sorry, he's not," Theresa said. "He left a while ago, and he hasn't come back yet."

Phyllis's hand tightened on the phone. Consuela had assumed that Tom was at home with their girls, and so he couldn't have had anything to do with Sheldon Forrest's murder.

"How long has he been gone?"

"I don't know, let me look at the clock . . . an hour and a half or maybe two hours, I guess."

Phyllis closed her eyes for a second. She had no idea what sort of evidence the police had found that pointed to Consuela as the killer, but it appeared that Tom might not have an alibi, either.

Neither did he have any motive, Phyllis reminded herself . . . but that hadn't stopped Chief Clifton and his daughter from taking Consuela into custody.

"Do you know how I could get ahold of him?" she asked Theresa, referring to Tom.

"Do you have his cell phone number?"

"It's not written here on the board." Phyllis reached for the dry-erase marker that was held by a clip on the other side of the frame from the fisherman's line. "Can you give it to me?"

"Sure." Theresa rattled off the number, then said, "Is something wrong at Oak Knoll? You sound like you're upset about something, Mrs. Newsom."

Theresa was a grown woman—even though someone in her early twenties still seemed like a kid to Phyllis—and Phyllis knew she ought to tell her what had happened.

But she wanted to speak to Tom first, so she said, "I just need to talk to your father for a minute."

"Oh. Okay. Anything else I can do for you?"

"No, that's all. Thank you for your help."

"Fine. I'll go listen to Bianca whine some more about how unfair everybody is to her."

Phyllis hung up and dialed the number of Tom Anselmo's cell phone, aware that everyone in the kitchen was watching her. The phone buzzed quite a few times on the other end, and she was just about to decide that Tom wasn't going to answer when she heard a click and then a loud burst of Tejano music. "Yeah?" Tom said.

"Tom, it's Phyllis Newsom. From the bed-and-breakfast."

"Oh, yeah. What can I do for you?"

His voice was a little slurred. He'd been drinking, Phyllis thought. Upset over what Bianca had done, he had probably gone out to a bar somewhere. That might give him an alibi for Sheldon Abbott's murder, anyway.

"Tom, have you been here at Oak Knoll since you left earlier when Consuela did?"

"What? What are you talkin' about? I haven't been there since one thirty, two o'clock." He had to raise his voice to be heard over the music, and Phyllis wished that wherever he was, he would just step outside.

"Tom, listen to me. Something has happened—"

"More trouble? *Ay, Dios mio!* What is it now?"

"Sheldon Forrest, one of the guests here, has been killed. Murdered."

An explosion of Spanish too rapid for Phyllis to keep up with came from the phone. She let Tom go on for a moment, then raised her own voice to speak over his.

"Tom, listen to me. Listen to me. The police have arrested Consuela. They think she killed Sheldon."

A loud thump made Phyllis jerk the phone away from her ear. She realized that Tom must have dropped it. But he snatched it up again, and when he spoke the drunken slur was gone from his voice. Phyllis's news had shocked the liquor right out of him.

"Consuela . . . arrested?"

"That's right. Chief Clifton and his daughter took her

to the police station a little while ago. Consuela said that she would call your family lawyer and asked me to call you at home. She said for you to stay there with Theresa and Bianca."

She couldn't keep a faint note of disapproval out of her voice. Tom wasn't home, so he couldn't very well stay there.

Just as she expected, he said, "The hell with that. Sorry, Mrs. Newsom. I gotta go." Then the line went dead as he ended the call.

Phyllis sighed and hung up the phone on her end. From the kitchen table, Sam said, "Let me guess. He was takin' off for the police station."

"That's right," Phyllis said with a nod. "He'd been drinking, too. I just hope that he gets there safely and doesn't have a wreck on the way."

"That would be all that family needs right now," Carolyn said.

Nick stood up and came over to Phyllis. "Well, at least you did what Consuela asked you to do. You can take some comfort from that. You did what you could."

Phyllis nodded again. "Yes, I suppose so," she said.

But that wasn't all she could do, she told herself.

She could find out who really killed Sheldon Forrest and clear Consuela's name.

Phyllis had one more phone call to make, this one to her cousin Dorothy. When Dorothy answered her cell phone, the connection wasn't good. "Hold on," she said. "I'm in the hospital. Let me walk down to the other end of the hall and see if the reception's better."

Phyllis waited tensely for several seconds until Dorothy asked in a much clearer voice, "How's that?"

"Just fine. You're in the hospital, you said? How's the baby? Are they going to do surgery?" For the moment, the untimely end of two lives took a backseat in Phyllis's worries to the medical woes of the new one.

"They already did," Dorothy replied. "Early this

morning. Once these doctors make up their minds what needs to be done, they don't waste any time doing it. But they repaired the baby's defective heart valve, and they say that she's doing fine. She's out of the recovery room and in intensive care."

Phyllis heaved a sigh of relief. "That's wonderful news. I know it's terribly nerve-racking having a little one in the hospital like that—"

"But it's better that they can go ahead and fix things like this now," Dorothy said, completing the point that Phyllis had been about to make.

"Amen to that." She hesitated. "I know you have an awful lot on your mind right now . . ."

"Something else has happened down there?" Phyllis heard the catch in her cousin's voice. "Something bad?"

"I'm afraid so. One of the guests, Sheldon Forrest, was killed today."

"Sheldon? Oh, my Lord! How terrible! That poor man. Was it a car wreck, or some other sort of accident?"

"No. He was murdered. And the police have arrested Consuela."

For the second time in the past few minutes, Phyllis winced as she heard the thump of a phone being dropped. She supposed that people who were in the habit of delivering bad news probably got used to it. But she hoped she never would.

A clatter came over the line as Dorothy picked up her phone. It was a good thing those little gizmos were sturdily built. Breathing heavily, Dorothy said, "Murdered? Sheldon?"

"Yes. He was stabbed, upstairs in the room he and his wife shared." Feeling uncomfortably like a gossipmonger but knowing that she needed to find out as much as she could if she was going to have any chance of finding the real killer, Phyllis continued, "How much do you know about what goes on between the Forrests and the Blaines?"

"Goes on? What do you mean? All I know is that

they're friends and they always come to the bed-and-breakfast together each year."

Well aware that Sam, Carolyn, and Eve were watching and listening intently, Phyllis said, "I think that Sheldon Forrest and Jessica Blaine were having an affair. Either that, or the couples were . . . swapping spouses."

Carolyn's eyebrows shot up. Eve looked scandalized, but intrigued. And Sam just took it in with an unreadable expression.

Dorothy said, "Good Lord, Phyllis, I never knew anything about that! I never pried into the guests' personal lives. As long as they kept their rooms fairly clean and didn't cause a racket, I . . . I just never . . . I wouldn't have ever suspected such a thing." She paused. "Sheldon and Jessica? Are you sure?"

"No, but I saw some things that led me to believe that."

"I wouldn't think he'd ever have an affair with anything except maybe a slide rule. Wait a minute, they don't use slide rules anymore, do they? Good heavens, what am I saying? What are you saying? *Sheldon?*"

"Never mind," Phyllis said wearily. "I just thought you might know something about it."

"I'm sorry. I don't. And to be honest with you, I have a hard time believing it. I'm not saying that you're imagining things, just that maybe you're mistaken."

"Maybe," Phyllis said, although after seeing Sheldon putting his shirt back on in the same room where Jessica had been red-faced and breathing heavily, she didn't really think she was wrong.

"You said Consuela's been arrested?"

"That's right. I don't know why the police think she killed Sheldon, but they seem to."

"That's just crazy. Consuela would never hurt anybody."

Dorothy didn't know about what had happened between Bianca and Leo Blaine. She might think differently if she were aware of everything that had been going on around here in the past thirty-six jam-packed hours. The whole thing was too complicated to go into over the phone, though, especially when you threw in all the corporate intrigue going on over McKenna Electronics.

"Listen, if Consuela's been arrested, she's going to need a good lawyer," Dorothy went on. "It's not enough to just know that she's innocent. She'll have to have somebody fighting on her side."

"I feel the same way," Phyllis said.

"If she needs help with hiring someone, I'm committed to doing everything I can. Nobody could ever ask for a stronger, better right hand than she's been to me in running that place, and whatever it takes, Ben and I will do it."

Phyllis had known that Dorothy would feel that way. Unfortunately, Dorothy had problems of her own and might not have the resources to do as much as she wanted to for Consuela. Once the news got around that someone else had been murdered at Oak Knoll, no one was going to want to stay there. The business was slipping away like a beach being eroded by the tide, and Phyllis was sickened by the fact that it was happening on her watch, so to speak.

"You'll tell her that, won't you?" Dorothy went on.

"Of course I will," Phyllis promised. "As soon as I get a chance to speak to her. I don't know when that will be. The police can hold her for up to forty-eight hours without actually charging her, I think."

"We'll be heading that way as soon as the baby is well enough to be released from the hospital. Until then . . ."

"I'll hold down the fort," Phyllis vowed . . . even though she felt that she hadn't been doing a very good job of it so far.

The cousins said their good-byes and hung up. As Phyllis turned toward the kitchen table, Carolyn demanded, "What's all this about orgies going on upstairs?"

"She didn't say there were orgies going on, dear," Eve pointed out. "She said the Forrests and the Blaines were wife-swapping."

"What's the difference?" Carolyn snapped.

Eve frowned in thought for a second, then said, "Quantity?"

Sam leaned forward and clasped his hands together on the table. "You sure about this hanky-panky goin' on?" he asked Phyllis.

"No, not really. I just saw Sheldon Forrest and Jessica Blaine alone together in the Blaines' room yesterday afternoon, and they looked like . . . well, they looked like *something* had been going on. And they acted like they knew exactly where Leo and Raquel were, and I took that to mean that they were together the way Sheldon and Jessica were together . . ." Phyllis sank into one of the empty chairs. "Oh, I don't know what anything means anymore. All I know is that I thought this would be a chance for the four of us to get away and have a nice vacation while I helped out my cousin at the same time. I didn't know we were going to land smack-dab in the middle of more murders."

"Nobody expects the Spanish Inquisition," Sam said.

Phyllis had no clue what he meant by that, unless it was the idea that terrible things often came out of nowhere, with no warning. Even though she had just sat down, she stood up again and said, "I'm going to the police department. I want to see Consuela, if they'll let me."

"They probably won't," Carolyn said. "They've probably got her locked up in some little room with bright lights and rubber hoses."

Eve said, "I don't believe the police do that anymore, dear, if they ever did."

Sam got to his feet as well and said to Phyllis, "I'll go with you."

She started to tell him that wasn't necessary, but then the prospect of venturing into the police department without his strong presence at her side seemed too much to contemplate. She nodded instead and said, "Thank you."

Carolyn said, "It's nearly time for supper. If anyone wants to eat, there's a pot full of tamale soup I can have finished in a few minutes."

And it probably still smells delicious, Phyllis thought as she went out the back door with Sam at her side. But not to her.

Two murders in two days had pretty much ruined her appetite right now.

Chapter 17

$\mathcal{A}$ late-afternoon breeze ruffled the fronds of the tall palm trees along the road. Tall, ungainly-looking gray herons stood in the shallow waters of the bay, waiting for fish to venture unwisely close. Seagulls floated in the sky with apparently effortless grace. To the west the thick clouds that had hung over the area earlier had begun to break up, letting shafts of orange sunlight slant through them. Everything was as beautiful as ever around here . . .

Except the police department. There was nothing beautiful about it.

Sam parked the pickup and they went inside. The officer on duty at the reception desk asked if he could help them. The name tag on his shirt read KINCAID.

"We'd like to speak to either Chief Clifton or . . . Assistant Chief Clifton," Phyllis said, wondering if the two top officers in the department having the same last name ever got awkward.

That didn't appear to be a problem, because the officer said, "Dale's not here, but Abby still is." He reached for a phone. "Who are y'all?"

"Just tell her that Phyllis Newsom and Sam Fletcher would like to talk to her," Phyllis said.

The officer nodded, punched a button on the phone,

and relayed the message after saying, "Couple folks out here to see you, Abby." Obviously, they didn't stand on formality around here ... at least, Officer Kincaid didn't.

When he hung up the phone, he said, "She says for you to come on back. Her office is—"

"We know where it is," Phyllis said, remembering how she and Sam had come here to give their statements that morning. It seemed a lot longer ago than that now. "Thank you, Officer."

"My pleasure, ma'am."

They found Abby Clifton standing in the door of her office, waiting for them. She smiled as she said, "I didn't expect to see you again this soon. Come on in. What can I do for you? Did you remember something that could be important to the investigation?"

"Actually, we just came to see Consuela and make sure she's all right."

Abby's friendly smile disappeared. "We haven't been working her over with a rubber hose, if that's what you mean."

Sam said, "Carolyn's gonna be disappointed."

"That's not what I meant," Phyllis said. "I'm sorry ... Do I call you Chief, too?"

"Why don't you just call me Abby, like everybody else around here? And Consuela's fine. She declined to answer any questions until she talks to her lawyer, which is her right. But he can't get here until tomorrow morning."

"So you're going to hold her overnight."

Abby shrugged. "It was Consuela's decision. I don't like it any more than you do, Mrs. Newsom. I've known Consuela practically since I was a little girl."

"And yet you believe she could have stabbed a man in the chest. Murdered him."

"What I believe or don't believe doesn't matter," Abby said with a sigh. "Around here we go by what the evidence tells us."

"What evidence?"

Abby opened her mouth to say something, then stopped abruptly. Her smile came back, but it wasn't completely friendly.

"You know better than that, Mrs. Newsom. I can't divulge details of the investigation. But I'll tell you what . . . I was just about to go out and grab a bite to eat while I've got a chance. Why don't you and Mr. Fletcher come with me, and if you've got any ideas about the case, I'd be glad to listen to them."

"You mean an unofficial interrogation?"

Abby shook her head. "Nope. Just a conversation. I know you've done some investigating in the past, and I'd love to pick your brain about this mess."

Phyllis hesitated. She wasn't hungry, and she suspected that the assistant chief was really fishing for more evidence that could be used against Consuela, but it was always possible that Abby would let her guard down enough that something important might slip, something that could *help* Consuela instead of hurting her. Phyllis glanced over at Sam to see what he thought about the invitation.

"Where'd you plan on goin'?" he asked Abby.

"A place called The Dancing Pelican."

Sam nodded. "I've seen it when we were drivin' by the water. Wouldn't mind checkin' it out."

"All right, then," Phyllis said. "I don't suppose it would hurt anything."

"I'm glad," Abby said as she pulled the door of her office closed. "Actually, I think we could be friends, Mrs. Newsom, if you'll just give it a chance."

"We'll see about that," Phyllis said, her voice cool. She wasn't sure she wanted to be friends with someone who could arrest an obviously innocent woman such as Consuela.

But then she realized that she was falling into the trap of jumping to conclusions of her own. As much as she wanted to believe that Consuela couldn't be a killer, it would certainly be nice to have some proof . . .

Phyllis and Sam followed Abby in Sam's pickup. The assistant chief drove along the waterfront until she came to a point of land that jutted out into the bay near the boat basin. At the very end of that point was a weathered-looking building with a rear porch built on pilings, so that it extended out over the water, and a pier that stuck out even farther. Old fishermen's nets and floats hung on the walls, giving the place a nautical look. A large wooden sign on the roof proclaimed THE DANCING PELICAN, and in addition to the words, the sign also depicted a cartoon pelican who seemed to be dancing an enthusiastic jig.

Abby parked the police cruiser in the crushed-shell parking lot, and Sam pulled the pickup to a stop beside it. As they all got out of the vehicles, Abby grinned and asked, "What do you think of it?"

"Very picturesque," Phyllis admitted.

"I have an ulterior motive for asking," Abby admitted. "I own the place. Inherited it from my uncle Dave, my mother's brother."

"The assistant chief of police owns a bar and grill?"

Abby shrugged. "Yeah, I know what you mean. It looks sort of odd. That's why I've got a good manager, the same one who ran the place for Uncle Dave. Come on in."

Quite a few cars and pickups were parked in the lot, so Phyllis wasn't surprised to see that The Dancing Pelican was doing a brisk business. The interior was dimly lit, with a bar across the back and tables covered with mismatched tablecloths scattered over the floor. A jukebox in one corner blared loud music. The interior walls were decorated with nets and floats, like the exterior ones.

"Good Lord," Sam said as he looked around. "It's 1972 all over again."

Phyllis leaned closer to him and asked over the music, "Is this what they call a honky-tonk?"

He looked at her. "You've never been in a place like this before?"

She shook her head.

"Well, I guess it's part honky-tonk," Sam said. "Part biker bar, part fisherman's bar, part hippie bar, and pure beer joint. Some of my, uh, misspent youth was misspent in places a lot like this."

Phyllis clutched his arm. "I'm not sure I like it."

"You'll be fine," he told her as he patted her hand. "Just don't throw a drink in anybody's face and start a brawl."

She frowned at him, thinking that he was joking. He had to be joking.

The plank floor seemed to be vibrating a little from the loud music as Abby led them over to the bar, where a huge man with a bushy salt-and-pepper beard was filling beer mugs for his customers. Nobody seemed bothered by the fact that a police officer had just come in, so Phyllis supposed that Abby was a regular visitor.

"Hey, Boaz," she said to the massive bartender, "couple new friends of mine, Phyllis and Sam." She jerked a thumb over her shoulder at them. Evidently everybody was on a first-name basis around here.

"Howdy," Boaz rumbled as he nodded to them. White teeth gleamed in a grin partially hidden by the beard. "What can I get you folks?"

"Cheeseburgers and beers all around," Abby ordered for them, then shook her head. "Deep-six the beers. I'm still on duty. Better make it Dr Peppers instead." She glanced at Phyllis and Sam. "That all right?"

"Sounds good to me," Sam said, and Phyllis didn't want to be a problem so she nodded, too.

"Comin' right up," Boaz promised.

Abby led them over to a booth upholstered in red Naugahyde that showed cracks of age. The dark wood table was scratched and bore countless ringed stains where condensation had dripped off of icy beer mugs. She slid in on one side, Phyllis and Sam on the other. The song on the jukebox changed from "In-A-Gadda-Da-Vida" to "Dust in the Wind."

Phyllis leaned forward and said, "Calling it picturesque doesn't really do the place justice, does it?"

Abby grinned. "I practically grew up here and at the police station. Not your normal upbringing for a little girl, I know. But I turned out all right . . . I hope."

"I'd say that bein' assistant chief of police is turnin' out all right," Sam said.

"My dad plans on me taking over the department when he retires in a few years." Abby shrugged. "We'll see." Those pleasantries aside, she got down to business. "You're convinced that Consuela is innocent, aren't you, Mrs. Newsom?"

"That's right," Phyllis answered without hesitation.

"Then who do you think killed Sheldon Forrest? Give me something else to go on."

"First I'd like to know why you arrested Consuela." Phyllis had been pondering that very question, and when Abby hesitated and didn't answer, she went on, "I suppose it was because the murder weapon came from the kitchen at Oak Knoll."

If she had hoped to startle Abby into agreeing with that theory, she was disappointed, but the sudden look of surprise in the assistant chief's eyes was enough to convince Phyllis she was on the right track.

"If that's all you've got to go on, it's not very much," she continued. "I'm sure you'll find Consuela's fingerprints on the knife. It came from her kitchen. She used it all the time. And she had absolutely no reason to kill Sheldon Forrest."

"Then who did?" Abby asked. "Who had a motive to murder Mr. Forrest?"

It was Phyllis's turn to hesitate. All she had to go on was speculation, but if she wanted to help Consuela, she was going to have to share that with Abby.

"If I were you," she said, "I'd take a close look at Raquel Forrest, as well as Leo and Jessica Blaine."

"The spouse is always one of the first people we look at in a murder," Abby said. "We'll question Mrs. Forrest as soon as she's recovered from the shock of finding her husband's body. Don't worry about that. But what motive would the Blaines have? It's my understanding that they're all good friends."

"Sheldon and Jessica may have been very good friends." Again, Phyllis felt like a gossipmonger, but it couldn't be helped.

"As in, they were having an affair? Now, that's interesting. I hadn't heard that."

"Well, I didn't actually . . . you know . . . catch them in the act." Phyllis felt her face warming. "But I saw enough yesterday to suspect that it might be possible."

They were interrupted then by Boaz, who brought a huge platter containing their cheeseburgers and Dr Peppers over to the booth. He set the food and drinks on the table with an easy grace unusual in such a big man and asked, "Anything else I can do for you?"

Phyllis and Sam shook their heads, and Abby said, "No, we're good. Thanks, Boaz."

He lumbered off, and Abby went on, "I don't know what I'd do without him." She gestured toward the burgers. "Dig in."

The cheeseburger was huge, dripping with grease, and surrounded by potato chips. Phyllis was rather intimidated by the size of it, but she managed to pick it up and take a small bite.

That was enough to convince her that she did have an appetite, after all. It was probably terrible for her health, but the first bite of burger tasted so good that she immediately wanted more. Fire speared into her mouth with the second bite, and she knew that the burger had jalapeño slices on it. She reached for the big glass of crushed ice and Dr Pepper and gulped some down to quench the fire.

"Mighty good," Sam said as he crunched on some chips. "Almost decadent."

"Sin on a plate," Abby agreed.

Now that the burning from the pepper had subsided a little, Phyllis was ready for more. She might pay for this later with a fine case of heartburn, she told herself, but it might be worth it.

They devoted themselves to their food for a while. The pounding rhythm and incomprehensible lyrics of "Louie, Louie" came from the jukebox, followed by the catchy but almost-as-incomprehensible "Incense and Peppermints." Phyllis began to enjoy herself.

It was too bad they were here to talk about murder.

Eventually they got back to the topic, though, as Abby asked, "What else do you think about Sheldon Forrest's death? If he was carrying on with Jessica Blaine, that would give both his wife and Leo Blaine a reason to plant that knife in his chest, but what about Jessica herself?"

"Lovers' quarrel," Sam said. "Been known to happen."

Phyllis nodded. "And any of the three of them could have had a chance to take the knife out of the kitchen. Whoever it was could have worn gloves, too, to make sure that only Consuela's prints were found on the knife."

Abby still didn't confirm that that was the case, Phyllis noted. Instead the assistant chief asked, "What about the other people in the house?"

"None of us who came down from Weatherford ever met him until we got here. As far as I know the same holds true for the other guests, Nick and Kate Thompson."

Abby took a drink of her Dr Pepper and then asked, "If Sheldon was enough of a dog to be carrying on with Jessica Blaine—even though he sure didn't look like the type—maybe he made a pass at Mrs. Thompson, too. She could have told her husband about it."

"That seems awfully unlikely to me," Phyllis said. "Anyway, they were together in their room when Sheldon was murdered."

"Husbands and wives alibiing each other . . . not the strongest evidence in the world."

"Probably not," Phyllis agreed. "But if it was me, I'd be checking to find out exactly where Leo, Jessica, and Raquel were during the afternoon."

Abby nodded. "That's on the agenda. One thing at a time. You can't think of any other motive for Sheldon's murder other than jealousy over his possible playing around?"

Phyllis hesitated. She didn't want to tell Abby everything she had found out about the corporate intrigue going on between McKenna Electronics and the Jefferson-Bartell Group, because they were only linked indirectly to Sheldon Forrest. But if there *was* a connection, it went right through Sheldon, whose father-in-law headed Jefferson-Bartell and who worked for NASA, which did business with both companies.

"What about Ed McKenna?" she finally said. "Could Sheldon's death have anything to do with McKenna's murder? Maybe Sheldon found out who was responsible for that and threatened to turn them in."

"Or tried to blackmail them," Abby suggested.

Sam shook his head. "The fella didn't strike me as a blackmailer."

"He didn't strike me at first as a philanderer, either," Phyllis said. Sam shrugged in agreement with that point. Phyllis went on, "If you've made any progress in solving Ed McKenna's murder, it might lead you right to Sheldon's killer, too."

Once again, Abby didn't rise to the bait. She didn't say anything about how well the investigation into McKenna's murder was going. Instead, she swallowed the bite of cheeseburger she had been chewing and then said, "You wouldn't think that there would be two separate murderers at work in a single bed-and-breakfast, would you?"

"Especially not within two days' time," Phyllis said. She hoped she had planted a seed in Abby's mind. If the police investigation turned up the resentment Oliver McKenna felt for his father, or the fact that Ed McKenna had been trying to block Charles Jefferson's takeover of his company, well, then, *she* couldn't be held responsible for bringing all that out into the open, Phyllis told herself.

"What we're going to have to do is just carry out a thorough investigation of everybody in that house," Abby said. "I hope that won't offend you or your friends, Mrs. Newsom. But the more people we can eliminate as suspects, the more sure we can be that we've got the right person under arrest."

"You *don't* have the right person under arrest," Phyllis said, "at least not right now. But I'm glad that you're not going to concentrate just on finding evidence that implicates Consuela and ignore anything else."

"We're just after the truth, whatever it turns out to be. My dad taught me that." Abby smiled. "And Boaz taught me how to grill burgers. What did you think?"

Phyllis looked at her half-eaten cheeseburger. "I think I've eaten so much already that I won't need another meal for a week."

"Not me," Sam said with a nod toward his empty plate. "That just about hit the spot, Abby. My compliments to the chef."

"I'll tell him you said so." She started to slide out of the booth. "Food's on the house, folks, but you can drop a tip in the jar on the bar if you want."

"I'll do that," Sam said as he stood up and reached for his wallet.

While he was doing that, Phyllis said, "What about us seeing Consuela?"

"Sorry. Tom's already been to see her, and we're

just waiting for her lawyer to show up in the morning now."

"How long are you going to keep her there? You have to either charge her or release her—"

"Within forty-eight hours. I'm hoping it won't take that long."

"So do I," Phyllis said with a sigh. "I'm sure she must be scared."

"Probably not as scared as Sheldon Forrest was when he saw that knife coming at his chest," Abby said.

Chapter 18

Phyllis couldn't bring herself to dislike Abby Clifton, especially after the trip to The Dancing Pelican. Abby had certainly had a colorful childhood.

But neither could Phyllis really warm up to the assistant chief, at least not as long as Consuela was locked up for a crime she hadn't committed. Phyllis clung to that belief, even though she knew she didn't have any real evidence to support it. All of her instincts told her that the two murders were connected, though, and for the life of her she couldn't think of any reason why Consuela would have wanted to kill either of the victims.

As she and Sam headed back to the bed-and-breakfast in Sam's pickup, she said, "I feel a little bad about going off and having supper at that place when we left everybody else to just fend for themselves."

"We had a good reason," Sam pointed out. "You were tryin' to get information out of Abby so you could solve these murders."

"Was it that obvious?"

"No more obvious than it was that she was tryin' to get information out of you."

"But that's her job," Phyllis said. "And she admitted that she wanted to pick my brain."

Sam chuckled. "I'd say you two are a pretty good match. Neither one of you is liable to outwit the other by too much. You were pretty sly yourself, tryin' to put her on the trail of Charles Jefferson and Oliver McKenna. You think both killin's are tied together somehow, don't you?"

"I'm sure of it," Phyllis said. "There's something out there, some part of the puzzle that I'm not seeing yet . . . But I've gone over it and over it in my head and can't come up with it."

"You will," Sam said without hesitation. "I got plenty o' confidence in you."

Phyllis appreciated that, but she wasn't sure she had that much confidence in herself. Even though this case wasn't yet forty-eight hours old, she had run into brick wall after brick wall so far.

"Anyway," Sam said, going back to what Phyllis had been saying a moment earlier, "we left 'em with a pot full of tamale soup on the stove, so nobody should've starved unless they wanted to." He paused, then added, "Speakin' of that tamale soup, I might just have a bowl of it when we get back, if it's still warm."

Phyllis looked over at him. "My God, you can't still be hungry after eating that enormous cheeseburger."

"I've been accused of havin' a hollow leg when it comes to food," Sam said with a grin.

Phyllis just rolled her eyes and shook her head. For someone who bordered on downright skinny, Sam had an impressive capacity for eating, all right.

A police car was still parked in front of the bed-and-breakfast when they got back, but other than that everything looked normal again. The ambulance and the crime-scene vans were all gone. Carolyn and Eve sat in two of the rocking chairs on the front porch, while Nick Thompson sat on the steps and Kate perched on the railing around the porch.

Sam drove around back to park; then he and Phyllis walked up the side of the house to the front porch. Nick stood up to greet them and asked, "Did you get to talk to Consuela? How is she?"

Phyllis shook her head. "They wouldn't let us in to see her, but Abby Clifton said that Tom had been there and that Consuela's lawyer is supposed to be there in the morning."

"So they're going to keep her locked up overnight?" Carolyn said. She sniffed in disgust. "Typical."

Phyllis and Sam took the other two rockers. "I take it there's still an officer upstairs outside the door to Raquel's room?" Phyllis asked.

"Yeah," Nick said. "I guess that even though they arrested Consuela, they don't want Raquel running off just in case they want to arrest her, too."

"Well, they still have to question her," Phyllis pointed out. "She was too incoherent this afternoon after she found Sheldon's body to make any sense out of anything." She paused, then asked, "Do any of you happen to know how it came about that Raquel found him?"

"From what I gather," Eve said, "the four of them all went their separate ways this afternoon. Jessica was still angry with Leo, so she spent the afternoon in some of the boutiques in Rockport. Leo went to a sports bar out on the highway. They came in at almost the same time, but not together, not long after you and Sam left, dear."

"So maybe they have solid alibis, and maybe they don't."

"And of course we don't know what Raquel was doing or where she was," Carolyn said, "because no one's really talked to her. I'm not sure that police officer would let us speak to her, even after the sedative they gave her wears off."

Nick spoke up. "I heard Leo say that he asked Sheldon to come with him to the bar, but Sheldon didn't want to. Maybe Sheldon was already worried that Leo knew about him and Jessica."

"If there's really anything to know," Kate said. "I still have a hard time believing that."

"Well, I'm sure it'll all get sorted out in the end," Nick said. "I just hope it doesn't ruin the place's business." He grinned. "Not everybody is as tolerant of people dropping dead around them as Kate and I are."

She shivered. "Speak for yourself, Dracula. I'm seriously creeped out by the whole thing. I'd cut this trip short and just go home if this wasn't the first real vacation we've taken together. Business trips don't count."

"The two of you have to travel together on business?" Phyllis asked.

"Not really, but sometimes, since we work for the same company, one of us will have to go somewhere and the other one will tag along ... usually me," Kate explained. "Since most of what I do is crunching numbers, I don't get out in the field that much, but Nick is my dad's top property scout, so he has to travel quite a bit, locating suitable places for development."

Nick laughed and held up both hands, saying, "That's enough business talk. We're on vacation, remember? Even if it *has* been interrupted a couple of times by murder."

"At least it wasn't another poisoning this time. I really would have been afraid to eat anything if somebody else had died that way."

"Speakin' of that ..." Sam said.

Kate looked at him. "You mean poison?"

"No, eatin'. Was there any of that tamale soup left?"

Carolyn said, "Oh, that's right. You two haven't eaten."

Phyllis and Sam exchanged a glance, but neither of them said anything. By mutual agreement, they would keep their visit to The Dancing Pelican to themselves for now.

"There's plenty of soup left," Carolyn went on. "I took the liberty of putting it in the refrigerator after everyone had eaten. The Blaines even ate some of it."

"And none of us died," Eve added.

Carolyn gave her a look and went on to Phyllis and Sam, "I can heat some of it up for you, if you'd like."

"I'm not hungry," Phyllis said honestly, without going into the reason why she felt that way.

"I could use a bowl, I reckon," Sam said, "but I'm perfectly capable of heatin' it up myself."

Carolyn shrugged. "Suit yourself."

Nick said, "You know, if you're heating it up anyway, Sam, I might be able to eat a little more, too."

"Good grief," Kate said. "You men are bottomless pits, you know that?"

Nick grinned. "Part of our manly charm, eh, Sam?"

"You said it, son, not me," Sam said as he stood up and headed into the house.

Phyllis went into the house, too, but she headed for Dorothy's office. When she got there she called the Anselmo house again, as she had earlier in the day. She wasn't breaking bad news this time, but she wanted to talk to Tom.

He answered, sounding subdued and worried. When Phyllis identified herself, he said, "Oh, hey, Mrs. Newsom, I don't know how much of the work I'm gonna be able to do around the house for the next few days—"

"For goodness' sake, Tom, don't worry about that!" Phyllis broke in on his explanation. "The only thing you need to be concerned with is Consuela's situation. Sam Fletcher and I went by the police station a while ago, but they wouldn't let us see her. How's she holding up?"

"That was nice of you, even if it didn't work out," Tom said. "Consuela's scared, of course. She knows she didn't hurt nobody, but convincing the cops of that may be hard. Once they make their minds up, you can't get 'em to change. I know that from experience." He sighed. "Of course, in my case it was a little different, because I was guilty. But I guess you don't know about that."

"Actually, Consuela told me," Phyllis admitted.

"Oh." Tom sounded embarrassed, and Phyllis wondered if she should have lied. He went on, "I give you my word, Mrs. Newsom, I been walkin' the straight and narrow ever since I did time, and your cousin Dorothy, she knew all about it. I wouldn't ever lie to her."

"I know that, too," Phyllis assured him. "And I have a bit of good news to pass along."

"What's that?" Tom asked. He sounded desperate for any sort of good news.

"I spent quite a bit of time talking to Abby Clifton this evening, and she assured me that the police are going to conduct a thorough investigation of everyone involved in this case. They're not going to be wearing blinders when it comes to the evidence. If they find something that points to someone else, or that clears Consuela, they'll follow up on it."

"You really think so? You trust her, Abby Clifton, I mean?"

Phyllis thought about it, but only for a moment, before she answered. "Yes, I do." She went on, "I spoke to Dorothy, too, to let her know what's going on, and she was as outraged as the rest of us that Consuela was arrested. She said that if you need financial help for the lawyer or anything else, you should just let her know."

"Dorothy's a wonderful lady, and I sure do appreciate her and Ben. But they should keep their money," Tom said. "They're liable to need it when the bed-and-breakfast goes belly-up."

"I'm sure that's not going to happen," Phyllis protested.

"I dunno. With people dying there, nobody's gonna want to spend their vacation there."

"Once the murders are solved, people will forget all about that. You know how they are. People have short attention spans these days."

"I hope you're right, Mrs. Newsom."

"Is there anything *I* can do to help? Are your girls all right?"

"Yeah, I guess," he replied, and she could hear the weariness in his voice. "They're like me . . . scared. The sooner their mom's out of jail, the better." He laughed humorlessly. "Not gonna be a very festive SeaFair weekend for the Anselmo family this weekend, is it?"

"Who knows?" Phyllis said, trying to make her own voice sound bright and optimistic. "Maybe it'll all be over by then, and you can enjoy the fair like always."

Even as she said it, though, the hope sounded hollow.

A short time later she went into the kitchen and saw the refrigerator door open. Her first thought was that Sam was rummaging around for something else, and she was about to make some comment about that when she realized that the blue-jean-clad rear end she could see past the door was much too broad to belong to Sam Fletcher.

"Excuse me," she said. "Can I help you?"

Leo Blaine stood up quickly and swung the refrigerator door closed. "Mrs. Newsom," he said with a curt nod. "Hope I'm not out of line looking in here. Jessica doesn't feel very well, and she thought some warm milk might settle her stomach."

"I'm sorry to hear that," Phyllis said. The possibility of another poisoning sprang unbidden into her mind. "Does she need to go to the emergency room?"

"Oh, heck no," Leo said, and he managed to smile. "Spicy food always gets her that way, and that soup we had for supper was just spicy enough."

This solicitous, friendly Leo was certainly a change from the angry, blustery Leo he had been for so much of the time Phyllis had known him, which admittedly hadn't been very long. She supposed that most people, even the generally unpleasant ones, had their good points. Leo's concern over Jessica's queasy stomach didn't seem like the reaction of a man who was upset because he'd found out that his wife was cheating on him.

"I'll be glad to warm up a cup of milk for her," Phyllis offered.

"That's mighty nice of you." Leo put a hand on the

back of a chair at the kitchen table. "Mind if I sit down while I wait?"

"Go ahead," Phyllis told him. She got a pan out of the cabinet, took a carton of milk out of the refrigerator, poured some of it into the pan, and set it on the stove.

As Phyllis was lighting the burner under the pan, Leo said, "Yeah, mighty nice, especially considering that I wouldn't be surprised if you wanted to boot us out of here. After what happened this morning, I mean."

"I don't have anything against Mrs. Blaine." Well, other than the fact that she'd been carrying on an affair in the bed-and-breakfast, Phyllis added to herself.

"Right. I'm the one who screwed up. I admit it. What happened with Bianca, it was out of line. Way, way out of line."

"We're in agreement about that," Phyllis said.

"I'll be lucky if Jess doesn't leave me over it," Leo said, and she thought she could hear genuine pain in his voice. That came as something of a surprise to Phyllis. Could a man genuinely love his wife and still be disgusting enough to do what Leo had done? She supposed anything was possible.

She got a silicone spoon from a drawer and stirred the milk as it heated. At the table, Leo mused, "Man, this has been a really messed-up vacation. First old Ed McKenna drops dead. Then the sh—uh—the stuff hits the fan about me and Bianca, and then poor Sheldon gets killed." His voice caught a little as he went on. "Him and me, we were pretty good buddies. I know it doesn't seem like we would be, me being in business and him being, well, a rocket scientist and a little weird to boot, but we had some pretty good times together. Poor old Sheldon."

Was he going to get maudlin and start crying? Phyllis wondered. Leo Blaine seemed to be a man of extremes, most of them unpleasant. She wondered how he would react if she told him she knew about the affair Sheldon had been having with his wife.

If Leo *didn't* know about the affair, he would as soon as the police began questioning him in earnest about Sheldon Forrest's murder, Phyllis thought.

"Yeah, the guy just couldn't catch a break," Leo went on. "Having to put up with all that pain would be enough to make anybody a little weird."

Phyllis frowned and looked around at him. "Pain? What sort of pain?"

Leo looked surprised by the question. "You didn't know that Sheldon had a really bad back?" He shrugged. "No, I guess you wouldn't unless you happened to notice the stiff way he sometimes carried himself when it was really hurting. He had a slipped disk or something . . . I couldn't tell you the medical details, all I know is that he had surgery on it a couple of times and the operations just made it worse. Thank goodness Jess was able to help him when it got really bad."

"Jess . . . you mean Jessica, your wife?"

"Yeah. She used to be a nurse and a physical therapist. She was able to massage Sheldon's back and get his spine straightened up so that it didn't hurt him so much. It wouldn't last, of course, but he was grateful for any relief he could get. I've seen him in so much pain that he couldn't move, and Jess would work on him for fifteen or twenty minutes and get him up and around again."

As she muttered, "Oh, my word," Phyllis realized that she was staring at Leo. She couldn't help it.

Leo frowned. "Something wrong?"

"I just didn't realize . . . Was Sheldon having trouble with his back down here, too?"

"Sure. He never goes more than a few days without it going out on him, and then Jess has to straighten him up again. She was working on him yesterday, in fact."

Phyllis closed her eyes for a second and heard her pulse beating inside her skull. Sheldon had been buttoning up his shirt, and Jessica had been red-faced and out of breath . . .

"Fifteen or twenty minutes, you said?"

"Yeah. Sheldon kept trying to pay her for what she did, like you would with a physical therapist, but of course Jess wouldn't take any money. Hey, Sheldon and Raquel are our friends. And she says she likes keeping in practice, in case she wants to go back to work at the hospital one of these days, or maybe even open up her own business."

"She's still a licensed physical therapist?"

"Sure."

That would be easy enough for the police to check out, Phyllis thought. And when they did, it would confirm what an utter fool she had been. She had looked at Sheldon and Jessica and seen a couple who had just been making love, not a man with a bad back and a friend trying to ease his pain. Phyllis rubbed her temples.

"Are you okay, Mrs. Newsom?" Leo asked.

"Yes, I suppose so. Why?"

"The, uh, milk is boiling over."

Phyllis smelled it now. She turned around quickly, snatched the pot off the burner, and exclaimed, "For heaven's sake!" She had made a real mess of things, and she wasn't thinking just about the burned milk. "I'll fix some more for you."

"Really, I hate to put you out . . ."

"It's no bother," Phyllis told him.

Fixing some warm milk was the least she could do, she thought, since she had told the police that Leo Blaine had a motive for murder . . . a motive that apparently existed only in the mind of a suspicious old woman.

Chapter 19

Just because she had been wrong about Sheldon and Jessica, though, didn't mean that Leo was in the clear, Phyllis reminded herself. There was still the matter of the connection between Ed McKenna's company and the Jefferson-Bartell Group, the corporation that Leo worked for. And since Leo seemed to be in a talkative and friendly mood—rare for him—she wanted to take advantage of that.

As she set aside the pan with the burned milk and began looking for another pan in the cabinet, she said, "I thought you didn't really know Ed McKenna all that well."

"I didn't," Leo said, the change of subject not seeming to bother him.

"Your boss, Mr. Jefferson, certainly knew him."

Leo scowled. "Yeah, and that bothers me. I get the feeling that Charles had some sort of business deal going on with old McKenna, and I should've known about that, blast it. If you're gonna have a vice president in your company, don't you think you ought to trust him enough to let him in on what you're doing?"

"You'd think so," Phyllis agreed. Leo appeared to be sticking to his story about being unaware of the pending deal between McKenna Electronics and Jefferson-Bartell.

"When we get back to Houston, I'm gonna have to have a long talk with Charles. I don't want to work for anybody who doesn't trust me."

He sounded awfully self-righteous for a man who had paid an eighteen-year-old girl to pose for indecent pictures, Phyllis thought. But she supposed that one thing really didn't have anything to do with the other. Business was one thing; Leo Blaine's perversions were another.

"And after the way I've tried to help out with Raquel, too," Leo went on.

Phyllis found another pan, poured milk into it, and started heating it again, vowing to keep a closer eye on it this time. But that didn't stop her from asking, apparently casually, "What do you mean, you've helped out with Raquel?"

"Taken her under my wing. You know, tried to teach her everything I know about the company."

"That's what you've been doing?"

"Sure. She wanted to know all the details." Leo gave a curt, unpleasant laugh that sounded more like his usual arrogant self. "Daddy's girl never could get Daddy to pay enough attention to her, so she figured she'd impress him by learning all she could about his business. She even had some crazy notion that Charles might give her a position in the company one of these days. I could've told her that was never gonna happen, but what would be the purpose in that? I didn't figure it would hurt anything to give her a few pointers."

So Jessica had been helping Sheldon with a bad back, and Leo had been giving Raquel a crash course in the business of designing and selling electronic guidance control systems to the space program. Phyllis sighed as she stirred the warming milk. It appeared that she had been pretty far off base with her deductions this time.

Did that mean she'd been wrong about everything else? Maybe Consuela had poisoned Ed McKenna and stabbed Sheldon Forrest after all . . . even though Phyllis still couldn't see any reason why she would have committed either crime.

Obviously, she wasn't seeing everything.

She stirred the milk and asked, "How did Raquel wind up married to Sheldon, anyway? They don't really seem the sorts who would have paired up, even though they got along all right as far as I could tell."

"They got along fine," Leo agreed. "I think she went after him because right then she was looking for somebody as unlike her father as she could find. And Sheldon and Charles were different as night and day, that's for sure. She met him at a reception the company was giving for some of the NASA engineers and administrators on the project they were working on at the time. This was like fifteen, sixteen years ago. Raquel latched on to Sheldon right away. She swept him off his feet, instead of the other way around." Leo smiled, and fondness and sadness were mixed in the expression. "I really did like the guy, but he was a real nerd, no two ways about it. He'd probably never had a date, let alone a real girlfriend, and suddenly here was this . . . well, you've seen her. Raquel's still a pretty hot babe, but she was really something back then. Sheldon never had a chance once she set her sights on him."

"But it worked out all right," Phyllis said.

"Yeah," Leo agreed. "Yeah, it did."

And then, to Phyllis's amazement, he reached up and knuckled a tear out of his eye.

Of course, he could be acting, she reminded herself. His grief could be completely phony, even though it seemed real to her. She no longer trusted her instincts one hundred percent.

"The cops have to find out who killed him," Leo went on after a moment, when he had regained his composure. "I've done plenty of things in my life I'm ashamed of. If somebody wanted to plant a knife in my chest, they might have a good reason for it. But poor Sheldon didn't have it coming. He never hurt anybody."

202 · LIVIA J. WASHBURN

"I'm sure the police will solve the case," Phyllis said. "They'll probably be talking to all of us again. I take it that you'll cooperate with them?"

Leo sighed. "Yeah. I will now. I still don't like that old chief's high-handed attitude, but if I can help them find Sheldon's killer, I'll do anything I can."

Phyllis got a glass from the cabinet and carefully poured the milk into it. As she handed the glass to Leo, she said, "It's hot, so tell your wife to be careful. She might want to let it cool for a minute, so that it's just warm."

"I will. And thanks, Mrs. Newsom. I'm sorry about the mess."

"That was my fault for not watching the first batch closely enough, Mr. Blaine, not yours."

Leo nodded. "Well, good night."

"Good night," Phyllis told him.

Leo left the kitchen, and Phyllis started cleaning up the mess she had made earlier. While she was doing that, Sam came into the room.

"Finished questionin' Leo?" he asked, keeping his voice low. "I just saw him headin' upstairs with what looked like a glass of warm milk."

"That's what it was. His wife has a bit of an upset stomach from the tamale soup, and she thought it might help her sleep."

Sam frowned. "You sure that's all it is?"

"That's all it could be. Everyone else here ate the soup, too," Phyllis pointed out, "and they're all fine."

"Yeah, I guess so."

"And I wasn't questioning Leo," Phyllis went on. "I was just talking to him."

"Uh-huh."

Sam always saw right through her, especially since they had grown closer over the past year. "Oh, all right," she said with a touch of exasperation. "I guess I *was* questioning him . . . but I tried to be subtle about it."

Sam nodded. "You always are."

Phyllis couldn't keep what she had learned to herself. "Oh, Sam, I was completely wrong about them," she said. "Sheldon and Jessica weren't having an affair at all! He had a bad back, and she was helping him with it because she used to be a physical therapist. She even still has her license."

Sam's bushy eyebrows rose in surprise. "You don't say! So that explains what he was doin' in her room, and both of 'em lookin' like things had been a mite hot and heavy."

Phyllis nodded and said, "That's right. There was something going on between Leo and Raquel, too, just as I suspected, but it wasn't an affair, either. He was helping her learn about her father's business so she could impress him. Impress her father, I mean."

That drew another frown from Sam. "Isn't she a little old to be worryin' about something like that?"

"As long as your parents are alive, Sam, you never outgrow being their child and wanting their approval, no matter how old you are."

"I suppose that's true," he said with a nod. "Now that I think about it, I always wanted my dad to think I was doin' the right thing, and I was still askin' his opinion about important decisions when I was in my fifties. He's been gone for ten years, and every now and then I *still* think to myself that I'm gonna ask him about somethin'."

"I know the feeling."

"So you were wrong about what was goin' on between the Forrests and the Blaines," he mused. "But you got to remember one thing . . . you've got only Leo's word for all of this."

Phyllis's eyes widened as she realized that he was right. "That's true," she said. "Why would he lie about those things, though? He didn't know what I suspected about them."

"Maybe he's used to lyin' to everybody, if he's been coverin' up an affair," Sam suggested. "Could be just a habit by now."

It was possible, she admitted to herself as she considered the theory. Maybe she didn't need to rule out Leo as a suspect just yet. Actually, she couldn't rule out anyone except herself, Sam, Carolyn, and Eve.

It was a good thing after all that she had told Abby Clifton about her suspicions. The police would get to the bottom of it. If there had really been an affair, or affairs, they would be exposed by the investigation.

Milk had burned on the bottom of the first pan. She put some water in it and left it in the sink to soak overnight. "I've thought about murder enough today," she told Sam. "I'm going to turn in and get a good night's sleep. I have a lot to do tomorrow."

There was only one more day before the SeaFair and the Just Desserts competition, and she still had to bake the cookies she was going to enter. She planned to spend the next day doing that and let the police worry for a while about catching the murderer, or murderers.

"Yeah," Sam said. "A lot to do . . . like hope nobody gets killed for a third day in a row."

She glared at him. She could have done without having that thought in her head.

Phyllis slept surprisingly well, with no dreams of murder to plague her. If she had hoped that the solution to the crimes might come to her in her slumber, though, she was disappointed. When she woke up she was no closer to knowing who killed Ed McKenna and Sheldon Forrest than when she went to sleep . . .

But a nagging thought lingered in the back of her head. She had seen or heard *something* that ought to put her on the trail of the killer. She just couldn't think of what it was.

She was up early enough so that she was the first one in the kitchen. With Consuela still in police custody, Phyllis knew that the responsibility of preparing breakfast fell to her. She was mixing some pancake batter when a key rattled in the back door lock. The door swung open, and Theresa and Bianca Anselmo came in. Both of the young women were hollow-eyed, as if they hadn't slept much the night before.

"Good morning," Phyllis greeted them. She didn't attempt any artificial cheer. "Is there any news?"

Theresa shook her head. "No, it's too early. Mama's lawyer probably won't even show up for a couple of hours yet."

"But *Papi's* already gone down to the police station," Bianca said. "He's going to wait there. He told us to come on over here and do our work like normal. He said that's what Mama would want."

Phyllis nodded. "I think he's right about that. No one else is up yet, so you can start downstairs since your mom's not here to do it."

"All right," Theresa said. The two of them left the kitchen, heading for the front of the house.

While the pancakes were cooking, Phyllis began setting out some of the ingredients for her Oatmeal Delight cookies. Might as well get an early start on the baking, she thought. She pulled the butter out of the refrigerator and set it out to soften, then set out the other ingredients she had bought at Wal-Mart with Sam.

Carolyn came in while Phyllis was flipping the pancakes and saw the other preparations. "You're making cookies?" she asked, evidently surprised.

Phyllis nodded. There was no reason to keep her entry a secret now, especially since she knew that Carolyn planned to bake a pie. Unless, of course, Carolyn changed her mind and decided to make cookies out of sheer contrariness, and if she wanted to do that, Phyllis couldn't very well stop her.

"Well, that's . . . fine," Carolyn said. "Somehow I just assumed that we'd be competing against each other, but I plan to make my chocolate strawberry pie."

"Why, I think that's a wonderful idea," Phyllis said. "I've always thought that pie was delicious. Who knows, maybe we'll both win."

"Yes, that would be a nice change, wouldn't it?"

Phyllis noticed that Carolyn refrained from making any comment about how she usually won and Phyllis was one of the runner-ups. Maybe the laid-back atmosphere of this coastal area was making her more mellow.

Although she wasn't sure how laid-back anything could be with two unsolved murders hanging over the place.

Carolyn pitched in to help with breakfast, and so did Sam and Eve when they came into the kitchen a short time later. By the time the guests began coming downstairs, they had plenty of food prepared. Nick and Kate were the first ones down, followed by Leo and Jessica.

"Are you feeling better this morning?" Phyllis asked Jessica.

She smiled and nodded. "Yes, I am. Thank you so much for fixing that warm milk last night. It always settles my stomach. I'm sure Leo would have made a huge mess if he had tried to do it."

Leo caught Phyllis's eye and gave a little shrug. The mess she had made would remain their secret, he seemed to be saying. At the same time, Jessica turned and frowned at him, making it clear that she was still angry with him over the whole Bianca debacle the day before.

"I was glad to help out," Phyllis said.

Tentative footsteps on the stairs made them all turn and look in that direction. They saw Raquel Forrest descending slowly, followed by the uniformed officer who had spent the night in a chair in the hallway outside the door of her room. The officer looked a little bleary-eyed and gratefully accepted the cup of coffee Phyllis offered him.

"I've already called and checked in with the station," he said. "Chief Clifton will be here in a little while."

"He'll be welcome to join us for breakfast if he wants to," Phyllis said. "For that matter, so are you, Officer."

"Well, ma'am, maybe I'll just, uh, take one of those

flapjacks with me and eat it out on the porch while I wait for the chief."

Sam said, "Suit yourself, son," and gave the officer one of the pancakes from a platter piled high with them.

The cop said to Raquel, "The chief will want to talk to you, ma'am, so if you'll do like we talked about and wait for him . . ."

"Don't worry," Raquel said in a voice seemingly dulled by grief and the hangover from the sedative she had been given. "I'm not going anywhere."

Everyone sat down at the table and began to eat, passing platters of food around with a minimum of talk. No one seemed to be in much of a mood for conversation. Approximately forty-eight hours had passed since Ed McKenna's death. That wasn't much time, and the shock of Sheldon Forrest's murder was still fresher and more painful.

Nick tried to perk things up by saying, "Kate and I thought we'd go through that big mansion up the road this afternoon. Anybody want to come with us?"

"I've been meanin' to take one of the tours through there myself," Sam said. "I like historical sites, since I was a history teacher myself before I retired."

Nick said, "I thought you told me you coached basketball."

"I did, but coaches have to teach an academic subject, too, at least in most places. In my day, most of 'em taught history. Texas history was my subject, so I know a little about the Fulton mansion already."

"Why don't we go, too?" Leo suggested to Jessica. "All the times we've come down here, we must've driven by the place a hundred times, but we never stopped and went in to have a look around."

"I suppose we could," she said with a shrug, still not being very friendly toward him. "If you want to."

Raquel gave a wan smile. "I think I'll pass. I have . . ." She paused and drew a deep breath. "I have arrangements to make."

Jessica reached over to pat her hand. "Oh, dear, I'm so sorry. I should have thought . . . Here we are talking about taking some stupid tour . . . I'll stay here with you today."

"No, no, that's all right," Raquel said. "There's really nothing you can do, Jess . . . nothing anybody can do. Anyway, I'm sure the police wouldn't let you stay with me. The chief will want to talk with me alone."

Phyllis knew that was true. Still, she felt bad about abandoning Raquel, too. But she would be finished with her baking by the time the others left, and she was interested in the mansion because she had been a history teacher like Sam, although she had taught world history and American history rather than Texas history.

Sam turned toward her and asked, "Are you comin' along?"

"We'll see. But I think I might."

"I hope you do," he said with a nod.

The conversation might have continued, but at that moment the uniformed officer returned from the front porch where he had been waiting. Chief Dale Clifton was with him. The chief gave everyone around the table a smile and a nod and said, "Good morning, folks." He looked at Raquel. "Mrs. Forrest, you have my deepest sympathy on your loss. I'm really sorry to intrude on you at a time like this, but I have a few questions that I need to ask you."

Raquel nodded, put her hands on the table, and pushed herself to her feet. "Of course. I understand, Chief. Let's get this over with."

Chapter 20

Phyllis had a hard time concentrating on cleaning up after breakfast and then getting her cookies in the oven, because she knew that Chief Clifton was questioning Raquel Forrest in the parlor. She didn't think that Raquel would break down and confess to stabbing her husband, but anything was possible. She might even admit that she had poisoned Ed McKenna, although Phyllis couldn't think of any possible motive for her to have done such a thing.

Clifton surprised her by coming to the kitchen door and saying, "I have some questions for you, too, Mrs. Newsom."

"Me?" Phyllis said. She glanced at the timer attached by a magnet to the refrigerator door. It was counting down the minutes and seconds until the first batch of cookies was supposed to come out of the oven. "I thought you were talking to Raquel."

"Mrs. Forrest and I are finished for now. And you and Mr. Fletcher *were* the first ones on the scene after she discovered her husband's body."

"But . . . but I have cookies in the oven," Phyllis protested.

Carolyn was sitting at the table. She and Phyllis had

been chatting aimlessly. Now she said, "I'll take them out and put the next batch in for you, Phyllis."

"I really ought to check them when they come out and make sure they're done." It wasn't that Phyllis was worried about being questioned by Chief Clifton. She really was concerned that the cookies she was going to enter in the contest be as good as they possibly could be.

"I can tell when cookies are done, and I know how long to bake the next batch," Carolyn said as she got to her feet. "For goodness' sake, I've even watched you make this particular recipe before. I won't mess them up. I give you my word on that."

"You don't have to give me your word," Phyllis said. She didn't want Carolyn to think that she didn't trust her. She did ... especially since they weren't competing directly against each other this time. If they had been ...

But they weren't, Phyllis reminded herself, so it wasn't necessary to even think such things. She went on, "Thank you, Carolyn." Then she turned to Chief Clifton and said, "I suppose you'd like to talk in the parlor?"

"That'll be fine," he said. "I'll try to have you back out here before that next batch of cookies needs to come out of the oven." As they left the kitchen and started down the hall toward the parlor, he added, "Are you baking them for the guests here?"

"No, for the Just Desserts contest at the SeaFair tomorrow."

"Ah." He nodded. "The SeaFair. Just what we need around here ... more excitement. It actually starts tonight, you know. My men will be busy keeping up with all the extra traffic, not to mention the fights and the drunk-and-disorderly calls."

"Goodness. Is it really that bad?"

"No, by and large the SeaFair visitors are a really well-behaved bunch. But you put a large number of people together with beer and you're going to have a little trouble here and there. You shouldn't have to worry about it tomorrow during the contest. That's during the middle of the day, right?"

"One o'clock, I think."

They went into the parlor. "I know you talked to my daughter yesterday," Clifton began, "and Abby said she even went to The Dancing Pelican with you and Mr. Fletcher for supper. I appreciate any help you gave her. Right now I just want you to tell me in your own words what you saw when you and Mr. Fletcher got back here yesterday afternoon and found Mrs. Forrest coming out of the room where her husband's body was."

Phyllis went through it again, knowing that her story hadn't changed from the other times she had told it. Chief Clifton nodded a lot and made a few notes in a little notebook, then asked her if she could account for the whereabouts of everyone else connected with the house during the half hour or so previous to that time.

That had to mean Sheldon Forrest had been stabbed during that half hour, she thought. And she couldn't truthfully account for the whereabouts of anyone just then except her and Sam. They had been on the Copano Bay Causeway fishing pier with Oliver McKenna, Charles Jefferson, and Roger Fadiman. She hadn't mentioned that little detail the day before, though, so she kept quiet about their companions now and crossed her fingers for luck that her deception wouldn't be discovered. She didn't want to be charged with obstruction of justice. Mike would be very disappointed in her. She regretted now trapping herself in that lie of omission.

Finally, Chief Clifton nodded and said, "I guess that's all. Thank you for your cooperation, Mrs. Newsom."

"You've arrested the wrong person, you know." Phyllis couldn't resist saying it.

"Oh?" Clifton's white eyebrows rose. "Is that right? You think Consuela Anselmo is innocent?"

"I'm convinced of it."

"Then who do you think is guilty?"

Feeling a little like she was—what was the expression?—throwing Raquel under the bus, Phyllis said, "I thought that a spouse was always the first suspect in a murder."

"That's true. By all accounts, though, the Forrests were happily married. Nobody says that they quarreled recently. In fact, they seem to have been very much in love, despite the differences in their background."

"But why would Consuela want to hurt him? You can't just go by the fingerprints on the murder weapon. It came from her kitchen, after all."

Clifton looked surprised again. "Abby told you about the fingerprints, eh?"

"Your daughter didn't confirm or deny anything, Chief . . . but you just did."

Clifton frowned at her for a moment, then burst out in a laugh. "Son of a gun! I sure did . . . But as for motive, did you ever stop to think that maybe Sheldon Forrest wasn't Consuela's intended victim?"

Now he had totally lost her, and Phyllis said as much.

"Maybe she took that knife and went upstairs intending to stick it in Leo Blaine's chest," the chief suggested. "She could have known that Blaine's been spending a lot of time with Raquel Forrest—"

"That's completely innocent, from what I've heard," Phyllis said. "He was teaching her about her father's business." If Clifton didn't already know about that, he would as soon as he questioned Leo.

Clifton nodded. "That's what Mrs. Forrest told me. But what if Consuela went upstairs looking for Leo, intending to settle his hash for that business with Bianca? She didn't find him in his room, so she looked in the Forrests' room, and Sheldon Forrest saw her with the knife and guessed what she was up to. He could have threatened to tell Leo that she was gunning for him, so to speak, and then Consuela lost her temper and struck out with the knife . . . and when she saw what she'd done, she got scared and hurried back downstairs."

"Leaving the knife in Sheldon's chest? Do you really think she could kill a man and then calmly go downstairs and start cooking a pot of tamale soup?"

"Well, when you put it like that," Clifton said with a grudging frown, "it does sound pretty unlikely."

"It certainly does!"

"Unfortunately, we have a limited amount of forensics evidence to go on."

"I don't mean to lecture you, Chief, but there's more to it than forensics evidence. You have to know the people involved. People have to have a *reason* to commit murder. If Leo Blaine was the one with the knife in his chest, then Consuela might have thought she had a reason to do that."

"Like I said, it could have been an accident."

Phyllis shook her head. "I can't believe the scenario you laid out. I just can't." She lifted a hand to her mouth as a thought occurred to her. "Oh, good grief. I'm arguing crime-solving with a chief of police."

Clifton grinned. "And arguing quite well, I must say."

"Why did you let me go on like that?"

"Because I'm interested in your point of view, Mrs. Newsom. You've solved murders before. You know more about this sort of thing than the average citizen. To tell you the truth, I was sort of hoping you'd read me the riot act and come up with another viable suspect for me. But . . ."

"I didn't, did I?" Phyllis sighed. "Chief, there was no affair between Sheldon Forrest and Jessica Blaine. No one had any reason to kill him. Just like no one who was actually here in the house had any reason to poison Ed McKenna. These are . . . are senseless crimes."

A frown of concern appeared on Clifton's face. "You think maybe we're dealing with some sort of deranged serial killer? Somebody who kills for the thrill of it?"

"That seems impossible. That sort of murderer is usually, well, some sort of squalid little man who just wants to feel powerful."

"Studied profiling, have you?"

Phyllis shook her head. "No more so than anyone else who's watched the news on television and read a few books. But no one involved in this case ... no one! ... strikes me as a thrill killer."

Clifton nodded. "For what it's worth, I agree with you. There's a motive, or motives, behind both killings. We're just not seeing it." He got up from the armchair where he had been sitting. "But Abby and I will keep poking around until we find it. You can be sure of that."

Phyllis stood as well. "We're finished, then?"

"For now. Unless I think of anything else." Clifton held out his hand, and as Phyllis took it, he went on, "Thank you for talking things over with me, Mrs. Newsom. It's sort of like having an unofficial consultant whose business is murder."

She shook her head firmly. "My business is being a retired schoolteacher. And right now, it's also baking cookies for that contest tomorrow ... Oh, dear. I forgot about the cookies!"

"Darn it, so did I. But at least you had Mrs. Wilbarger out there in the kitchen backing you up."

"That's true. I assume you'll be around for a while, questioning the others who are staying here?"

"That's the plan," Clifton said.

"Stop by the kitchen before you leave. I think I can spare one or two cookies."

A grin spread across his face. "I'll sure take you up on that offer."

My business is murder, Phyllis thought as she headed back to the kitchen. It sounded like the title of some silly old tough-guy paperback. How ridiculous.

While Phyllis was talking to Chief Clifton, Carolyn had taken the first batch of cookies out of the oven, put in the second batch, taken *them* out, and put in a third batch, which used up more than half of the dough Phyllis had prepared. That third batch was now baking. When Phyllis checked the cookies that had already come out of the oven, she saw that they were perfectly done.

Carolyn was putting spoonfuls of cookie dough on the pan when she stepped aside to let Phyllis take over.

"I feel like this should be a team entry now," she told Carolyn.

"Nonsense. I didn't do anything. All the credit for them goes to you."

"I'd be glad to help with your pie," Phyllis offered.

"I appreciate it, but that won't be necessary. I'm not going to bake it until tomorrow morning, so that it'll be nice and fresh for the contest."

"You're not going to the SeaFair before then?"

"Wander around in a crowd of people swilling beer and smelling of insect repellent and sunblock? No, thank you. I don't plan to get there until right before the contest, although I'll probably check out some of the arts and crafts exhibits afterward. Let's face it, though, Phyllis, this is the same sort of thing as the Peach Festival, and we already go to that every year."

Carolyn had a point, but the SeaFair certainly wasn't exactly the same as the Peach Festival. For one thing, you couldn't stand in the town square in Weatherford and see the surf rolling in on the beach or smell the salt air or hear seagulls calling to each other. As much as she loved her hometown, it was good to get away and see some different things sometimes, too.

Like the Fulton Mansion, which she planned to join the others in touring later that afternoon. She had read a little about it and knew that the waterfront mansion was well over a hundred years old. Like many of the other historic old buildings in Rockport and Fulton, it had survived for so long because the occasional hurricanes vented most of their fury on the barrier islands offshore, rather than roaring in with full force.

While Phyllis was getting the last batch of cookies out

of the oven, Chief Clifton stuck his head in the kitchen door. "Looks like I'm just in time for those cookies you promised me," he said with a smile.

"These are too hot," Phyllis said, "but you can have a couple off that plate over there on the counter."

"Much obliged," the chief said as he moved over to the counter. He picked up two cookies from the pile on the plate and took a bite out of one. Making a face of pure pleasure, he said, "Oh, now, that's really good. I always try all the entries, and I think you're going to be one of the favorites in the contest tomorrow."

"We'll see," Phyllis said with a shrug. "You'll have to try Carolyn's pie, too."

"Oh, I will, you can count on that. But I want to be sure and get the recipe for these cookies for Boaz. Of course, he'll come up with something crazy to put in them and ruin 'em, but he'll have fun with it."

When the chief was gone, Phyllis and Carolyn started getting ready for lunch. Without looking at Phyllis, Carolyn commented, "I'm not very fond of the police, you know, ever since they tried to arrest *me* for murder, but I have to admit, Chief Clifton is a rather handsome man."

"Really?" Phyllis replied, smiling to herself. "I hadn't noticed." She couldn't remember the last time Carolyn had commented on a man's looks.

"In a weather-beaten sort of way, of course."

"Of course."

Carolyn didn't say anything else, but still, Phyllis thought, it was progress of a sort. Maybe one of these days Carolyn would find someone she wanted to spend the rest of her life with. If she did, that was fine. If she didn't . . . well, she would always have her friends. Thank goodness for that, Phyllis thought, because she knew that the same thing applied to her.

Tours began every hour at the Fulton Mansion, Sam had found out from looking at the mansion's Web site. At

two o'clock that afternoon, he and Phyllis were waiting in front of the massive three-story house, which sat
facing the water over a long, narrow lawn dominated
by four towering palm trees and several of the picturesque bent oaks. Eve was with them, along with Nick
and Kate Thompson and Leo and Jessica Blaine. Jessica
seemed to have warmed up a little to Leo, although it
would probably be a long time before she forgave him
for what had happened with Bianca. Phyllis knew that
Jessica had to be wondering what other unsavory activi-
ties her husband had gotten up to over the years.

A historical monument and marker along the walk
that led to the house had explained that it was built between 1874 and 1877 by George W. Fulton, an early-day
settler and cattle baron for whom the town was named.
It was constructed in the mansard style, and the latest
technological advances of the time had been installed in
it, including running water, central heating, and gaslights.
What would now be considered the bare necessities of
life had been the height of luxury back in 1877 when the
Fulton family moved in, Phyllis thought.

But it was that way with everything, she mused. People got used to having certain things, and they didn't
want them taken away.

There were other visitors to Oakhurst, as the mansion was named, besides the group from Oak Knoll.
When one of the volunteers who conducted the tours
opened the front door at two o'clock, everyone trooped
up the rather steep set of stairs to the porch and filed
inside. Phyllis was struck immediately by how ornate
the furnishings were. The rooms were crowded with
overstuffed furniture, thick rugs on the floors, and crys-
tal lighting fixtures. The guide pointed out not only the
obvious luxuries, but also things like the pipes that conducted heat from room to room. She also talked about
the life of George Fulton, who had fought in the Texas
Revolution as a young man, long before becoming a
successful rancher and financier.

For someone interested in history, it was a fascinating forty-five minutes, Phyllis thought. She and Sam both took it in avidly. Eve didn't care much about the historical aspects, but she was impressed by the furnishings and the elaborate garden behind the house. So was Jessica Blaine. Leo looked bored at times, Phyllis thought, but he made an effort not to, especially when Jessica was looking at him. Maybe he really did want to clean up his act and earn his wife's forgiveness. Phyllis hoped that was the case.

When she and Sam finally wandered back out onto the mansion's front porch, they found Nick and Kate standing there looking across the long front lawn to the bay. Nick's hands were thrust in the pockets of his cargo shorts, and he sighed as he said, "You know, if you knocked down those palm trees and those funny-looking oaks, you could put up condos in that space, or some sort of club."

"That's terrible!" Kate said. "It's a perfectly beautiful view, and you want to spoil it?"

Nick laughed. "Hey, just force of habit. You know me, can't let go of the ol' work mentality." He took his hands out of his pockets and slipped an arm around Kate's waist. "But you're right, it *is* a beautiful view. Romantic, even."

"Yeah," she agreed as she rested her head on his shoulder, stooping a little to do so. She put an arm around Nick.

They stood there like that, taking in the view, seemingly oblivious to Phyllis and Sam, until finally Nick turned his head and gave Kate a kiss. It was a little more than a peck but didn't turn too passionate, for which Phyllis was grateful. She had never quite gotten used to the way young people sometimes demonstrated their affection for each other in public. Some things needed to be reserved for more private moments.

Still, Sam had a certain wistful look in his eyes, too, as he gazed out over the lawn and the trees, she noted, and she couldn't help but ask, "What are you thinking about, Sam?"

"Well . . . if those trees weren't there, like Nick said . . . that yard's just about the right size and shape to play football on."

She stared at him in disbelief for a moment, then took hold of his hand and squeezed it. "Once a coach, always a coach, I guess," she said with a laugh.

"See?" Nick said to Kate. "It's hard to break old habits."

Chapter 21

*A*ll day long, the thought that there might be another murder had nagged at Phyllis, even when she was busy with other things. But it was actually a rather pleasant day, what with Chief Clifton talking to her more like a fellow detective rather than a suspect, and the cookie-baking, which always made Phyllis feel better, and the visit to the Fulton Mansion, where she could forget about murder for a while and just be a tourist again.

And of course, most important, no one died.

But when she got up Saturday morning, even though Phyllis's thoughts were full of the SeaFair and the Just Desserts competition that would be coming up in a matter of only hours now, she still couldn't forget that Ed McKenna and Sheldon Forrest weren't here to enjoy the festivities. And as far as she knew, the police were no closer to finding out who had killed them, despite the fact that Consuela remained in custody.

Phyllis had talked to Tom Anselmo the night before. "Our lawyer says they'll have to release Consuela tomorrow. It'll be the weekend, so they won't be able to arraign her, and they can't keep her until Monday without charging her." The relief had been evident in his voice as he went on. "So she'll be coming home."

Phyllis was glad of that, but she knew that the police could take Consuela back into custody on Monday and charge her with murder if they wanted to. The physical evidence against her was only circumstantial, though, so she thought that the district attorney might decide not to press the case.

That would be a foregone conclusion if only Phyllis could figure out who was really responsible for the murders, but that didn't seem likely to happen. That brick wall was still as solid as ever.

Meanwhile, she boxed up the cookies in a plastic container after breakfast and went to find Sam. "I'm going to ride to the SeaFair with you, if that's all right," she told him. "Carolyn wants to come later, and I told her she could borrow my car."

"Sure, that's fine," Sam agreed, as Phyllis had known that he would. "Were you wantin' to go on now? Those young people have already left, and I think the Blaines are about to."

Raquel wouldn't be going to the celebration, of course. The local funeral parlor was shipping Sheldon's body back to Houston today, and his funeral would take place on Monday. Raquel had made the arrangements the previous afternoon. Chief Clifton was allowing her to return to Houston for the funeral, as well as Leo and Jessica, but he had asked all of them to stay where he could get in touch with them after that.

"I'm almost ready to go," Phyllis told Sam. "Let me get some sunblock and my hat."

She had a straw hat with a wide brim that would shield her face, and she rubbed sunblock on her arms since the day was warm and she was wearing a short-sleeved blouse over capri-length jeans. It would be a long day, a lot of it spent in the sun, and she was dressing for comfort, not style. However, she thought she looked pretty good, too, as she glanced at the mirror over the dressing table in her bedroom.

She went down to the kitchen and got the cookies,

then found Sam and Eve waiting for her just outside the back door. Eve wore jeans, too, although as usual hers were considerably tighter than the ones Phyllis wore.

Sam nodded toward the house next door, where a large moving van was backed up. "Looks like the neighbors are movin' out," he said.

"I knew they were going to," Phyllis said. She saw Darcy Maxwell standing beside the moving van, supervising as the movers loaded furniture into it. "I suppose I should go over there and say good-bye on behalf of Dorothy and Ben, since they were neighbors for a long time." She handed the container of cookies to Sam, who took them without complaint. "I'll be right back."

Darcy saw her coming and smiled. "Good morning," she said. "On your way to the SeaFair?"

"That's right. I'm surprised you're not going."

"No, we're done with Rockport. We're going inland, where the humidity isn't as bad. My husband's arthritis can't take it anymore. Thank goodness for Garrett Development."

"What's that?" Phyllis asked with a puzzled frown.

"The company that bought our place," Darcy explained. "They made us a very generous offer, too."

"Oh. For some reason I thought you'd sold it to some other family, that Dorothy and Ben would be getting new neighbors."

"Could be," Darcy said with a shrug. "Garrett may have bought the place as an investment with an eye toward reselling it. Flipping it, you know."

Phyllis nodded. She had heard the term before.

With barely a pause for breath, Darcy went on, "Isn't it terrible about Consuela? I never would have dreamed she would do such a thing! I'm glad now that I wasn't able to hire her away from Dorothy. It's sure going to be a blow to the bed-and-breakfast when word gets around that the cook killed at least one of the guests."

"Consuela didn't kill anybody," Phyllis said, her voice stiff with anger now. She wanted to be polite because

Darcy Maxwell had been her cousin's neighbor for a lot of years and because, well, it was her nature to be so. But she was irritated enough to add, "I don't see how anyone could ever believe that Consuela is a murderer."

Darcy shrugged. "Well, the police arrested her, didn't they? And the wild stories I've heard about those daughters of hers and the way they carry on with the male guests . . . Dorothy should have sold out when she had the chance."

Phyllis resisted the impulse to give the woman a piece of her mind. Instead she just nodded and said as briefly as possible, "Well, have a nice trip."

"Sure. Say good-bye to Dorothy and Ben for us, will you?"

"Of course," Phyllis said. What she wanted to say to Darcy Maxwell was good riddance. The woman really did have a wagging tongue, as Consuela had said.

"What's wrong?" Sam asked when Phyllis walked back over to the pickup. "You look a mite annoyed."

"Some people just get on my nerves, and that woman is one of them," Phyllis said. She took the cookies back from Sam. "Let's go."

What Chief Clifton had said about the traffic was right. The cars on the highway slowed to a crawl as they approached Rockport Harbor. The SeaFair was held in a large grassy, parklike area adjacent to the water. Cars filled the parking areas around the harbor and the Maritime Museum, and they lined the shoulders of all the surrounding roads as well. Huge awnings with brightly colored stripes on them were arranged to form tents that were laid out in a rough rectangle around the outside of the fair area, with smaller tents in the center of the open area. And everywhere there were people, also as Chief Clifton had predicted.

Even though it was relatively early, Sam had to park far enough away so that they had a good walk to reach the fair. There was a nice breeze off the water, though, so it wasn't unpleasant. Phyllis enjoyed seeing all the families with young children. The kids all looked so happy and excited. They would remember these good times for the rest of their lives, she thought.

Music from one of the center tents filled the air, along with the hubbub of the crowd. Local bands would be playing there all day and on into the evening.

Phyllis, Sam, and Eve paid their admission fees at a ticket booth and were given plastic wristbands that were good for the rest of the weekend. Eve frowned at hers and said, "They could have made these more colorful and stylish, couldn't they?"

"Maybe you should suggest that to someone," Phyllis said. She looked around for one of the volunteers, located a lady with a SeaFair Staff tag on her shirt, and asked where the entries for the Just Desserts competition were being taken. The woman pointed her toward the front part of the group of tents.

Phyllis had filled out an entry form on the Internet and had been given a number, which she had taped to the side of the container of cookies. "Judging will be in the yellow-striped tent at the front of the fair area at one o'clock," the woman told her.

She glanced at Phyllis's entry form, which included her address, and continued, "My goodness, you didn't come all the way down here just to enter our little contest, did you?"

"No, my friends and I were down here anyway," Phyllis explained without going into detail. She didn't want to have to tell the woman that they were temporarily running the bed-and-breakfast where all the murders were taking place.

"Well, good luck, dear," the woman said with a smile. "These cookies certainly look good, and presentation is part of the judging."

"Got that taken care of?" Sam asked a few minutes later, when Phyllis emerged from the yellow-striped tent, where she had left the cookies with the other entries, watched over by several volunteers.

"Yes, all we have to do now is wait for one o'clock." She looked around. "Where's Eve?"

Sam waved toward the center tents, where arts and crafts and various sorts of merchandise were displayed. "She headed off over yonder to have a look around. Said she'd catch up to us later."

"That's fine," Phyllis said with a nod. There was no reason they all had to stay together. "What would you like to look at first?"

"I'm game for anything you want to do," Sam said. "Or we can start at one end and just look at everything until we get to the other end."

"Sounds like a plan," Phyllis said as she slipped her hand in his.

They spent the morning wandering along the wide, grassy aisles formed by the tents, with Tejano, country, and rock music from the groups playing in the big center tent providing a sound track. The areas underneath the tent awnings were divided up into booths selling all sorts of merchandise from T-shirts to sculptures made of seashells to driftwood carvings. Nautical motifs dominated, along with fish, pelicans, seagulls, palm trees, and anything else you could think of connected with life along the coast.

Phyllis enjoyed herself, but the unsolved murders continued to nag at her brain, even in these festive surroundings. More than ever, she felt like the answer to all the questions she had was within reach, if only she could grasp it.

"Mrs. Newsom!" a familiar voice called from behind her and Sam. They turned to see Leo and Jessica coming toward them. The Blaines were actually holding hands, which was something of a surprise to Phyllis. She wouldn't have thought that Jessica was willing to go that far toward forgiving Leo just yet. But in the middle of a celebration like this, she supposed it was hard to stay mad, especially when Leo seemed to be making an effort to earn Jessica's trust again.

"What do you think?" he asked with a grin as he and Jessica walked up. "Quite a shindig, isn't it?"

"Yes, it is," Phyllis said. "Are the two of you enjoying yourselves?"

"It's been fun so far," Jessica admitted. "I feel sort of bad about saying that when we have to drive back to Houston tomorrow and go to poor Sheldon's funeral on Monday, but . . ."

"Life goes on," Leo finished for her. "I don't mean that in a callous way, but it's true. Nothing we can do will bring Sheldon back." He gestured toward one of the tents with the soft drink that he held in his hand and went on, "Sign over there says they're gonna be starting the gumbo cook-off in a few minutes. I've got to check that out."

"Me, too," Sam said.

"Why don't you go on with Leo and Jessica?" Phyllis suggested to him. "I see a display of homemade quilts over there I want to look at."

"All right," he said with a nod. "Where'll we meet up again?"

"I'll come to the center tent in a little while. That's where you'll be anyway."

"It's a deal," Sam said. He set off with the Blaines for the gumbo cook-off.

Phyllis looked over the quilts, which were all elaborately stitched and beautiful. They reminded her poignantly of her late friend Mattie Harris, who had been an expert quilter.

She was standing in front of the display when a voice said behind her, "Well, hello, Mrs. Newsom. We seem to run into you wherever we go."

Phyllis turned and saw Charles Jefferson and Roger Fadiman standing there. The business mogul and the lawyer both wore expensive suits and looked totally out of place in the middle of this casual, fun-loving crowd.

"No offense, but what are you two doing here?" she asked. "This doesn't seem like the sort of thing you'd attend."

"They're here to meet me," Oliver McKenna said as he stepped up. "We're going to settle this deal between us . . . and I didn't exactly feel comfortable about meeting these two unless it was in a public place." He gestured at the crowded surroundings. "You can't get much more public than this."

"You're paranoid, Oliver," Jefferson said. "Why would Roger and I wish you any harm?"

"I haven't forgotten what happened to my father," Oliver replied with a darkly ominous frown.

"I had absolutely no reason to want to hurt your father," Jefferson pointed out.

"Other than the fact that he might have killed the deal we worked out, if somebody hadn't killed him." An oily smile appeared on Oliver's face. "I've done some more research. The Jefferson-Bartell Group isn't quite as secure as it seems on the surface. You need this acquisition."

"And so do you," Jefferson snapped. "You can't keep McKenna Electronics afloat without an influx of new capital, which I'm willing to provide. It's the proverbial win-win, so let's get it done."

"Fine by me." Oliver gave Phyllis a curt nod. "Mrs. Newsom."

The three of them walked off into the crowd without Jefferson or Fadiman giving Phyllis even a perfunctory good-bye. Just as well, she thought. She didn't like any of them. They could do their business and go away, as far as she was concerned.

But she was interested, a moment later, to spot Oscar McKenna and Frances Heaton moving through the crowd as well. From the looks of it, they were following Oliver, Jefferson, and Fadiman. The other two siblings clearly didn't trust Oliver and wanted to know what he was up to. Phyllis was glad that she didn't have to be in the middle of that mess.

She was making her way toward the center tent to look for Sam when she saw several more familiar figures walking through the fair. "Consuela!" she called. All four of the Anselmos were together again.

Impulsively, Phyllis threw her arms around Consuela and gave her a hug. "Thank goodness they let you go!"

Consuela's answering smile was tinged with worry. "Yes, but it may not last. Our lawyer warned me that they may take me into custody again first thing Monday morning."

"Surely not," Phyllis said. "Dale and Abby Clifton aren't fools. They have to know that you couldn't possibly be a killer."

Tom said, "Of course she couldn't. That's why I insisted that we come to the SeaFair. Everything's going to get back to normal now."

He didn't look or sound like he was totally convinced of that, however. Neither did his wife or daughters. Worry still lurked on all their faces.

"You'll stop at the dessert competition and try my cookies, won't you?" Phyllis asked.

"Sure," Tom said. "We'll be there."

They lifted hands in farewell and moved on. Phyllis went into the big center tent and found that the gumbo cook-off was over, with winners in several different categories having been declared. But now cups of all the entries were available to be purchased, and she found Sam doing his best to try each and every one.

"Want some gumbo?" he asked with a grin.

"That sounds all right. Something that's not too spicy, though. Can you recommend one of the varieties you've already tried?"

"Sure." He threw away the cup he had just emptied and took her arm. "Let's try that table right over there."

The gumbo was excellent, just spicy enough without being too hot for Phyllis's taste. It was good enough that she had a couple of cups of it, in fact, washed down with swigs from a canned Dr Pepper that came out of a barrel of ice. When she was finished eating, she and Sam sat at one of the tables and listened to the music for a while. While they were sitting there, she told him about running into the Anselmos, along with Jefferson, Fadiman, and Oliver McKenna, as well as seeing the other two McKenna siblings.

"Sounds like the whole gang's here," Sam commented. "The whole gang of suspects, I reckon I ought to say."

"That's true," Phyllis said. "The only person involved with the case who isn't here is Raquel."

Sam frowned. "You don't reckon that means something, do you?"

"I don't know what it could be, if it does. Her husband hasn't even been dead for forty-eight hours. No one could expect her to attend a big celebration like this."

But if Raquel was innocent—which she didn't know for a fact, Phyllis reminded herself—that meant the killer, or killers, likely *were* in attendance. Whoever had poisoned Ed McKenna and stabbed Sheldon Forrest could be in this very tent. Once again she began going over in her mind everything she had seen and heard over the past few days, and the music filling the air and the hustle and bustle of the crowd around her seemed to fade away. She didn't really know how much time had passed when she finally gave a little shake of her head.

"You looked like you were thinkin' mighty hard," Sam said. "I didn't want to interrupt you, so I kept my mouth shut." He leaned toward her with an excited look on his face. "You know who killed those two, don't you? You've solved the case."

"I don't have any earthly idea," Phyllis said honestly as she looked at her watch. "Come on. We have to get to the dessert contest."

Chapter 22

When she and Sam reached the tent where the competition would take place, she saw that the entries had been brought out from the trailer and were now placed on folding tables in the shade of the awning for people to look at before the actual judging began. Carolyn was there, standing proudly near her pie, and Eve was with her.

Phyllis was surprised to see that Dale and Abby Clifton were there as well. Dale was sitting at a small table with another man and a middle-aged woman. A folded cardboard sign set up on the table in front of them read JUDGES ONLY, and they had a stack of scoring sheets in front of them.

Phyllis went over to Abby, who greeted her with a smile. "Hello, Mrs. Newsom. I was just checking out all the goodies. They look mighty good."

"I didn't know your father was going to be one of the judges."

Abby laughed. "Neither did he until a few minutes ago. One of the regular judges couldn't make it, so Dad got volunteered to take his place."

"I wonder who volunteered him."

"I'll never tell," Abby said with another laugh. "Anyway, it's a good thing we're here. We'll be on hand if a riot breaks out. People take their desserts seriously around here."

Phyllis wanted to dislike Abby and her father because of what Consuela had been put through, but she couldn't quite bring herself to do it. The Cliftons were just doing their job as they saw fit, whether Phyllis agreed with it or not. They didn't really bear any ill will toward Consuela. In fact, Phyllis had gotten the distinct impression that they would have preferred not to bring her in for questioning.

Phyllis felt like pointing out to Abby that all the other suspects in the murders were on hand here at the SeaFair, but she wasn't sure it would do any good. The police had their hands full with the celebration this weekend. The mystery of who had killed Ed McKenna and Sheldon Forrest had been put on the back burner for now, she supposed.

But it wouldn't hurt to ask, so she said to Abby, "Is there anything new on the murders?"

"Not really. We plan to question Charles Jefferson on Monday, although that lawyer of his is going to try to make it as difficult as possible. We've already checked him out, though, and he has a solid alibi for the McKenna killing."

"What about Sheldon's murder?"

Abby shook her head. "Sheldon Forrest was Jefferson's son-in-law. They got along all right, and so did Sheldon and his wife, so Jefferson wouldn't have had any motive there. I just don't see it."

Neither did Phyllis. Several different people had had reason to want Ed McKenna dead, but none of them had been at the bed-and-breakfast when the crab cakes were poisoned. And Sheldon's murder just made no sense at all. Once Phyllis had discovered that there hadn't been any affair between Sheldon and Jessica Blaine, the only reasonable motive for anyone to kill him had disappeared as well.

Then there was the matter of the two deaths occurring so close together. Either there were separate murderers, which would be a coincidence almost beyond belief, or there was some connection between Sheldon and Ed McKenna that she just wasn't seeing . . .

She was so deep in thought that she almost didn't notice that the judging had begun. Each of the judges was presented with a sample from each entry. Phyllis sat down on one of the folding chairs that had been set up in several rows and watched as the judges went about their work with serious demeanors. One of the local ladies served as mistress of ceremonies, announcing each of the entries but not the names of the contestants. She kept the large audience laughing with her comments about the cookies, pies, cakes, brownies, and puddings.

Somebody sat down behind Phyllis and leaned forward to put a hand on her shoulder. "Hi, Mrs. Newsom," Kate Thompson said. "Have they announced any of the winners yet?"

Phyllis turned half around on the metal chair. "No, I guess they're going to sample the entries in all the categories and then announce all the winners at the same time." She looked along the row of metal chairs and saw Leo and Jessica sitting a few yards away. Kate seemed to be alone, though. "Where's Nick?"

She made a face. "The heat got to him. He had to leave. Poor baby gets queasy when he gets too hot. I thought maybe I could catch a ride back to the bed-and-breakfast with you and Mr. Fletcher."

"Both of our vehicles are here. I'm sure someone can take you home, dear . . . although it's not really your home, is it?"

"I sort of wish it was," Kate said with a wistful expression on her face. "I really like it down here. I was sort of hoping that if the deal went through, we could move to this area."

Phyllis frowned. "Deal? What deal?"

"Your cousin didn't tell you about it?"

"All right," the mistress of ceremonies said into the microphone attached to the portable public address system she was using, "we're ready to announce the winners, including the grand prize winner!"

"I'll tell you about it later," Kate said. "Right now we want to see who won."

But Phyllis didn't care anymore. Her hand shot out and grasped Sam's arm. "Take me back to Oak Knoll," she said.

"Right now?" he asked with a frown. "But they're about to tell who won—"

"I have to go now, Sam!"

His eyebrows shot up as he realized what was going on. "Son of a gun! Come on!"

They got to their feet and hurried out from under the shade of the tent. Phyllis heard Kate calling after them in confusion but didn't stop. There was no time to explain.

"Who is it?" Sam asked when they were in the pickup and he was turning the key in the ignition.

"Nick," Phyllis said.

"Nick Thompson? That kid? Shoot, Phyllis, he's harmless!"

She shook her head as he pulled out onto the highway and gunned the truck toward Fulton Beach Road. "When I was looking through the files on Dorothy's computer, I saw all the registration information on the guests, including the scans of their driver's licenses. The name on Kate's license is Katherine Garrett Thompson. Her father owns Garrett Development, the company that Nick works for. The company that bought Darcy Maxwell's house next door for what she called a very generous offer. I'll bet Garrett owns the empty house on the other side, as well. But the company needs Oak Knoll, too, in order to tear all those old places down and put up a new multimillion-dollar resort."

Sam sent the pickup veering onto the beach road. "You don't know that."

"Kate mentioned some sort of deal in this area that didn't work out. What else could it have been? Nick probably scouted out the location and recommended it to his father-in-law, but then Dorothy and Ben refused to sell because this is their home and has been for so long. That ruined everything ... and you heard what Nick said about his father-in-law. He said that Garrett would even fire Kate if she fouled up. He must be afraid for his job."

Phyllis had been talking rapidly, fitting the pieces of the theory together in her mind at the same time she was putting it into words. She paused, and Sam said, "So he starts murderin' folks?"

"We said it over and over ... murder would ruin the bed-and-breakfast business for Dorothy and Ben. They'd have to sell out to Garrett, but probably for a lot lower price now. Nick would come out all right after all."

"How in the world did you put this together?"

"Because there's no connection between the murders except for the fact that Ed McKenna and Sheldon Forrest *were both staying at Oak Knoll.* The murders weren't directed at them, but rather at the bed-and-breakfast."

Sam shook his head. "Darned if it doesn't fit together," he admitted, "but would somebody really kill a couple of strangers over a real estate deal?"

"Every killer has a reason that makes sense to him or her, whether it does to anybody else or not."

"So why are we rushin' back there now?" Sam asked as the pickup slewed around a curve in the road next to the water.

"Because Nick left the SeaFair claiming that he didn't feel well. Raquel's alone at Oak Knoll."

"Good Lord," Sam muttered. "He's gonna kill her, too."

"And then pretend to discover her body, just like he would have pretended to discover McKenna's body on the pier if we hadn't come along. Remember, he and Kate were heading in that direction."

Sam glanced over at her. "You reckon Kate knows what he's been doin'? Is she part of it?"

"I don't think so. If she was, she wouldn't have mentioned that failed deal to me just now. That's what made it all click for me. That's when I remembered seeing her maiden name in those computer files."

They were in sight of Oak Knoll now. Everything looked all right at the bed-and-breakfast ... but that didn't mean that it was.

"Stop in front," Phyllis said. "I want to get inside as quickly as possible."

"Well, that's where you're wrong," Sam said as he steered the pickup toward the side of the road in front of the house. "You're not goin' in. I am."

"Sam, this is my responsibility. I'm looking after the place for Dorothy—"

"And I'm lookin' out for you, whether you like it or not." He brought the pickup to a stop and killed the engine. "Stay here."

With that he had the door open and was out of the pickup, his long legs taking him up the steps to the porch and inside in several bounds. Phyllis wanted to call after him to be careful, but she didn't want to warn Nick that someone was coming. She thought Sam could overpower the younger man if he took him by surprise.

But there was no way she could just sit there and wait in the pickup, she realized. Since the driver's door was still open, she slid across the seat and stepped out.

Sam had left the wooden door open when he went inside. Phyllis eased the screen door back and stepped into the foyer, listening intently. She didn't hear anything ... then suddenly there was a heavy thump from upstairs, like something had fallen on the floor.

Something ... or someone.

She wanted to call Sam's name, but instead she kept her mouth shut and moved to the stairs. She had just started up them when Nick Thompson appeared at the second-floor landing.

"Oh, hell," he said with what sounded like genuine regret. "Not you, too, Mrs. Newsom." He sighed. "I guess that all three of you will have to die in the fire that burns this place to the ground. I didn't really want to do that, but you're not leaving me much choice."

Phyllis stared at him in horror. She knew that Sam was hurt or even dead, and she wanted to go to him, but on the chance that he was still alive, she couldn't help him if she allowed Nick to kill her, too.

She spun around and lunged for the front door.

She reached it while Nick was still only halfway down the stairs, cursing as he came after her. Flinging the screen door open, she raced toward the pickup, but as she slapped her hands against it to stop herself, she glanced in and saw that the ignition was empty. Out of habit, Sam had pulled the key and taken it with him when he got out. The houses on either side of Oak Knoll were empty, and there were gaps of several vacant lots in either direction before there were more houses.

And Fulton Beach Road was empty at the moment.

Everybody was at the SeaFair.

"Come on, Mrs. Newsom," Nick said as he came down the walk toward her. "Let's don't make this any worse than it has to be."

"Why, Nick?" she said, trying not to gasp from fear. "For a real estate deal?"

His affable look disappeared as his face twisted in a grimace. "You don't know what it's like to work for that bastard. He never thought I was good enough to marry Kate in the first place. If I don't deliver this place to him, he's gonna make my life a living hell. I'm sorry, but I don't have any choice."

"Everybody . . . everybody always has choices . . ."

He shook his head. "Not me. And not you, anymore."

He was right about that. The only thing Phyllis could do was turn and run.

She headed straight across the street toward the pier,

and a second later her shoes slapped the planks as she ran out onto it. Someone would come along Fulton Beach Road and see him chasing her, she told herself. Someone would stop and help.

But as she glanced desperately in both directions, she saw that the road was still empty.

She backed away as he came on inexorably. "Maybe this will work out," he said. "You walked out onto the pier by yourself, slipped and fell in, and drowned. A real tragedy. But it probably happened when you saw that the house was on fire and tried to run back in. I'll still have to burn it down to take care of Sam and Mrs. Forrest and make it look like an accident, too."

"Three accidental deaths in one day, less than a week after two murders?" Phyllis shook her head as she continued backing toward the end of the pier. "The police will never believe it."

"Maybe not, but there's nothing to tie me to any of it. I don't have any motive."

"You can't get away with this in broad daylight!"

Nick shook his head. "Oh, you'd be surprised what you can get away with. The people on the other side didn't want to sell, either, but their heirs were willing to after they were killed by a hit-and-run driver. Another damned shame."

A cold chill went through Phyllis as she realized that Ed McKenna wasn't the first person Nick had murdered. He was a serial killer, all right, but he wasn't doing it for the thrills.

He was doing it to impress his father-in-law.

"I still say this doesn't have to be hard . . ."

"Yes," Phyllis said. "It does. The police are here."

Nick looked like he was about to say something about not falling for that old trick, when the squeal of tires coming to a skidding stop at the end of the pier made him stiffen. He turned his head and stared as Abby Clifton lunged out of the cruiser and ran out onto the pier, gun in hand. "Get down, Mrs. Newsom!" she called.

Phyllis dropped to the wet, clammy planks just in case Abby had to fire. Nick wasn't going to put up a fight, though. His shoulders drooped in defeat. He turned and Abby took him down with expert ease, pulling his wrists behind him one-handed and fastening them together with a plastic restraint without ever holstering her gun. Then she stepped back, hauled Nick to his feet, and prodded him toward shore while Phyllis was climbing to her feet again. Abby glanced back and asked, "Are you all right?"

"I am now," Phyllis said, because she had just seen Sam step out onto the porch with his cell phone held to one ear while blood trickled down the other side of his face from a gash on his head. But Phyllis could tell from the grin on his face that he wasn't hurt too badly.

"Move over and let the lady by," Abby said, tugging Nick to the edge of the pier. Phyllis went past them and broke into a run again.

Toward Sam.

"If I'm gonna be the brawn of this detectin' outfit, I got to get better at it," Sam said an hour or so later as he sat on the porch at Oak Knoll with Phyllis, Carolyn, Eve, Abby Clifton, the Anselmos, and Leo and Jessica Blaine. "Nick must've heard me comin' and hid behind the door of Raquel's room, because he walloped me a good one when I came in. Lucky for me he didn't take the time to finish me off then and there. I guess he heard you come in, Phyllis, and that was all that saved me."

"Well, you regaining consciousness and calling the police was all that saved me," she said.

"Not necessarily," Abby put in. "I was already on my way here when Mr. Fletcher was patched through to me and told me that Nick Thompson was trying to kill you. When I saw you leave the dessert contest in such a hurry, I had an idea that maybe you had figured something out. And, of course, you had. But I might not have hurried as much as I did without Mr. Fletcher's call."

Leo said, "Hey, I know what it's like to work for a tyrant, but I can't imagine killing people over a business deal."

"Poor Raquel," Jessica said.

"She may pull through yet," Abby said. "Thompson thought he had killed her by smothering her with that pillow, but he's no expert on things like that, even if he did manage to murder four people and get away with it . . . for a while."

"Mrs. Newsom, what do you think Dorothy and Ben will want to do with the bed-and-breakfast now?" Tom asked. "Will they try to keep it going?"

"I hope so," Phyllis said. "Once everyone knows that one of the guests was responsible for the murders, not someone who works here, I don't see any reason why people won't want to stay here."

Carolyn sniffed. "As morbid as most people are, it may even *increase* their business."

"Bed-and-breakfast as the notorious Murder House," Eve said. "It might make for some catchy advertising."

Carolyn rolled her eyes and shook her head.

"I feel sorry for Kate," Phyllis said. "She and Nick seemed like such a nice young couple. Now her life may be ruined, too, through no fault of her own. I don't think she knew anything about it."

"She didn't," Abby said. "Thompson's already admitted that he'd been drugging her to keep her sleepy all the time, so he could slip out and do his dirty work."

"You mean they really were *napping*?" Eve asked. "I thought they were—"

"We all know what you thought," Carolyn said.

At that moment, another police car eased to a stop in front of the house. Chief Dale Clifton unfolded his long-legged form from the front seat and came up the walk toward them. As he climbed the steps, he asked, "How are you, Mrs. Newsom?"

"I'm fine. Sam's the one who was hurt."

Sam touched the bandage taped to his head. "I'll be

all right. Takes more than one wallop to dent this old noggin of mine."

Clifton turned to Phyllis and went on, "You forgot something, Mrs. Newsom. You left before the awards were handed out." He extended a painted plate toward her. "First place in the cookie category went to the Oatmeal Delights, baked by Mrs. Phyllis Newsom."

Phyllis put a hand to her mouth and said, "Oh." She looked at Carolyn. "You didn't tell me. You said your chocolate strawberry pie came in third, but you didn't tell me the cookies won."

Carolyn smiled and shrugged. "The chief said that he would deliver your trophy plate later. Who am I to argue with the police?"

Phyllis almost laughed at that sentiment, but instead she reached out to take the plate from Clifton. "Thank you, Chief," she said.

"Thank you," he replied with a grin. "Those were mighty good cookies." He leaned a shoulder against one of the pillars supporting the porch roof. "I hope all this unpleasantness hasn't soured you on our little part of the world. We want everybody who visits the coast to come back again."

"We certainly might," Phyllis said as she slipped her hand into Sam's. "It's beautiful here, no doubt about that."

"Paradise," Chief Clifton murmured as they all looked out at the water gently rolling in from the bay.

But there was a serpent in paradise, Phyllis reminded herself, and that had been true here, too. Murder could happen anywhere, even in surroundings like this.

She wasn't going to think about that now. Not with a warm breeze blowing and the golden light of late afternoon fading toward dusk and the cry of a seagull in the air as it sailed above the waves. Right now she held tightly to Sam Fletcher's hand and thought only good thoughts.

Recipes

Sweet Peach Rolls

Jam:
1 cup chopped fresh peaches
½ cup sugar
4 teaspoons liquid fruit pectin

Rolls:
2 packages dry yeast
2½ cups warm water
1 package yellow cake mix
5 cups all-purpose flour
½ cup dried cranberries

Glaze:
½ cup confectioners' sugar
1 teaspoon lemon juice
½ teaspoon vanilla extract
½ to 1 teaspoon water

Jam: In a saucepan combine peaches and sugar. Heat over medium-high heat until mixture comes to a boil, stirring constantly to dissolve sugar. Add liquid pectin, and then bring to a full rolling boil. Boil hard for 1 minute, stirring constantly. Remove from heat. Refrigerate overnight.

Rolls: In a large bowl combine the yeast and warm water. Let stand 5 minutes. Stir in the cake mix and then the flour one cup at a time. Cover the bowl with a cloth and let the dough rise in a warm place about 2 hours, or until doubled in bulk.

Roll out the dough onto a floured surface into a rectangle about ½ inch thick. Spread with peach mixture and sprinkle with cranberries. Roll up the dough, starting from the long side. Chill 1 hour.

Preheat the oven to 350 degrees Fahrenheit. Grease a 15-x-10-inch jelly-roll pan.

Slice the chilled dough roll into ½-inch pieces. Place each slice on the prepared pan. Bake 23 to 25 minutes.

Glaze: In small bowl, mix sugar, lemon juice, and vanilla, adding the water until the glaze is the right consistency. Drizzle glaze over warm rolls.

Note: You can use a small jar of peach jam instead of the homemade jam.

Peachy Bread Pudding

6 to 7 slices bread
¼ cup melted butter
4 eggs, beaten
1 can skim evaporated milk
½ cup milk
1 teaspoon vanilla
1 cup sugar
1 tablespoon cinnamon
2 cups fresh sliced peaches

Cut bread in cubes and allow to dry overnight. Put bread cubes in large bowl. Drizzle butter over bread. Mix eggs, milk, vanilla, sugar, and cinnamon. Pour over bread-and-butter mixture. Add sliced peaches and toss mixture. Put in baking dish and let set for 15 minutes.

Preheat oven to 350 degrees Fahrenheit. Bake for 30 minutes.

Killer Crab Cakes

1 small white onion, finely chopped
2 tablespoons butter, divided
¼ cup whole milk
2 eggs
½ teaspoon white vinegar
1 teaspoon Old Bay seasoning
1 teaspoon salt
1 tablespoon spicy Dijon mustard
1½ cups panko (Japanese bread crumbs), divided
1 pound fresh crabmeat
½ cup finely chopped pecans
2 teaspoons lemon pepper

Sauté chopped onions with 1 tablespoon butter over medium heat until barely limp, about one minute. Transfer to a small bowl to cool.

In medium bowl whisk milk, eggs, vinegar, Old Bay seasoning, salt, and mustard until well blended. Add ½ cup bread crumbs, onions, and crabmeat and mix thoroughly.

In a shallow bowl or pan mix 1 cup bread crumbs, pecans, and lemon pepper.

Divide crab mixture into 8 equal piles and form cakes, or fill a ⅓ measuring cup until almost full, pack down into cup to form patties, dump, and then flatten them lightly into cakes. Turn cakes in the bread crumb mixture until well covered.

Place cakes on a large baking sheet covered with parchment paper, cover pan with plastic wrap, and chill 2 to 4 hours.

Preheat oven to 400 degrees Fahrenheit. Put about ½ teaspoon butter on each crab cake. Bake around 20 minutes.

Note: If you like spicy crab cakes add ⅛ to ¼ teaspoon cayenne pepper with the milk/egg mixture.

Seafood Quesadilla

1 cup cooked crab (can use imitation crab)
1 cup cooked small shrimp, peeled and deveined
8 ounces softened cream cheese
½ cup green chile enchilada sauce, mild or hot
⅓ cup green onions, chopped
Salt and pepper to taste
2 cups shredded mozzarella cheese
8 10-inch flour tortillas
Oil for pan

In a medium bowl blend crab, shrimp, cream cheese, green chile sauce, onion, and salt and pepper. Place ¼ of the mixture and ½ cup cheese on a tortilla, and cover with second tortilla. Brush skillet with oil and lightly brown each quesadilla on both sides. Cut into fourths and serve with salsa.

Serves 6–8.

Tamale Soup

1 pound ground pork or beef
1 pound ground chicken or turkey
1 chopped onion
2 tablespoons oil
2 beef bouillon cubes
2 cups water
1 tablespoon chili powder
1 teaspoon salt
½ can green chile enchilada sauce (about ½ cup)
1 15-ounce can diced tomatoes
1 15-ounce can tomato sauce
1 15-ounce can pinto beans, drained
10 fresh tamales, frozen
Grated cheese

Brown ground meat with onion in oil in a large skillet. Drain off grease. Add bouillon from cubes that have been dissolved in water. Add other ingredients, except tamales and cheese. Cook on low heat until flavors are blended. Ten minutes before serving, cut the frozen tamales into one-inch pieces and add to soup. If tamales are not frozen, they will fall apart after a short time. Top servings with cheese and serve with tortilla chips.

If fresh tamales are not available, use canned. Drain, remove paper, and slice into one-inch pieces. Add at last minute to soup to heat through.

Makes 8–10 bowls.

Oatmeal Delights

2 cups flour
1 teaspoon baking soda
1 teaspoon baking powder
1 teaspoon salt
1 cup oatmeal
1 cup unsalted butter (2 sticks), softened
1 cup sugar
1 cup brown sugar
1 teaspoon vanilla
2 eggs
1 cup chopped pecans
1 cup chopped shredded coconut
1 12-ounce bag white chips

Preheat oven to 350 degrees Fahrenheit. Sift together flour, baking soda, baking powder, and salt. Add oatmeal; set aside. Mix butter and sugars in a large bowl until creamy. Add vanilla and eggs, one at a time. Gradually mix in flour mixture until well blended. Chop pecans and coconut in food processor until finely chopped. Then add to dough. Fold in white chips.

Drop by tablespoon 2 inches apart on cookie sheet.

Bake 12 to 14 minutes. Allow to cool 5 minutes on cookie sheet before transferring to wire rack to cool completely.

Makes 5–6 dozen.

Chocolate Strawberry Pie

Butter Crust:
1½ cups all-purpose flour
1½ teaspoons sugar
½ teaspoon salt
½ cup (1 stick) cold unsalted butter
¼ cup very cold water

In a large bowl combine the flour, sugar, and salt and mix well. Cut the butter in ¼-inch pieces and scatter over the dry ingredients. Toss to mix. Using your fingers, two knives, or a pastry blender, rub or cut the butter into the flour until it is broken into pea-size pieces. Sprinkle half of the water on top. Toss with a fork to dampen the mixture. Add the remaining water in two stages. Continue tossing the mixture until it seems packable. If it's still too dry, add 1 teaspoon of cold water at a time until the dough is the desired consistency, working in the water with your fingertips. Using your hands, pack the dough into a ball. Then flatten into a disk, wrap with plastic wrap, and refrigerate for 30 minutes to 1 hour before rolling. Try not to handle the dough too much.

Filling:
¼ cup butter
2 squares (1 ounce each) unsweetened chocolate
1½ cups sugar
1 tablespoon flour
pinch of salt
½ cup milk
2 eggs
1 teaspoon vanilla extract
1 unbaked 9-inch butter pastry shell
1 pound washed, hulled, and halved strawberries

Melt butter with chocolate in a saucepan, or microwave in a small bowl. In a mixing bowl, combine chocolate and butter mixture with sugar, flour, salt, milk, eggs, and vanilla; beat with electric mixer at medium speed until well mixed. Pour filling into prepared pastry shell. Bake at 350 degrees Fahrenheit for 40 to 45 minutes, until set. Cool. Arrange halved strawberries on top of pie.

Drizzle:
4 tablespoons butter
1/8 cup cocoa powder
1/3 cup sugar
1 tablespoon milk

In a small saucepan, melt butter. Add cocoa, sugar, and milk, stirring constantly. Bring to a good boil for one minute. Drizzle the warm fudge sauce over the strawberries.

Author's Note

Rockport and Fulton are real towns on the Texas Gulf Coast, and they're every bit as charming, picturesque, and friendly as I've tried to describe them in this novel. I've taken a few minor liberties with the geography of the area for dramatic purposes, and none of the characters in this book are based on any real people who reside there. The SeaFair, including the Just Desserts competition, takes place at Rockport Harbor every fall, and if you ever find yourself in the area at that time of year, I highly recommend that you pay it a visit. But really, any time of year is a great time to visit these wonderful towns.

It's a Thanksgiving feast in Weatherford, Texas!

Read on for a special sneak peek at the next

Fresh-Baked Mystery from Livia J. Washburn

The Pumpkin Muffin Murder

Now available from Obsidian.

One thing you never forgot about being a parent, Phyllis Newsom thought, is the feeling of helplessness that comes over you when your child is sick. Of course, Bobby was her grandson, not her son, but that didn't matter. He felt miserable, and she had done everything she could to make him feel better, but he still sobbed in pain as she held him and carried him back and forth across the living room of her house, trying to calm him down.

"It'll be all right, Bobby," she told the four-year-old. "Don't worry. Everything will be just fine. You'll be all well soon."

Not soon enough to suit her, though. The pediatrician had said that it might be a week or more before Bobby's ear infection cleared up. And it would have to heal on its own, because this wasn't like the old days when doctors prescribed antibiotics for such ailments. Phyllis remembered giving her son, Mike, the wonderful pink liquid when he was little and came down with something like this. That stuff seemed to cure anything.

Now the doctors claimed that it really didn't, and Phyllis supposed that they ought to know what they were talking about. They were doctors, after all. But she missed being able to feel like she was accomplishing something, like she was helping her child get well sooner.

Ah, well. She sighed and held Bobby closer, letting him rest his head on her shoulder. She was wearing a nice thick robe over her pajamas, so she supposed it almost felt like a pillow to him.

The sound of footsteps made her glance toward the stairs. Sam Fletcher's long legs came into view, followed by the rest of his lanky form. He was dressed in pajamas, robe, and slippers, too, although his were a nice manly brown rather than the purple of Phyllis's nightclothes.

"Thought I heard the little one carryin' on," Sam said as he came from the foyer into the living room.

"I'm sorry, Sam. He just can't rest comfortably with his ear hurting that way. I gave him some pain reliever like the doctor said, but . . ."

Sam nodded. "Yeah, I reckon it must hurt, all right." He held out his arms. "Here, let me hold him for a while."

Phyllis hesitated. Not because she didn't trust Sam, of course. In the nearly two and a half years that he had rented a room in her house here in Weatherford, Texas, she had grown to know him very well. He was both strong and gentle—just the sort of man who wouldn't think twice about offering to comfort a sick child. But Bobby was her responsibility, not his.

"It's the middle of the night," she told Sam. "You should be sleeping. I'll be all right."

A smile spread across Sam's rugged face. "Shoot, I wasn't asleep anyway. Seems like the older I get, the less easy it is for me to sleep. I was on the computer lookin' at YouTube. You know they got clips on there from all the TV shows I used to watch back in the fifties? I haven't seen George Burns and Gracie Allen in a long time."

Phyllis couldn't help but smile back at him. They were roughly the same age, in their late sixties, and it wasn't unusual for either of them to discover something new and wonderful on the Internet that most younger people had probably known about for years.

"I'll have to check that out," she said. "Are you sure you don't mind . . . ?"

Sam motioned with his fingers to indicate that she should give Bobby to him.

"Well, all right." She handed the whimpering youngster over.

Bobby immediately threw his arms around Sam's neck and buried his face against the man's shoulder. His sobs began to subside.

"I think I'm jealous," Phyllis said with a laugh. "He appears to like you more than he does me."

"Oh, I wouldn't say that. He just senses that we're kindred spirits."

Phyllis raised an eyebrow. "How so?"

"Normally, I sleep like a baby, too. I kick and fret all night."

"I wouldn't know," Phyllis said as she arched an eyebrow.

Sam chuckled as he started walking slowly back and forth across the living room. Bobby quieted even more. Within a few minutes, he appeared to be sound asleep.

Sam looked at the boy, then grinned at Phyllis. "Say good night, Gracie," he whispered.

"Good night, Gracie," she responded. She held her arms out. "I'll put him in bed."

"No, I got him. We start passin' him around like a football, he's liable to wake up again."

Sam left the living room and started carefully up the stairs. A couple of days earlier, when Bobby had come to stay with Phyllis, Sam and Mike had climbed up in the attic of the old house and brought down the crib Mike had slept in twenty-odd years earlier. Bobby had complained that he wasn't a baby and shouldn't have to sleep in a crib, but that was really the only place Phyllis had for him to sleep. They had compromised by leaving the sides down when they put the crib in Phyllis's bedroom.

She was in the kitchen brewing some herbal tea when Sam came back downstairs. "Figured I'd find you in here," he said.

"Did he keep on sleeping?"

"Like a rock. I reckon that medicine finally caught up with him and made him conk out."

"You want some tea?"

"Is it made from flowers and stuff?"

"Well, I'm not going to drink regular tea at this time of night. I never would get to sleep."

"All right, sure. I guess I don't need anything else keepin' me awake, either."

Phyllis poured the tea when it was ready, and they sat down on opposite sides of the kitchen table. She sipped from her cup, then said, "I wish Bobby had been able to go to California with Mike and Sarah. This may well be Bud's last Thanksgiving."

"That's Sarah's dad?"

"Yes."

"At least she's gettin' to spend this time with him."

"Yes, and that's a blessing."

Phyllis thought about her daughter-in-law. She knew from experience how terrible it was to have to face the impending end of a loved one's life. She had lost her husband, Kenny, a number of years earlier. And Sam had gone through the same thing when cancer claimed his wife. But Phyllis also knew that the last days spent together could be some of the most precious of all, easing the passing of the one who had to leave and creating memories that those left behind would carry with them for the rest of *their* days.

So when Bobby had come down with the ear infection the day before Mike and Sarah were supposed to leave to spend a week in California with Sarah's parents and the doctor told them they couldn't take him on the airplane, Phyllis hadn't hesitated. She had urged them to make the trip and leave Bobby with her. "I'd love the chance to spend that much time with him," she had told her son and daughter-in-law. "That way you can make your trip without having to worry about him."

"Oh, I'll worry about him," Sarah had said, and Phyllis knew exactly what she meant. Worrying was a parent's permanent job. Mike was a grown man, and not a day went by that Phyllis didn't spend some of the time wondering where he was and what he was doing and worrying about whether he was all right.

The fact that Mike was a deputy in the Parker County Sheriff's Department didn't make things any easier. But Phyllis knew she would have worried about him no matter what he did for a living.

Phyllis realized that she'd been sitting there quietly, musing over the events of the past few days, without saying a word. Sam had been silent, too. Yet she didn't feel the least bit awkward or uncomfortable because of the silence, and from the looks of him, neither did Sam. It had been a good thing when she'd had a vacancy open up in the house a couple of years earlier, she thought. Her old superintendent, Dolly Williamson, had suggested that she rent the room to Sam, and even though there had been some rough patches at first, caused by having a man in a house full of retired female teachers, it hadn't taken long for Sam to become a member of the family.

And that was the way she thought of him and Carolyn Wilbarger and Eve Turner, the other retired teachers who lived here with her. They were all family now.

"This tea's not bad," Sam said. "Bein' a good Texan, though, I'm not sure I'll ever get used to drinkin' any kind of tea without a bunch of ice cubes in it."

Before Phyllis could say anything to that, a key rattled in the lock of the back door.

She and Sam looked at each other in puzzlement. Who in the world could be coming in at this hour? It was after midnight, and anyway, no one had a key to her house except the people who lived here and Mike. Carolyn and Eve were upstairs asleep, and Mike was in California. . . .

Phyllis felt a little twinge of apprehension. Maybe someone was actually trying to break in. They could be attempting to pick the lock. But would a burglar do that when the lights in the kitchen were on and someone was obviously in here?

Sam was on his feet, facing the door. He had braved danger to protect Phyllis in the past, and she wasn't surprised that he would do it again. She wouldn't let him do that alone, though. She stood up as well and started looking around for some sort of weapon.

The door swung open, and Carolyn said, "I'm sorry. I didn't mean to disturb anybody."

Sam, bless his heart, didn't miss a beat. He crossed his arms, frowned at Carolyn, and said, "Young lady, do you have any idea what time it is?"

Carolyn looked flabbergasted for a second, but then she glared as she closed the door and said, "I don't need any sass from you, Sam Fletcher. I'm tired."

"Well, I'd imagine so, what with you out gallivantin' around until the wee hours of the morning."

Carolyn looked at Phyllis, who came around the table to get between them. "I thought you were upstairs asleep," she said to her old friend.

"I would have been if I hadn't gotten a call from Dana Powell," Carolyn said as she took off her coat. "Logan was supposed to help her with some decorations for the Harvest Festival, but you know how undependable *he* is. I've been over at Dana's house all evening, giving her a hand."

Phyllis shook her head. "I didn't hear the phone ring."

"She called me on my cell. Anyway, you were busy with Bobby."

Like seemingly everyone else in the world these days, Phyllis carried a cell phone, but after living for decades before the things were even invented, she sometimes forgot how ubiquitous they were. Occasionally she had to remind herself when she was out that she didn't have to look for a public phone if she wanted to make a call.

"Like I said, I didn't want to disturb anyone," Carolyn went on. "So I just slipped out and went on over there."

Dana Powell was about twenty years younger than Carolyn—and Phyllis and Sam, for that matter—but she and Carolyn had taught together at the same school before Carolyn retired, and they were still friends. Phyllis liked her as well, although she thought sometimes that Dana was a little too skinny and a little too blond for an elementary-school teacher. But there was no denying that Dana was good with the kids and was also heavily involved in the community, including being in charge of some of the plans for the upcoming Harvest Festival.

In recent years, that term had been co-opted in a lot of places for Halloween celebrations, but this year, in Weatherford, the festival was taking place the Saturday before Thanksgiving, which as far as Phyllis was concerned was a more traditional and appropriate time for it, anyway. The festival was being held on the south side of town in a city park that surrounded a small lake known for the flock of ducks that lived there most of the year. The ducks would be gone now, having migrated south for the winter, but the park was still a pleasant, picturesque place with playground equipment for the children, hiking trails, picnic areas, and a couple of old settlers' cabins that had been moved in from farther west in the county. Phyllis remembered taking some of her history classes to the park on field trips so the students could see the bullet holes in the walls left behind by Indian battles and check out the interiors, which were furnished in pioneer fashion.

A couple of days from now, on Saturday evening,

the park would be full of games and rides and craft displays, along with an assortment of food and drink vendors, much like the Peach Festival held in Weatherford every summer. There would also be a cooking contest centered around traditional Thanksgiving foods like pumpkin pies, creative uses of cranberry sauce, unusual stuffings to go with turkey, and things like that.

The cooking contest was especially interesting to Phyllis, who entered nearly every such contest that came along, usually in competition with Carolyn. There wouldn't be any rivalry this time, however. Carolyn had already agreed to serve as a judge in the contest, instead of entering it. That was fine with Phyllis, although in a way she would miss their friendly competition.

She might miss the contest entirely, she thought, depending on how Bobby was doing. She might not have the time to prepare her entry.

"What were you working on with Dana?" she asked Carolyn now, as she got another cup from the cabinet and poured some tea for her friend without asking. She knew Carolyn loved herbal tea.

"Scarecrow costumes, of all things," Carolyn said as she took the cup. "Thank you."

Sam said, "I thought they were tryin' to get folks to come to this festival, not scarin' them off."

"Oh, there are going to be scarecrows and bales of hay scattered around the park as decorations," Carolyn explained. "Logan was going to pick up the supplies to make the costumes, but then he had some sort of business emergency, so Dana called me and we went to Wal-Mart together to get what she'd need. When I saw how much work she had in front of her, I said I'd stay and help." Carolyn stifled a yawn. "I didn't expect to be quite so late, though. But we got to talking while we worked, and well, you know how that goes."

Phyllis nodded. "Yes, of course. I hope Logan was at least properly apologetic when he got home."

Carolyn took another sip of tea. "He didn't get home. At least, he hadn't when I left."

"Wasn't Dana worried? I would have been."

"I suppose she's used to it," Carolyn said with a shake of her head. "She should know by now that her husband is as much married to that real estate business as he is to her." She looked back and forth between Phyllis and Sam. "Enough about the Powells. What are the two of you doing up at this time of night?"

"Bobby's ear was hurting and he had trouble sleeping," Phyllis said. "Sam was able to get him to doze off, though."

"Well, I'm not going to have any trouble falling asleep. I'm exhausted." Carolyn stood up, drank the rest of her tea, and put the empty cup in the sink. "Good night, both of you. Don't stay up too late."

"We won't," Sam said, then added, "I'm gonna go look at YouTube some more."

He started to follow Carolyn out of the kitchen, but Phyllis stopped him with a hand on his arm. "Thank you for helping with Bobby."

"Anytime," he said with a smile. "He's a good little fella. Hate to see him hurtin'. You think he'll feel good enough to go to the festival on Saturday?"

"I hope so. We could all use some good times."

"Yeah." Sam nodded. "Hope it goes well."

"Why wouldn't it?"

"Well, you never know. . . ."

"Yes, you do," Phyllis said firmly. "I know. There's not going to be any trouble at this festival. Nothing unusual is going to happen."

"That's right." Sam leaned over and planted a quick kiss on her forehead. "Good night."

She told him good night and watched him go up the stairs, wishing he hadn't brought up all the things that had happened in the past. He hadn't meant anything by it, of course.

It was hard to forget, though, that for a while there, murder had seemed to make a habit of following her around.

But more than a year had passed without any sort of trouble, she reminded herself. There was no reason to think it would crop up again now.

With that thought in her head, she turned off the light in the kitchen and went upstairs.